TWO MAN STATION

LISA HENRY

RIPTIDE PUBLISHING

Riptide Publishing
PO Box 1537
Burnsville, NC 28714
www.riptidepublishing.com

Cover art: Natasha Snow, natashasnowdesigns.com
Editors: Rachel Haimowitz, Carole-ann Galloway
Layout: L.C. Chase, lcchase.com/design.htm

ISBN: 978-1-62649-711-5

First edition
January, 2018

Also available in ebook:
ISBN: 978-1-62649-710-8

TWO MAN STATION

LISA HENRY

RIPTIDE PUBLISHING

To the real-life Andrea.
For her friendship, and her inspiration . . . and for her rum.
Bingo!

People who truly live in the outback listen to it. What they hear I do not know . . . What the country says is beyond words.

—Ian Parkes, "A Youth Not Wasted"

TABLE OF CONTENTS

CHAPTER ONE

The dusty ribbon of the Flinders Highway stretched west from the Coast, frayed edges crumbling into the red dirt that clumped in the wheel arches of Gio's Mazda 3, and packed hard as clay into the tread of the tyres. The drive from the Gold Coast took two days. Gio had started out on Monday, and overnighted in a cheap hotel in Emerald, sharing the shower stall with a dead cockroach before falling asleep with the TV blaring. Tuesday had been more of the same: another ten hour stretch behind the wheel, the dull ache of homesickness tugging at him with every kilometre that clicked over on the odo.

Gio stopped every hour or so to stretch, to pace for a while, to break the hypnotic power of the never-ending highway. He'd never seen country like this before. Never been this far west. Slow, lazy flies buzzed around him, drowsy with heat.

The drive was red dirt, chips in the windscreen that caught the blazing sunlight, and mirages that shimmered on the dips in the road. The car shuddered whenever a road train roared past in the other lane.

Gio reached his destination just after four on Tuesday afternoon.

At the edge of Richmond, the road branched. The highway continued left, bypassing the centre of town. The road curved right and swelled into a main street. Gio drove past a bank, a supermarket, two pubs, and the RSL. There wasn't a single building over two storeys high, as though the weight of the endless blue sky had squashed everything flat. No clusters of steel and glass towers, their floor-to-ceiling windows facing the beach and reflecting the thin stretch of sand and the breakers that rolled in endlessly from the ocean.

This—the dust, the heat, the small town, and the empty sky—was a different planet.

Gio turned left at the tiny hospital, following a sign, and found the police station a block back from the main road. A riotous crimson bougainvillea bush half obscured the sign out front of the low-set cement building.

Gio pulled over and turned the ignition off. He tapped his fingers against the steering wheel, drawing a deep breath as the heat bled into the car. He'd been running from his nerves since leaving the Gold Coast, and now that he'd finally stopped, they'd caught up with him.

He could still remember his first day in the job. Four years ago now, Southport station. It was a big station, always busy no matter the time of day or night. Gio had been so nervous he hadn't trusted himself to eat breakfast before starting his shift. Better getting light-headed than throwing up, right? Caffeine and adrenaline had carried him through to lunch.

Gio was nauseated now as well, his stomach roiling. He sat for a moment longer, until the heat became unbearable, and then opened the car door to let the breeze in. His hand shook as he unclipped his seat belt, and he drew another deep breath of hot dry air before getting out of the car. The sun burned his shadow onto the cracked cement path as he walked towards the front entrance of the station. The doors rolled wide when he reached them, and a chill blast of air-conditioning ushered him inside.

The small foyer was empty. There was nobody behind the counter. The grill was pulled down.

Gio pressed the buzzer and heard it sound somewhere out the back. Moments later, the door behind the counter opened, and a woman appeared. She was short, round, and middle-aged, and she wore her grey hair in a pixie cut.

She peered at Gio over the half-moon glasses perched on her nose. "Can I help you?"

"Hi." He slid his badge under the grill. "Gio Valeri."

The woman's expression faltered for a moment. The smile that followed seemed forced. "I'll get Sergeant Quinn."

"Thank you." Gio pulled his badge back and shoved it into his pocket again. He studied the posters on the noticeboard. Domestic Violence. Child Safety. Drugs. The usual stuff.

"Jason?" the woman called as she headed into the back rooms of the station. "The new guy's here."

The door behind the counter *snick*ed closed, muffling any response.

The new guy.

Gio had no doubt that his reputation had preceded him here. And he didn't kid himself that it was a good thing. He fixed his gaze on the curling edges of a Police Recruiting poster, and on a thin crack in the paint job on the wall underneath it.

The new guy.

It wasn't the worst thing she could have called him.

Gio had told himself all the way from the Gold Coast that he was a good copper, and that none of the shit that had happened on the Coast mattered out here. Which was total bullshit, just like Gio's reputation.

Gio straightened up when he heard the *click* of a lock disengaging. A moment later the door to the foyer swung open and the sergeant stepped through. Gio moved forward and stuck his hand out, his heartbeat quickening.

Sergeant Quinn had a firm handshake. "Giovanni?"

"Gio," Gio corrected.

"Jason," Sergeant Quinn said. He was in his mid to late thirties, maybe. He was an inch or so taller than Gio, and in good shape. Tanned too. The faint lines at the corners of his blue-grey eyes deepened when he smiled. He had light-brown hair, the tips sun-bleached. He was younger than Gio had expected. Hotter too, but Gio was careful not to let his appreciation of that particular trait show in his expression as he shook the sergeant's hand. The sergeant gestured at the middle-aged woman. "And this is Sandra."

Gio looked past him to where the woman stood in the doorway. She twisted her chequered lanyard around her finger. Her ID card jiggled against her bosom.

"Come on through," Sergeant Quinn said. "I'll give you a tour of the place."

There wasn't much to the Richmond Police Station. A holding cell, a narrow storeroom, and an even narrower armoury. The small dayroom contained two desks. One was empty and, presumably, Gio's.

The other one was occupied by a kid wearing a faded maroon Richmond State School polo shirt, with his homework spread out around him. The kid was skinny, like a half-grown pup. He couldn't have been more than nine or ten.

"Finished your homework, mate?" Sergeant Quinn asked him.

The kid smiled at him around the pencil shoved in his mouth. He had tousled light-brown hair, eyes the colour of storm clouds, and a spray of freckles across his nose. A mini version of Sergeant Quinn. "Yep!"

"Sure you have," the sergeant said wryly, like a man who'd heard that lie a million times before. He glanced back at Gio. "This is my son, Taylor. Taylor, this is Gio, Dan's replacement."

"Hi," Gio said.

Taylor's smile grew into a wide grin. He ducked his head and the pencil dropped out of his mouth. It rolled off the desk and onto the floor, and Taylor scrambled to retrieve it.

The tour continued.

"My office," Sergeant Quinn said, gesturing to a door. "And the kitchen and showers and toilet are down the hall." He dug into the pocket of his blue cargo pants and pulled out a clump of keys. He flipped through them. "Station, armoury, cell, property room, your locker, the safe, and . . ." He turned the last one over. "Your house."

He dropped the keys into Gio's palm.

Gio closed his fingers around them tightly. The teeth dug into his flesh. He cleared his throat to find his voice. "Thanks, Sarge."

His house.

Shit.

He really was stuck here, wasn't he?

The highset house sat on a quarter-acre block behind the station. It was built on an elevated slab that made Gio wonder if flooding was a concern. Sergeant Quinn's house shared the block. There was no fence between the houses, just an expanse of scrubby grass that seemed to blaze like fire as the sun went down.

The house smelled musty. Gio opened the windows and turned on the ceiling fans. His furniture wasn't due to arrive until tomorrow, but he'd planned for that. He unrolled his air mattress out on the lounge room floor, and walked through the house again, opening and closing the cabinets and cupboards.

The three-bedroom house had been built for a family, not for a single guy. Gio didn't have enough furniture to fill this many rooms. It wouldn't feel like home here.

There were cleaning products under the kitchen sink that the last resident hadn't bothered to pack. Half a bottle of detergent. A pack of green scourers. Insect spray. A can of silver polish. Who the fuck had silver these days? And who the fuck polished it? Gio took the can out and set it on the bench beside the sink to remind him to throw it out as soon as he bought garbage bags.

His phone buzzed in the pocket of his jeans, and he dug it out. The number was blocked. Gio didn't answer it. Probably just a telemarketer, but he didn't feel like pushing his luck right now. He ignored the way his heartbeat picked up. Just a telemarketer. No need to answer and find out it wasn't. Gio had driven two days to get to Richmond. He wanted to believe, for as long as he could, that all the shit on the Gold Coast hadn't followed him.

Gio shoved his phone back into his pocket.

Jesus. What the hell was he even doing here? This wasn't his house. This wasn't his life. There was nothing here that resembled the future Gio had so carefully planned. He curled his fingers around the edge of the bench. Stared at the instructions on the back of the can of silver polish, as though he might find all the answers there. He'd searched in stranger places, hadn't he? Put his faith in dumber things. And look where it had got him. Still, he was somewhat unsurprised when the secrets of the universe failed to reveal themselves via a can of Silvo.

He smiled wryly.

Okay, so he was tired, and he was miserable, and he was homesick, but at least he wasn't totally crazy, right? That seemed like something worth holding on to.

He took his phone out of his pocket and unlocked the screen. He scrolled through his contacts. Hundreds of names there, and the only reason Gio hadn't deleted most of them was that he wanted some warning if any of them called him. He wanted to see a name instead of a random string of numbers. He wondered if any of them was the blocked number.

Probably just a telemarketer.

He should phone Sophie. Let her know he'd got here safely. Except a text would work as well, and that way he wouldn't get pulled into another argument about how selfish he was. It was Gio's fault they argued. He hadn't told her everything. He couldn't bring himself to admit to her that the transfer had been pretty much forced on him. He'd never told her how bad things had gotten. The late-night phone calls where nobody had spoken. The slashed tyres and keyed panels on his car. The can of dog food left on his desk. The threats. It had seemed somehow easier to pretend that moving to Richmond had been his own idea, and to bear Sophie's anger rather than tell her the truth and admit that he was scared, or to make her scared too. He needed some corner of his life that was still untouched by this shit-storm, and he wanted to keep his big sister in that corner too. He didn't want her to see how screwed up everything was now. How screwed up *he* was.

He texted. *Here safe. Call you in a few days.*

It wasn't enough, probably. It'd piss her off more than total radio silence, absolutely. Gio was used to being the bad guy though.

Fuck, he was tired.

He set his phone down on the countertop and twisted the tap on. A blast of hot water hit the bottom of the sink. It took a minute for it to run first lukewarm, and then cool. Gio splashed some over his face and wiped his face on his shirt.

Footsteps clomped up the back steps, and a moment later the handle on the security screen rattled. "Hello?"

Gio crossed to the door.

Taylor's face was smooshed against the screen. "Your door's locked."

"Yep," Gio agreed.

Taylor rattled the handle again. "Dad says he's taking us to the pub for tea."

Gio unlocked the door.

Taylor wrenched it open. "Do you want to come? I'm supposed to ask, not just tell you. In case you're tired."

Gio figured he was hungrier than he was tired. He pocketed his phone. "Yeah," he said. "That sounds good."

They ate in the restaurant attached to the front bar of the Royal Hotel. Occasional bursts of loud laughter drowned out the tinny electronic music of the pub's row of three poker machines. The pub did cheap, good food. Chicken schnitzel, chips, and salad for fourteen bucks, and it was better than anything Gio could have cooked up for himself.

Sergeant Quinn ordered them both a beer. A light.

Taylor got a Coke.

Sergeant Quinn went through the roster with Gio. There were only so many hours in a day that two blokes could fill. They wouldn't cross paths much between Sunday and Wednesday. One of them would work the day shift while the other was on a day off. From Thursday through until Saturday they worked overlapping shifts, trying to cover the afternoon until past midnight when it was more likely they'd have to deal with disturbances and domestics.

"Anything that crops up when you're rostered alone that you need backup for, you call me out," Sergeant Quinn said. "And I'll do the same to you. It's not like the city. This is a two-man station. If things turn to shit, it's just us. Even coming lights and sirens, the nearest backup is about two hours away. Longer than that if they're on the other side of their division."

"Yeah," Gio said. "That's gonna take some getting my head around."

The sergeant's mouth quirked at that, and Gio could hear the unspoken judgement: *city boy*.

Evidently, so could Taylor. The kid dragged a chip through a puddle of tomato sauce, and regarded his dad with a grin.

"It's a different style of policing out here," Sergeant Quinn told Gio. "Has to be."

Gio nodded. "It's, ah, it's a lot to learn."

He felt like a first-year constable again, earnest and respectful. Like he was performing a cheap pantomime, when he knew exactly what Sergeant Jason Quinn thought of him. Jesus. The assistant commissioner and the HSO had called Richmond a fresh start, but Gio knew what it really was: *"Get that fucking dog out of my sight."* Which had been a real kick in the guts especially coming from Jonesy, the boss who'd handpicked him for the team only eight months before. Richmond wasn't a fresh start. Richmond was punishment. *Banishment.* Richmond was seventeen hundred kilometres from the life Gio had built for himself on the Gold Coast. Seventeen hundred kilometres from civilisation. And Gio was stuck here for two years.

Two fucking years.

He ate his meal, and listened attentively while Sergeant Quinn spoke, and tried to remember why the hell he'd ever thought he was too proud to quit.

Thump.

Thump thump thump.

On Thursday, Gio awoke with aching muscles and a vague sense of unknowing. It took a moment for him to recognise the pattern of sunlight slanting through the blinds onto the wall, and a moment longer to remember what that meant. Richmond. This was his home now.

He'd spent all of yesterday shifting his furniture around. However he'd arranged it, it was too thinly spread. The third bedroom held nothing but his two bookshelves. Which was the closest Gio would ever get to a dedicated library, he supposed. Might as well enjoy it.

He had a couple more boxes to unpack today before he started his first shift at the station. He could have unpacked them last night probably, but he'd resisted. Didn't want to make it seem so real by having everything put neatly away, like he actually lived here now. Stupid, because he did actually live here now, and at some point he was going to need his plates and cutlery unpacked.

Thump thump thump.

Gio climbed out of bed, hitching his track pants up. He treaded down the hallway, into the kitchen, and then pushed open the screen door and stared out into the backyard. Taylor was standing there, smacking a cricket bat against one of Gio's discarded packing boxes. He must've dragged it out from under the house.

Thump thump thump.

Hell if Gio could figure out what he was doing.

"Hey," he called out.

The kid spun, wide-eyed, mouth open, the picture of guilt.

"What're you doing?"

Taylor shrugged his skinny shoulders.

"Where's your dad?

"Asleep." Taylor hefted the weight of the cricket bat from hand to hand and squinted worriedly up at Gio.

"Right." The sergeant had been working until two, hadn't he? And it couldn't be much past six now. "You're gonna wake him up if you keep bashing that box."

The kid's guilty expression intensified, and Gio wondered if that was what he secretly wanted. He was bored, probably.

"Aren't you supposed to be at school?" Gio asked him.

Taylor looked scandalised. "Not for *ages*."

"If you want something to do," Gio said, "you can help me finish unpacking."

Taylor's hesitation lasted for about half a second. Then he dumped his cricket bat and walked towards Gio's house.

"I am *great* at unpacking," he said confidently, climbing the steps.

After the third broken coffee mug, Gio begged to differ.

But it was better than silence, right?

CHAPTER TWO

When Jason Quinn woke up, Taylor was gone. There was a half-finished bowl of cereal in the kitchen sink and the milk had been left to slowly curdle on the table. The back door was open.

Jason was too tired to panic. He was still half sunk in sleep when he was climbing the new guy's back steps, and by the time he'd pulled himself into a state approaching wakefulness, he could already hear Taylor chattering away inside.

Boundaries.

Time to remind Taylor that boundaries were a thing that existed. He'd been the same with Dan and his family. At least Dan and Gabby hadn't minded having Taylor underfoot all the time. Taylor had liked coming over to visit Gabby and the baby. He'd been inconsolable when Dan had put in for a transfer to Cairns.

"Who's coming to live here now, Dad?" he'd asked one night, sniffling into his pillow.

"I don't know, mate."

Taylor had scrubbed at his eyes. *"Will they have kids maybe?"*

"Maybe," Jason had told him, tousling his hair. He'd hoped whoever got the spot did have kids, for Taylor's sake. Jason had just wanted someone he could work with as easily as he could with Dan. Someone he could trust to have his back.

Turned out they'd both been shafted, hadn't they?

Jason knocked on the screen door and then opened it. "Taylor? You in here, mate?"

Taylor poked his head around the kitchen doorway. "Dad! I'm helping Gio unpack!"

"You're supposed to be getting ready for school," Jason reminded him.

"What time is it?"

Jason squinted at his watch. "Eight thirty."

"Shit!" Taylor's eyes went owlishly wide.

And it was probably time for a refresher course on appropriate language while they were going over that boundary thing again.

"Go and get your bag and your shoes," Jason said. "And your lunchbox is in the fridge."

"Can I get money for tuckshop?"

"Maybe tomorrow."

Taylor's face split with a grin.

"Bye, Gio!" he yelled, pushing past Jason to get to the stairs. "Bye, Dad!"

Gio appeared in the kitchen doorway, leaning on the frame. He was wearing track pants and a faded Green Day shirt. "Sarge," he said, nodding.

"Morning. Sorry about . . ." Jason made a vague gesture that he hoped encompassed Taylor's lack of boundaries, Taylor's lack of polite language, and pretty much Taylor himself.

"It's no problem." Gio's expression was impossible to read.

"You settling in okay?"

"Yeah." Gio didn't hold his gaze. "Fine."

"Okay," Jason said. "First shift today, huh?"

"Yes, Sarge."

"I'll see you at two."

Gio lifted his gaze again. "Yes, Sarge."

Jesus. The guy was an absolute fucking delight, wasn't he? No wonder they hadn't been able to wait to see the back of him down the Gold Coast. Jason was tempted to ask him which telephone box they'd held his farewell party in.

"Okay," he said instead. "I'd better get Taylor to school."

He was halfway down the stairs again when he heard Gio locking the door behind him.

When Jason arrived at the station just before two, Gio was already there.

"How's it going?" Jason asked, pulling the back door shut behind him. The blast of air-conditioning chilled the sweat on the nape of his neck.

"He set the alarm off trying to get in," Sandra said, walking past with a stack of court briefs. "*Twice*."

Jason snorted out a laugh.

Gio ducked his head, but not before Jason saw his lips quirk in what might have been a tentative smile.

Jason grabbed the car keys off the board. "Time for a grand tour of town, Gio?"

"Yes, Sarge," Gio said, and Jason didn't think he was imagining the relief in Gio's voice. Sandra had probably ripped him a new one for setting the alarm off. She was . . . set in her ways. She'd been the AO in Richmond for the past twenty-three years. She ate coppers for breakfast.

Gio followed Jason outside to the LandCruiser.

"Don't drive these on the Coast, do you?" Jason asked.

"No." Gio settled himself into the passenger's seat, and then twisted around to check the gear in the back seat. "This is a lot of stuff."

"Wet season's coming," Jason said. "Last year I got stuck between two flooded creeks for three days. Fuck if I'm doing that again without camping gear and supplies."

"Are you serious?" Gio asked, eyes widening.

"You're a long way from Cavill Avenue now."

"Yeah." Gio's answering smile was a little hollow. "I'm starting to get that, Sarge."

Jason turned the key in the ignition, and the engine rumbled to life. He glanced at Gio as he checked for traffic before pulling out onto the road, and wondered exactly how this was supposed to work.

Giovanni Valeri.

On balance, Jason would prefer not to know what sort of cloud Gio came to Richmond under. Then again, given that Gio was the sort of arsehole who had Ethical Standards on speed dial, forewarned was forearmed, right? Jason didn't know the specifics of what had happened on the Gold Coast, but he knew enough. It could have been managed in-house, without bringing Ethical Standards on board, but Gio had apparently had an axe to grind. Because the guy whose career he'd sunk hadn't just been a colleague, they'd also been fucking. And the way the entire situation had been handled was bullshit. Jason had heard from at least three different sources that it was all bullshit, but Gio had pulled the discrimination card, and the bosses had been falling over themselves to prove how unprejudiced they were. Too scared they'd be called bigots and sued if they'd told Gio to go fuck himself. So some guy had lost his job and had his entire future ripped away from him, and Gio had got a promotion to senior constable out of the whole deal. Senior constable at twenty-six, and the guy had the audacity to look pissed off about it.

They drove slowly through town, and Jason pointed out the landmarks. The pubs, the motels, the supermarket, the banks, the post office, the hospital, the school. They went by the servo on the edge of town.

"The coffee's terrible," Jason told Gio. "But it's the only place open after midnight."

He stole glimpses of Gio's profile as he drove.

Gio was a good-looking guy. Probably got a lot of action some place like the Gold Coast. Probably wouldn't in Richmond. The girls would be all over him though, with his olive complexion, his dark eyes, and his generous mouth. There were going to be a lot of disappointed women in town when it turned out the new, hot, single copper was playing for the wrong team. Jason wondered if he was out, or if having fucked that bloke he worked with down on the Coast was supposed to be a secret.

Jason and Gio toured a few of the shit addresses in town, the ones that Gio would need to know, where there were disturbances and domestic violence incidents as regular as clockwork. They stopped in at the Ferguson house. It was early enough that everyone was still sober. Their welcome was grudging, but at least it wasn't hostile.

The house was a mess, which was par for the course with the Fergusons, but it wasn't the worst Jason had seen it. There were holes punched in the walls, and the broken window from last week still hadn't been fixed. The place stank of cigarettes.

"Janey, how come the kids aren't at school?" Jason asked, looking at the kids sitting in front of the TV.

Janey Ferguson tugged her threadbare dressing gown around herself, and glared at the kids as though she'd only just noticed them. "Hey! You kids! Go to fucking school!"

The kids scattered.

"Is Harvey around?"

"Not since last week when you locked him up." She chewed her cracked lower lip.

"I told you, you can't invite him around. That's what the order says. He's not allowed to come over." He kept his voice even.

Janey huffed and rolled her eyes, like Jason was the bad guy here.

"You know I'm keeping an eye on him," Jason continued. "If I find out he's breached the order while he's on bail, he'll be going to prison."

"Yeah, yeah." Janey lit a cigarette and looked Gio up and down. "This the new guy?"

"This is Senior Constable Valeri," Jason told her.

Gio nodded.

"Whatever," Janey mumbled, sniffing.

Gio was quiet while Jason asked after Janey's mum down in Gympie and about Janey's plan, the last time they'd talked, to move there with the kids. Gio's gaze took in the house: the cigarette burns on the peeling kitchen linoleum, the overflowing nappy bucket in the corner by the fridge, the loaf of bread mouldering beside the sink. Jason wondered what he was thinking, but his expression didn't give anything away. A professional mask or he just didn't give a shit?

Janey unfurled a little as she spoke with Jason, becoming less guarded, more animated. It was like pushing water uphill, but maybe one day he'd actually convince her to go, before she and Harvey killed one another.

"So," Jason said, stepping over the busted fence as they left, "that was Janey Ferguson. I'm sure you'll meet her other half soon enough. She's the aggrieved in the DV, but when she's drunk, she's as bad as Harvey. She's a biter too."

Gio cast a look back at the house.

"And there's usually a shitload of Harvey's family turning up to drink as well," Jason said. "Any callouts you get for the Fergusons, wake me up too."

"Right." Gio crunched a clump of red dirt under the toe of his boot. "How long ago did the last senior connie leave?"

"About three weeks." Jason climbed into the driver's seat of the LandCruiser and pulled the door shut behind him.

Gio sat in the passenger's seat and tugged his seat belt across his chest. "So how have you dealt with the Fergusons in the meantime?"

Jason hesitated for a moment. "Well, you just have to manage."

The largest place Jason had worked was Mount Isa. He'd been a country copper ever since graduating from the academy in Townsville. It was sometimes hard to remember that there were cities that had a constant stream of radio chatter, and their crews went from job to job to job, and had help only minutes away if it all went to shit. The pace was a lot slower out here, but so was the backup.

"Right," Gio said, squinting out the windscreen. He worried his lower lip with his teeth. "You manage."

Jason pulled the car off the wide dirt shoulder and back onto the road. "Yeah, you *manage*."

And if you don't, you can fuck off back to the Gold Coast.

But that was probably better left unsaid.

Jason left Gio at the station when he went to collect Taylor from after-school care.

"Can you put the siren on, Dad?" Taylor asked, slinging his school bag into the passenger seat and climbing up after it.

"Have I ever said yes to that?" Jason asked him.

"Today might be the day!"

"It isn't," Jason told him, but flicked the radio over to the Mount Isa channel so that Taylor could hear what was going on there. Not too much, as it happened.

"What's a three-one-four, Dad?" Taylor asked, listening avidly nonetheless. "A disturbance?"

"That's a three-one-three."

"Drunk!" Taylor exclaimed. "Is it a drunk?"

"It's a drunk," Jason confirmed.

Taylor raised his arms and cheered.

Jesus. The kid spent way too much time at the station, no question. And now with Dan and Gabby gone . . . *"You manage,"* he'd told Gio. You manage.

Sandra pursed her lips when Jason dropped Taylor off at her house, but she didn't say anything. She'd save it for when Taylor couldn't overhear.

"See you at ten, mate." Jason scruffed Taylor's hair.

"Okay," Taylor said, his face falling. "Bye, Dad."

Jason was managing. They both were.

The afternoon passed quickly, burning away into the sunset. The insects came out with the evening, shifting in glittering swarms around the streetlights. Jason did a few patrols through town, just to show the flag, and then returned to the station to take care of some paperwork before heading out again, this time with Gio.

Thursday night in Richmond. There was a fight at the pub that was the work of minutes to sort out—nobody seemed particularly invested in continuing once the coppers showed up—and someone smashed the front window of the bakery. The Fergusons were suspiciously quiet, but Charlie Grant and his brother George around on Racecourse Road picked up the slack for them by having a screaming match in the street. Jason watched the way Gio approached them. A little more aggressively than Jason would have—this was small-town policing, not riot control—but then Gio looked over at Jason and took his lead from him. Relaxed his posture, held one palm up in a conciliatory manner, took his other hand off his spray. It was easy enough after that to get the pair of them separated. They drove George to another relative's house in town for the night, and told him to come to the station tomorrow when he was sober if he still wanted to make a complaint against Charlie for punching him.

"Any reason we didn't bin him for drunk, Sarge?" Gio asked as they headed back to the station.

"Yeah," Jason said. "There is. It's almost ten o'clock, and I don't want to spend half the night watching a drunk snore in the cell. If that's how you want to spend your time off, feel free to arrest him next time."

Gio nodded curtly.

Fine. The next drunk job they got, Jason would let Gio take the lead. He'd figure out soon enough that the aim of the game out here was to *not* arrest anyone unless there was no alternative. The first time he had to drive a prisoner all the way to Townsville because Charters Towers was too busy to assist with the transport . . . well, that ten-hour round-trip would cure his enthusiasm for binning people. Gio would quickly learn to appreciate diversions, notices to appear, and arrests by appointment.

"You went in a little hard tonight," Jason said as they pulled up behind the station. "With the Grant boys."

Gio's expression shuttered.

A single spotlight attached to the back of the station illuminated the small car park. The spotlight created a wide column of light that was thick with long-winged flying ants and buzzing, iridescent Christmas beetles. Jason waved a few away from his face as he stepped out of the car.

"I'm not having a go." Jason dragged his vest out of the back seat, the plates in it heavy enough to pull his arm down. "But you go in like that, like you want a fight, you might get one. And this isn't the Coast. You don't have twenty other coppers right behind you ready to back you up."

Gio slung his backpack over his shoulder, and his vest over his arm. He slammed the door of the LandCruiser closed and snorted. His eyes narrowed. "Yes, Sarge."

Jason couldn't read his expression. "Gio?"

Gio straightened up. "Sorry, Sarge. Understood."

He followed Jason inside the station, and they finished up the rest of the shift in near-silence.

Taylor was a dead weight in Jason's arms as Jason carried him upstairs. He was getting too big to carry, but Jason didn't have the heart to wake him. He snuffled partly awake when Jason set him down on his bed and started carefully tugging his shirt over his head, and he wriggled out of his shorts himself, but was asleep again before Jason could get his pyjamas on him. It was hot enough that he didn't need them anyway. He could sleep in just his underwear. Their last trip to Charters Towers, they'd gone to Target, and Taylor had insisted on getting boxer briefs the same as Dad's. Although Jason's didn't have dinosaurs on them.

He eased Taylor's socks off as well, and spread the sheet out over him.

Jason leaned down and kissed Taylor on the forehead before turning the light off and leaving him to sleep.

He headed for the kitchen next, to make up Taylor's lunch for tomorrow. From the kitchen window, he could see across the yard to Gio's house. His kitchen light was on too, but Jason couldn't see him moving around.

Jason opened the fridge to hunt down the butter. He made Taylor a Vegemite sandwich for big lunch, along with an apple and some rice crackers. He threw in the revolting string cheese Taylor loved, a box of sultanas, and some SAOs—again with Vegemite, since Taylor refused to eat them any other way—for little lunch. In the morning, he'd add two juice boxes from the freezer, which would keep everything cold until it was time to eat.

He put Taylor's lunchbox back in the fridge, and then remembered too late that Taylor had asked about money for tuckshop. He went through his pocket, pulled out a dollar coin, and set it on the lid of the lunchbox so Taylor would find it in the morning. That'd be enough for an icy cup anyway, which was usually what Taylor wanted.

It was late by the time he'd finished up and then showered and changed. He slung his uniform pants and shirt over the end of his bed in case he was called out overnight. He'd throw them in the washing machine tomorrow.

He checked the house was locked up, that his phone was charging, and then crawled into bed. He reached for the book on his bedside table, but the words couldn't hold his interest, so he gave up and rolled onto his side and jammed his pillow under his neck.

Alana smiled at him from out of the frame on the bedside table.

Jason closed his eyes and drifted slowly off to sleep.

CHAPTER THREE

By his second week in Richmond, Gio was certain of one thing only: he was never going to get the hang of this place. Something of his worry must have shown on his face when they got the radio call that Thursday morning, because Sergeant Quinn's mouth twitched in a grin before he looked away.

"Can you say again, VKR?" Gio asked.

"The elderly caller has a snake in his bedroom." The voice on the radio sounded half-apologetic, and half-amused. "Unknown what sort of snake it is."

Gio stared at the radio for a moment while he waited for the punch line. And waited. And waited. Finally, he sighed. "Show us proceeding."

Sergeant Quinn's smile grew.

Gio shot him a worried look. "It's not a gee up, is it?"

"Nope." Sergeant Quinn flicked the indicator on, and slowed at the intersection of Wills Street to give way to traffic. Which, being Richmond, was a ute, a kid on a bike, and a blue cattle dog with only three legs. "If it's any consolation, if it was a gee up, they wouldn't do it over the radio."

"That's no consolation at all!"

Sergeant Quinn laughed, his eyes bright. "Are you scared of snakes, Gio?"

"Yes!" And Gio wasn't too proud to admit it either. "Isn't this a council job?"

"Nope." Sergeant Quinn turned the steering wheel, hand over hand before letting it go again as they rounded the corner and straightened up. He had strong hands, with tendons that stood out, and long fingers with blunt nails. Sunlight glinted off the gold of his wedding ring. "The council doesn't have any snake catchers. Their ranger, he'll take care of cattle, but he won't go near snakes."

"Smart bloke," Gio muttered, tearing his gaze away from the sergeant's hands.

Sergeant Quinn laughed again. "It's okay, I won't make you go in first."

The house they pulled up to was an old railway cottage with fibro walls. A cracked concrete path began at the sagging chain-link fence and cut a line through the patchy dry grass of the front garden. Three steps led up to the front door of the enclosed veranda. The wooden louvers were open to let the breeze through.

Sergeant Quinn took his heavy torch with him when he got out of the car. He pushed the squeaking gate open, and a lizard scuttled across the path in front of them, a flash of silver in the sunlight.

The occupant of the house—Jim Brown, Gio remembered from the details Comms had given over the radio—was waiting for them at the front door. Wisps of white hair stood out from his scalp like a halo of dandelion fluff. Toothpick legs protruded from his baggy shorts. The skin of his tanned, wrinkled torso appeared tough as old leather.

The steps groaned and shifted as Gio followed the sergeant up them.

"G'day, Jim," Sergeant Quinn said, taking off his hat. "This is Gio."

Gio shook the old man's hand.

"It's through here," Jim said, and led the way.

The house seemed dark at first, and the air smelled stale. It took a moment for Gio's eyes to adjust. There was a calendar hanging from a hook in the hallway, with the corners curling up. There was a bookshelf underneath it. One shelf was stacked with faded *National Geographic* magazines. The other two shelves were full of rocks.

Jim caught Gio's gaze. He reached out a bone-thin hand and picked up one of the pieces, then held it out to Gio. "You know what that is?"

Gio took the rock. It was an odd shape. It was striated. It looked more like plastic than a rock, but it was heavy. "A rock?"

"That's petrified wood," Jim said. "My daughter Trish found that back in '82. It's a good one."

Gio ran his thumb over the ridged edges of the wood, marvelling at the texture, and then handed it back to the old man.

"Used to take the kids fossicking all the time," Jim said, setting the petrified wood down again carefully. Then he nodded towards a closed door at the end of the hall. "I'll get a shovel."

Gio glanced at the door warily. There was a rolled-up towel wedged under the bottom of the door, presumably to keep the snake from vanishing elsewhere into the house.

"Any idea what sort it is?" Sergeant Quinn called as Jim vanished for a moment into one of the other rooms.

The old man reappeared a moment later, clutching the promised square-headed shovel. "I didn't get a good look at it, but it's brown."

The sergeant took the shovel and passed his torch over to Gio. "Where'd you see it last?"

"In the bottom of the cupboard," Jim said. "Gave me a hell of a fright."

"I can imagine." Sergeant Quinn put his hand on the doorknob, and drew a deep breath. "Okay."

He pushed the door open.

Gio followed him through, his hand instinctively going for his firearm. Which, *really*? Like he was going to shoot a *snake*? He shifted the heavy torch from his left hand to his right instead. The weight of it was almost comforting.

Jim's cupboard door was ajar. Gio hoped the snake was still inside, and not waiting under the bed or something, to strike out at him when he moved too close. Did snakes even do that, or had he been watching too many horror movies?

"Give us a bit of light, Gio," Sergeant Quinn said, edging nearer to the cupboard.

Gio stood shoulder to shoulder with him, angling the torch so that a shaft of light illuminated the nest of shoes in the bottom of the cupboard. Shoes, and—Gio's breath caught in his throat—a loop of shining flesh coiled around the top of a boot. The torchlight gleamed on the scales.

"Shit," Sergeant Quinn said. "Okay, so that is *not* a python. That's either a brown snake or a taipan."

"Taipan," Gio repeated, his voice flat, although a brown snake wasn't that much of a better option.

"Don't worry," Sergeant Quinn said with a smile. "I won't let you die before bingo night."

What?

"Okay," Sergeant Quinn said. "You're going to hold the torch there, and open the cupboard door for me."

Gio's stomach clenched. "I'm not liking this plan, Sarge."

Sergeant Quinn flashed him that quick smile again. "The hospital's only about four minutes away if we go lights and sirens."

"Who's gonna drive if we both get bitten?" Gio asked, inching forwards slowly. He couldn't see the snake's head, only that shining loop of scales. He had no idea how big it was, and no idea how it was actually situated in the bottom of the cupboard.

"We'll take turns," Sergeant Quinn said, and it was such a ridiculous answer that Gio huffed out a surprised laugh. The sergeant's eyes crinkled in the corners, his smile more protracted this time, and Gio's heart tumbled over a couple of erratic beats that he couldn't entirely blame on being in the presence of the world's most venomous snake. "Come on. Open the cupboard for me."

Fuck fuck *fuck*.

Gio's hand shook as he reached for the cupboard, as high up as he could without overbalancing—how high could an enraged taipan strike anyway? The only thing he could remember about taipans was the fact they didn't only bite once, they struck multiple times. Got their fangs in and just kept biting down. That, and the deadliest-snake-in-the-world thing. He kept the torch angled so that the light bounced off the scales of the snake.

"Okay," Sergeant Quinn said, his voice low. "Okay."

Gio tugged the cupboard open, and everything happened at once.

A shoe clattered out onto the floor, the snake moved, and Gio realised too late that he'd been expecting movement from the other end. The head of the snake protruded from underneath a crumpled shirt on the open side of the cupboard, and Gio hardly had a second to step back before the snake was following him at impossible speed.

Shoes and boots shifted and tumbled in the cupboard in its wake, and how the hell big was it?

There was a dull knock of pressure against Gio's left boot as the taipan struck.

Sergeant Quinn slammed the head of the shovel down, and missed. Then, regaining his balance quickly, he moved forward and stepped down on the back of the snake's head.

"Holy *shit*," Gio said, his heart thumping fast.

A good two metres of snake writhed angrily between Sergeant Quinn's boot and the cupboard, and the tail was still hidden somewhere underneath the pile of Jim's shoes and boots.

Sergeant Quinn brought the shovel down again. This time he didn't miss, neatly severing the snake's head from its body with a resounding *thunk*.

"Did it get you?" he asked, lifting his boot off the snake's head at last.

Gio looked down at his boot. There were indentations in the leather, and a shining trail of fluid sliding like a thick tear down towards the tread. Venom. "I'm okay. It got my boot, not me."

A bit higher though, and his uniform pants wouldn't have provided any protection at all.

"Show me," the sergeant said, and moved closer. He leaned the shovel against the cupboard door and went down on one knee. Gio tugged his pants up slightly, and Sergeant Quinn inspected the indentations in his boot. "Jesus."

"Yeah," Gio said as the light glinted on the venom. His heartbeat was quickening, as though his body was only now realising how close the snake had got to his skin, to his bloodstream.

Sergeant Quinn nodded, exhaling heavily. "You're good." He rose to his feet again, his hand resting briefly on Gio's knee for balance. "Jim?" he yelled. "You got a garbage bag?"

Jim produced a garbage bag, and Gio held it open as Sergeant Quinn dropped the snake in. It was heavier than he'd expected. The weight of it strained the plastic. Gio closed the bag tightly once Sergeant Quinn put the head inside, and held it at arm's length while he carried it out the back to Jim's bin.

His heart was beating fast now, adrenaline still coursing through him.

A taipan. *Shit.*

Gio clenched and unclenched his hands until they stopped shaking, and then went back into the hallway and picked up the petrified wood, just to feel something solid in his palm.

He was relieved as hell when he and Sergeant Quinn headed back to the car.

"Two-eight-nine, VKR," Gio said into the radio as Jim waved them off.

"Two-eight-nine, go."

"Show us back on," Gio said. "Job finalisation details when ready."

"Two-eight-nine, go."

"User 4028981, finalise as a job code six-zero-one," Gio said, and then put the handset back in place. He glanced at Sergeant Quinn and caught him grinning. "What?"

"You can't just leave them hanging like that," Sergeant Quinn said, and took the radio. "Two-eight-nine, VKR."

"Two-eight-nine, go ahead."

The sergeant's smile grew. "VKR, can you note on the job card that the taipan has been relocated from the premises?"

"Relocated?" the radio operator asked.

"Relocated to snake heaven," Sergeant Quinn said. "Courtesy of a shovel. I'll email the Comco the pictures."

"Ew, that's revolting," the radio operator said, sounding impressed all the same. "Send them to me as well. And I'll show you back on and patrolling, two-eight-nine."

At the end of the day, Gio sat on his front veranda with his feet up on the rail. The flies didn't seem too bad today, or Gio was getting used to them or something. He twisted the cap off his stubbie and chased a droplet of condensation that slid down the side of the bottle with his thumb. He drank the beer slowly. It was only a light, so he barely got a buzz. He wasn't on duty, and not on call tonight either, but that didn't mean he couldn't still be called out. There really was no such thing as off duty in a town where he was one of only two coppers. Gio would just add *getting drunk* to the to-do list for when he was back in civilisation. Right underneath *getting laid*. It'd been a while on both counts, and today's close encounter with the world's deadliest snake was making him acutely aware of the rut he was stuck in, or his own mortality, or YOLO or whatever. It was the sort of existential crisis that could be easily resolved by getting laid, and not by thinking about Sergeant Quinn's smile and the way his strong hands gripped the steering wheel or the radio, or the sudden warmth that had flooded through Gio when Sergeant Quinn had touched his knee.

The sound of a screen door slamming drew Gio's gaze to the Quinns' house. Taylor was heading down the front steps, barefoot, squinting into the sun from underneath a bucket hat. He was swinging his cricket bat wildly as he skipped down the steps. Sergeant Quinn followed him at a safe distance.

Taylor struck out across the yard, weaving through the tufts of scrubby grass and finally jabbing the blunt end of his bat into the dirt, sending up a puff of red dust. He scraped the bat back and forth, marking out a crease.

Gio's phone chimed and he glanced down. A text from Sophie. It was a picture of Chloe with a plate of spaghetti smooshed all over her face. The corner of his mouth tugged up as he studied it. Chloe might be a Cartwright, but she'd got the dark Valeri eyes and curls.

Gross, he sent back, and trusted that Sophie would translate it as *adorable*.

His homesickness wasn't as acute as it had been in the first week. Maybe he didn't miss the Coast anymore, though he missed Sophie and the family. He missed his dad.

The sharp *thock* of the cricket ball against the bat—and Taylor's crow of delight—pulled Gio's attention back to his immediate surroundings.

"I hit it, Dad! Did you see that? That's a six, right?"

"Yeah, mate." Sergeant Quinn laughed as he headed over to collect the ball from where it had landed against the side of their house. "That's a six."

Another smile tugged at Gio's mouth as he looked at them play. Sergeant Quinn bowled slowly, his form smooth, while Taylor swung wildly and was elated every time the bat connected. Gio watched them for a few minutes before he picked up his stubbie and walked inside again. He'd felt a little uncomfortable staring. He didn't want to risk Taylor spotting him and asking him to play. That seemed like something Taylor would do, and the last thing Gio wanted was to intrude on his boss's personal time with his kid. It was weird enough they lived in one another's pockets, wasn't it?

Fucking Richmond, seriously.

Two weeks down. One hundred and two to go.

For a small town hemmed in only by the boundless horizon, by the endless sky, Richmond was claustrophobic as hell. It was going to send Gio stir-crazy. It already was, probably. There was no other reason that Gio found himself drawn to the kitchen windows, where he could stare down unseen at the yard between the houses. Taylor had vanished from sight somewhere, but Sergeant Quinn was still standing in Gio's view, swinging the cricket bat from side to side. Gio had to lean forward to get a good look at him, and the edge of the bench pressed against his abdomen. Gio shifted back a fraction, and slid his hand underneath the waistband of his shorts to ease the dull ache. He stopped himself before he moved his hand lower, to his dick. He reached for his stubbie instead, drained the last few mouthfuls of beer in one long swig, and set the bottle down in the sink where it rattled against a lone teaspoon.

Gio stared out the window, and licked the bitter taste of the beer off his bottom lip.

Yeah, it'd been way too long since he got laid, but reaching for his dick as he watched his boss? That was not going to lead anywhere remotely healthy. Jesus. The last thing Gio needed was his boss reporting him for sexual harassment or inappropriate behaviour or whatever. Was that even what would happen out here? Maybe country coppers didn't believe in all that complaint bullshit. Maybe they sorted shit out the old-fashioned way, with their fists.

Gio snorted and turned away from the window. He dragged his hand through his hair and shook his head at his own paranoia. Sergeant Quinn had been nothing but decent to him. The problem was, he could say exactly the same thing about his colleagues down the Coast, right? Up until the moment they weren't decent anymore.

"Dog."

And why the hell would Gio think that it'd take a country copper to try to flog the shit out of him?

He clenched his shaking hands into fists.

It hadn't been a country copper last time, had it?

He closed his eyes and took a deep breath. From outside he heard the *crack* of the cricket ball against the bat again, and then Taylor's cheer, and Sergeant Quinn's laugh, and the screech of the cockatoos in the rain tree down the back. Somehow though, he could still hear Coop's voice loudest of all:

"What the fuck*, Gio? Why would you* do *that to Pete?"*

The look of betrayal had stung just as much as Coop's words, and in that moment Gio had known there was not a single fucking thing he could say to make Coop or any of the others understand. He'd thought they were his friends, but they were Pete's friends first, and they wouldn't . . . they wouldn't hear what Gio had to say. Not when they'd already decided who to blame. There had been nothing Gio could say, and then, after that, there had been no opportunity to say it anyway. Nobody talked to him after that. They'd frozen him out. Then they'd turned on him, and now here he was.

Sergeant Quinn had been nothing but decent to him, but that could change in a heartbeat. Gio didn't have friends anymore, and he sure as hell didn't have crushes.

That shouldn't have been so fucking hard to remember.

"Why would you do *that?"*

Gio took another stubbie from the fridge and headed for his bedroom, where he could close the door, crank up the rattling air-conditioning, and drown out the sounds of Sergeant Quinn and Taylor laughing outside.

CHAPTER FOUR

Gio seemed to pick things up pretty quickly: the names of the streets, businesses, and the landmarks around town. The property names outside of town still eluded him, but Jason saw him checking the maps at the station sometimes to at least try to place the larger properties. On a rare Monday day shift they were rostered together, Jason decided that now was as good a time as any to do a proper tour of the division.

"Weapons' audits," he explained. "Figured we'd do the rounds. Take you out to a few of the properties, and maybe the mine as well."

A few of the properties. That was no exaggeration. Most of the cattle properties were so vast they wouldn't be able to cover more than a few in an eight-hour shift. Jason phoned the owners first, not just to make sure they knew he and Gio were coming out so it wasn't a wasted trip, but also to check if there was anything the residents wanted brought out from town.

"You like scones, right?" he asked Gio when they were finally loaded up and ready to go.

Gio gave him a sideways look, and Jason laughed. There was no way they'd be allowed to leave any of these stations without being fattened up like poddy calves, and Gio was about to learn that. They'd probably come home stacked up with leftovers as well.

The tyres flung up waves of red dust as they headed north out of town. It billowed behind them, a plume, and then settled over the road again like a shroud.

Weapons' audits were a pain in the arse—and it wasn't like anyone was going to fail them, since Jason always gave them fair warning he was coming—but they needed to be done all the same. In the city, it might be possible to knock over fifteen or so on a dedicated shift. Here they'd be lucky if they managed five or six, but there were worse things than being paid to drive all over the division for a day.

Jason hadn't grown up in country like this, full of red dirt and spinifex, but it was home now. He'd been born in Cairns—mud flats and mangroves—and gone to university in Townsville where he'd met Alana. They'd got serious quickly. They'd moved in together by graduation. Jason had worked at Coles for a year after graduating, supporting Alana while she'd struggled through her first year of kindergarten teaching, and she'd supported him in turn when he'd applied to the academy. They'd got married the same week Jason had been sworn in as a police officer. Instead of a honeymoon, they'd packed up and driven to Mount Isa, neither of them with any idea what to expect. They'd figured they would go where their jobs took them and end up on the coast again one day. They'd only made it as far as Richmond.

Jason glanced at his wedding ring as he drove. He'd never taken it off. It had never occurred to him to do so, apart from a panicked moment a few days after Alana died when he'd suddenly been overwhelmed by the fact that he was no longer married. That she was gone and he'd never see her again. Worst of all had been how he'd kept having to explain it to Taylor, who'd been too little to really understand.

"I want Mummy! I want Mummy!"

Screaming it and thrashing in Jason's hold like Jason had been somehow withholding her from him. Like Jason was someone he could blame for this. Because up until that moment, Daddy had been the guy who could fix anything, right? He could repair busted toys, he could put Band-Aids on skinned knees, and he could even check under the bed for monsters, but he hadn't been able to fix this. He hadn't been able to bring Mummy back. Some days Jason wondered if that was the sort of loss of faith a kid could just bounce back from. It had to leave a scar, didn't it? Something that big. He looked at Taylor sometimes and worried he was damaged in places Jason couldn't see.

God knew Jason was. The ache in his chest when he thought of Alana, when he thought of Taylor growing up without her . . . that ache had never gone away.

Jason tightened his grip on the steering wheel and glanced over at Gio. Gio had his iPad out, checking the rego of the ute travelling in front of them. Well, it was probably the station iPad. Jason rarely used it, but Gio was from the Coast, where they were used to getting all the latest technology rolled out first. Jason was resisting using QLiTE until Comms started sending him jobs through the app. He was lucky to get two or three jobs dispatched to him via radio on a busy shift anyway. QLiTE wasn't going to streamline anything for him, or cut down on his already infrequent radio traffic. He'd still get most of his jobs the old-fashioned way: by people phoning the station directly, or turning up on his doorstep.

Gio slid the iPad back into the console between their seats. "There's not really much traffic to check out here."

"Not a lot," Jason agreed. "Bit different than on the Gold Coast, right?"

"Yeah." Gio's mouth twitched in a brief smile. "You ever worked down there?"

"Not my speed," Jason said. "I went to the academy in Townsville, did my first year in Mount Isa, then went down to Clermont, then here."

"You've been here a while?"

"Taylor was born here." *Alana died here.* "It's home."

Gio didn't seem to have anything to say to that. He avoided Jason's gaze and stared out at the flat, straight highway that cut through the red dirt and the spinifex.

It was home.

Eucalypts, thin bunches of leaves hanging, seemed to wilt in the heat. Brown and gold clumps of grass dotted the sides of the highway, dry as kindling. When the rains came, the plains would be flooded and vibrant green with new life once the water receded, but for now the land was parched.

The narrow highway north of town was two lanes, with hardly any shoulder at all. The edges of the bitumen just dropped sharply off into the dirt. On the rare occasions they met traffic coming the other way Jason hugged the left side of the road tightly. About half an hour out of town, an approaching road train drove a dust storm ahead of it, and Jason slowed to a crawl. Even then it almost shook the police LandCruiser off the road.

"Do you get a lot of accidents out here?" Gio asked, reaching for the handle above his seat.

"A few," Jason said, accelerating once the road train was behind them. "Tourists, mostly, who don't know how to drive for the conditions. Our roads are shit, and some of them are used to driving on the autobahn."

They bounced over a pothole, and everything in the back seat shifted.

Jason watched the odometer click over, and tried to remember if getting to know his previous partners had been punctuated by as many awkward silences. The only time Gio had seemed to loosen up a little was when they'd been about to go in and face the taipan in Jim Brown's bedroom. And no way in hell did Jason want to have to do something like that every shift just to bond with his new senior constable. Some things really weren't worth dying for.

"So what about you?" he asked as they passed a weather-beaten sign marking the turnoff to Hidden Creek. "You ever worked outside the southeast corner?"

Gio shook his head. "Academy at Oxley, then the Coast. This . . ." He released the handle above the door to drag his fingers through his dark curls. "This was never in the plan."

"Plans are overrated." Jason shrugged.

Gio didn't look convinced.

Baxter Mine was a little over two hundred kilometres from town. About three hours because of the condition of the roads. The mine, Jason told Gio as they approached, didn't have much to do with the town. Their workers weren't locals: they were from Townsville and Mackay, mostly, FIFO —fly in, fly out. The mine had its own runway. Apart from attending the occasional industrial accident or dispute between workers that mine security couldn't sort out, Jason didn't head to the mine often, but it was still a part of his more than 60,000-square-kilometre beat. The number did absolutely nothing to communicate the vastness of the division. That could only be learned by hours in the car, watching the dust paint a sunset vivid red, or the first stars come out in a sky that never ended.

Baxter was an open-cut gold mine, a gaping wound on the surface of the earth. Trucks inched up and down the steep inclines carved into the sides. Jason and Gio didn't make it as far as the actual mine today. Instead they looked at the framed pictures of it hanging on the walls of the administration building. The air conditioner hummed and buzzed. Condensation fogged up the windows. Jason's sweat chilled as the woman behind the desk made a call for someone to come and meet them. It was a few minutes before a guy appeared.

"John, right?" he asked. The guy was too clean to be anything but management. Shoes too shiny.

"Jason," Jason corrected him. "And this is Gio. He's new. I'm showing him around."

"Hi." The guy was young, with reddish hair and a smattering of freckles across his nose. He had a firm handshake and a gaze that lingered on Gio. Curious, maybe. He wasn't wearing a wedding ring, and Jason didn't really want to analyse the reasons why he'd noticed that, but it had something to do with the way the guy was *still* looking at Gio. "I'm Richard. Richard Hanna. Operations manager."

"Nice to meet you," Gio said, and flashed him a smile that was brighter than any Jason had seen. Faking it to appear friendly, or was that what his smiles were like when he wasn't stuck in a car with his boss? Another thing that Jason didn't need to analyse.

"You too," Richard said, leaning in a little closer towards Gio. "Do you want a tea or a coffee? Or something cold? It's another stinker out there."

"Thanks," Gio said, and his left cheek puckered with a dimple when his smile widened.

Was this flirting? And Jesus, was Jason so out of practice that he didn't even recognise it anymore? He was thirty-eight, not dead, but right now he felt exactly as old as Taylor had thought he was the day Taylor had discovered Jason had grown up without the internet. *And* mobile phones.

They drank their coffee in a small meal room past the main offices. There was a TV on the wall, and a stack of newspapers on the large laminate table. There was an open packet of Arnott's Family Assorted biscuits on the table. The packet had been looted, with only Scotch Fingers left behind.

Richard regarded the packet dubiously. "I think we've got, ah, some cake somewhere."

"I'm good, thanks," Gio said.

"Gotta stay in shape in your work, I s'pose," Richard said, and looked Gio up and down. "Not that you need to worry about that."

Gio's dimple appeared again.

Jason raised his eyebrows. That was definitely flirting. Pretty shithouse flirting, but flirting all the same.

The phone in his pocket began to buzz, and he turned away from them.

"Excuse me," he said, digging the phone out and stepping out into the corridor. It was a local number, but not one he had in his contacts. It was his personal mobile, and a few people around town had the number, but most work-related calls came through on the station mobile. He also had a satellite phone in the car. For a kid who'd grown up without a mobile, he had them coming out of his arse now, didn't he? He accepted the call. "Hello?"

"This is Leanne Fisher. I'm calling from the school. Is this Taylor's dad?"

"Yeah." Two hundred kilometres and three hours from town, Jason's blood ran cold. "What's happened? Is he okay?"

"He's fine," Sandra said when they made it back to town at last, and to the station. "He's in your office, reading."

He wasn't. When Jason found Taylor, he was curled up on the narrow bench in the holding cell, a blanket pulled around him and Jason's spare jacket bundled under his head for a pillow. He looked so small. Jason crouched down beside him and put a hand on his hot forehead. Smoothed his damp hair back.

Taylor snuffled awake. "Dad?"

"How you feeling, mate?"

Taylor wrinkled his nose and stretched. He was wearing a different shirt than the one Jason had sent him off to school in. This one was faded to almost pink, and at least two sizes too big. "I projectile vomited all over my desk. And all over Cassidy. She won't want to sit next to me anymore. It was really gross, Dad."

"I thought you sat next to Kane." Kane was Taylor's best friend.

"Cassidy sits on my other side." Taylor worried his lower lip with his teeth. "I probably should have thrown up on Kane instead."

"Probably." Jason fought a smile as he stroked Taylor's hair. "Do you feel better now?"

"Sandra took me to the doctor. I have a stomach bug." Taylor brightened. "Can I stay home from school tomorrow and watch TV?"

"We'll see how you feel in the morning," Jason said, but it was probably a given. He was supposed to be working again, but he'd take a day's leave. "Come on, mate. Let's get you home."

Jason avoided Sandra's gaze as he ushered Taylor out of the station. There'd be nothing in it he didn't already know.

Taylor grumbled about his sore stomach as they walked home.

When they got there, Jason put Taylor in a lukewarm bath and then headed down the back stairs and underneath the house. He very carefully untied the garbage bag the school had sent home with Taylor. Taylor's shirt was a stinking vomit-filled mess, and Jason held his breath while he dug it out of the bag, then retied the bag quickly and tossed it in the bin. He rinsed the shirt out under the tap in the laundry sink, then threw it into the washing machine.

When he got upstairs again, Taylor had left a trail of wet footprints from the bathroom to his bedroom. He was lying facedown on his bed wearing only a pair of dinosaur underpants.

"Taylor. You're not sleeping like that. Get into bed properly."

Taylor rolled onto his back and whined. "But, Daaad!" A wavering trill that would make an opera singer proud. "It's not even dark yet!"

Jason snorted. The kid who was so wrung out he'd face-planted on his bed thought he was staying up until his usual bedtime, did he? Right. "Get under the sheets. You don't have to go to sleep. You can read, or you can play Minecraft, and I'll make you some toast and Vegemite, okay? You should be able to keep that down."

"Okay. And a bucket, just in case?"

"Good thinking." Jason helped Taylor tug his sheets up, and then headed for the kitchen to put some toast on.

He loved his town and he loved his job, but Jesus, it wasn't fair on Taylor. It wasn't fair on Sandra, either, was it? Jason should have been the one to pick his sick son up from school and take him to the doctor, not Sandra. Jason had always told himself he was managing, but how much of that was bullshit? Because now that Dan and Gabby had left, he was seeing, for the first time, exactly how much he'd relied on them, particularly on Gabby. How many times had he collected Taylor from Dan and Gabby's house after a late shift, and carried him, still sleeping, across the scrubby yard between their houses? And how many times had he been called out in the middle of the night, and led a yawning, snuffling Taylor over to Dan and Gabby's house so that he didn't have to leave him alone? How many times had he and Dan arrived home from some shitty all-nighter of a job to find Taylor talking Gabby's ear off while they ate breakfast together? Jason had never actually been a single parent, had he? Not with Dan and Gabby right next door.

From the moment Dan put in his transfer to Cairns, Jason should have been looking for proper childcare for Taylor. As much as he tried to juggle between after-school care, between Kane's parents and Sandra, and letting Taylor hang out at the station, there were always going to be gaps. And it really wasn't fair to expect Sandra to step up every time, like she had today.

It wasn't fair on Taylor either.

Jason needed to sort out something permanent.

Like a nanny?

That sounded... expensive. And it wasn't as though Taylor needed round-the-clock childcare. He just needed there to be someone at home when Jason couldn't be there for him because of his job. The options in Richmond were hardly great, though. Ideally, Jason wanted someone who could watch Taylor at the house, but Richmond was not an environment rich with reliable people seeking housing options. Jason had lived in towns before where kids from rural properties lived in town during the week for school, rather than commute several hours a day for school, but Richmond State School only went as high as year ten. Kids went to boarding school after that, most to Charters Towers but some farther afield. Otherwise, a high school senior would have been ideal. It would be difficult to find someone other than a student who didn't already have their own family responsibilities, and it wasn't like Jason was going to hire a random procession of backpackers to sleep in his spare room and look after his kid. Although Taylor would probably enjoy that. He could learn to talk the ear off people in multiple different languages.

Jason wasn't comfortable with the idea of sending Taylor to someone else's house overnight when he was on call either, but that was his next best option. His only option, probably. He needed a retiree who had a flexible routine and a spare room, or a parent who could chuck a mattress on their kid's floor for Taylor. Jason had resisted looking so far though, since it felt like an admission of failure. Intellectually he knew it was no different than relying on Sandra or on Kane's parents, but emotionally it felt bigger than that.

Hadn't he promised Alana he'd look after their son?

Jason scraped Vegemite onto Taylor's toast. The knife clinked against his wedding ring.

It wasn't fair on Taylor. Not with the hours he worked. Maybe it was time to look into transferring, to going somewhere big enough that he could plant himself in an office and work eight to four, Monday to Friday for a couple of years at least. So that he could drop Taylor off at school and pick him up again. So that he wouldn't get called out in the middle of the night. So that he could be there for his son.

He screwed the lid back on the Vegemite, and swallowed down the ache in his throat. His son was the most important thing in his life, and today he'd been three hours away when Taylor had needed him. That wasn't right.

He poured Taylor half a cup of apple juice from the fridge and topped it up with water, hoping it wouldn't be too much for his upset stomach, and then carried the cup and the plate of toast into Taylor's room for him.

Taylor was already asleep.

Jason left the juice for him in case he woke up, and carried the toast back into the kitchen. He was eating it over the sink, the crumbs bouncing against the steel, when he heard footsteps on the back stairs. Moments later, someone rapped on the frame of the screen door.

"Sarge?"

Gio. Jason wiped crumbs off his shirt and headed to the back door to open it. Gio was still in uniform. Finishing up the shift that Jason hadn't.

"I'm going to do a patrol through town," he said. "Did you need anything from the chemist for Taylor?"

Jason tried not to let his surprise show. "No, we're good, I think. Thanks."

"Okay."

"I'm rostered an eight to four tomorrow," Jason said. "I won't be in."

"Okay," Gio said again, nodding. "Do you want me to change my shift, or still work my two to ten?"

"I'll keep you on your two to ten," Jason said. "But if you let Comms know you'll be on call tomorrow morning in case a job comes in?"

"No worries, Sarge." Gio stepped back out of the doorway. "If you think of something you need from down the street, give me a call."

"Thanks," Jason repeated, and closed the door after him.

Gio Valeri was a puzzle. If Jason didn't know his history, he wouldn't have hesitated to let his guard down around him and try to build a real friendship instead of just the basic courtesy they needed to be able to work together. Gio seemed like a decent guy—which was probably what his former colleagues down south had thought right up until the moment he'd stuck a knife in the back of one of them.

Jason moved into the living room. From the front windows, he could see across the yard to the rear of the station. He watched Gio walk across the scrubby grass. He had his phone out, and was texting someone. Jason wondered if it was a family member, or a friend—did Gio have any friends?—or if it was Richard Hanna from Baxter Mine. He'd given Gio his card before Gio and Jason had left in a rush.

Jason knew very little about Gio Valeri. But you kept your distance from a guy like that, right? You made sure the snake wasn't in striking distance when you inched open the cupboard door. Jason remembered the bead of venom that had slid down the side of Gio's boot like a shining teardrop. Or, if you couldn't keep your distance from the snake because it was your bloody job to deal with it, you made sure you were protected. That was common sense.

Jason sat down on the couch and turned the TV on. He flicked through the channels until he found the cricket, although he didn't actually give a fuck about the score, or even who was playing. The drone of the commentary was soothing.

He put his feet on the coffee table and rolled his shoulders in a vain attempt to get rid of some of the day's tension, and closed his eyes.

When he woke up later it was dark, and Taylor was cuddling into him, a little furnace pressed tightly against his side. His head was jammed under Jason's arm, like he'd burrowed in like a tick. Jason shifted carefully, and Taylor yawned and grumbled himself awake.

"How are you feeling?" Jason asked him.

"You were gonna make me toast," Taylor said, his face still screwed up as he blinked around the room. "What happened to my toast?"

Well, his appetite was back. That had to be a positive sign, right?

"I'll go and make you some now," Jason said. He tightened his arm around his son briefly. "With Vegemite?"

"Durr," Taylor said with an accompanying eye roll, which was probably a yes.

They'd talk about his attitude if he kept the toast down.

CHAPTER FIVE

By his third week in Richmond, Gio felt like maybe he was finding his feet. He could finally locate everything around the station without having to ask Sandra every time—like telling him where the envelopes were kept was such a hardship for her—and was starting to recognise a few of the more familiar faces around town. And not just the grubs either. He knew the publicans now, the woman at the bakery, the man at the newsagent, and of course Vicki, the ambo. She was divorced, in her late thirties, with a crooked smile and a riot of frizzy blonde hair that was usually trying to escape her bun. Gio spent most of his shifts, particularly those on a Friday or a Saturday, shadowing her around town, where he could make sure she didn't get into any shit. Or, if she did, that he was right there to dive in and assist. In an ideal world, nobody would punch the paramedic who was only there to help them, but it wasn't an ideal world, was it?

"You stalkin' me because I'm a sheila, Gio?" she asked him one night at the pub as she strapped the hand of some drunk who'd managed to put his hand through his beer glass.

"I'm stalking you because you work alone," he told her, "and you're surrounded by drunks."

"Fair enough." She shoved the guy's arm towards him. "Keep this elevated."

He was settling in, Gio supposed, or giving up the fight or something. It was a little hard to tell the difference. For a while he continued to avoid Sophie's calls—shift work was a good excuse for that—but he sent her a photograph of sunrise one morning, the river ablaze with light.

Not quite the hellish dystopia I was picturing, she sent back and whatever walls he'd put up in the last few months crumbled, and they were suddenly communicating again. It was good. He'd missed it.

I'm never going to get laid in this town, he sent her one night.

Talk to the hand, she sent back. *Yours, not mine.*

He fell into a routine with work, and at home. In the afternoons when he wasn't working, he'd sit out on the front veranda to catch the breeze, a mug of coffee in one hand and a book in the other. Catching the breeze also meant catching the flies though, and Gio learned very quickly to check there were none swimming in his coffee before he took a gulp.

Often Taylor was riding his bike in circles in the scrubby yard, or digging holes, or poking around with a stick, eking out the last of the golden light before the sun dipped below the horizon. Then he'd climb up the back stairs of his house, and the screen door would slam in the frame. Sometimes, if the breeze was right, Gio could hear the murmur of voices from the Quinns' house as they talked over dinner, and the scrape and *clink* of cutlery across plates.

There was obviously no wife in the picture. Not with the way Taylor hung around at the station at all hours if his dad was working. Not with the conversation Gio overheard one afternoon when he was starting his shift and Sergeant Quinn was finishing.

"I'm not his mother, Jason," Sandra said, her usual brusque tone tempered with something like pity. "I'm not yours either."

Gio froze with his hand raised to knock on the sergeant's office door. He hadn't noticed it was ajar.

"Sandra, I know it's not ideal, but—"

"You need to make other arrangements," Sandra said, cutting him off. "Babysitting Taylor is not part of my job description."

Gio slunk back to the dayroom, where Taylor was working on his homework and chewing on his pencil. Taylor scratched his head, and a small shower of red dirt rained onto the table. Jesus. Did he *roll* in it? Gio probably didn't want to know the answer to that.

It was Vicki who filled him in later that evening, when he stopped in at the ambulance station to see if she wanted him to pick up a coffee when he went past the truck stop. She elected to come with him instead, switching on her handheld radio in case she got a call, and climbing into the passenger side of the police LandCruiser.

They grabbed their coffee and an early dinner at the truck stop, sitting at the scratched laminate tables in the rundown café area, and watching the slow parade of trucks and cars and caravans pass through into the night. Vicki tore open three paper sachets of sugar and stirred them into her coffee.

"Thought it was Jason's turn to work tonight," she said, her spoon scraping against the side of her paper cup.

"He asked to swap," Gio said. "I don't mind."

"Right," Vicki said, thin mouth turning up in a smile. "Because you've got nothing better to do with your evenings than come to work?"

"I actually don't," Gio said, picking at his chips.

"Oh, please. I saw that backpacker girl flashing her tits at you last night." Vicki snorted. "You could pull without even trying."

Gio didn't know what to say. His hesitation said it all, he supposed.

"Jesus," Vicki said at last, and slurped at her coffee. "The poor women of this town. Two single cops, except you're not buying what they're selling, and Jason's still in love with his dead wife. And they were relying on you guys, Gio. We don't have any proper firemen!"

Gio jolted with surprise, both for the way that Vicki had picked up on his orientation and just rolled with it, and for the way she'd dropped the fact that Sergeant Quinn was a widower into the conversation as bluntly as she had. *"Jason's still in love with his dead wife."* But tact wasn't exactly Vicki's strong suit. Gio had figured that out within minutes of meeting her.

"I didn't know that," he said.

"Four years now," Vicki said, and then paused. Her forehead crinkled and she stirred her coffee again. "No. Five. Five years."

Outside, hydraulic brakes hissed as a B-double pulled off the highway.

Vicki pursed her lips and seemed to shake herself awake. "I'm gonna order some more chips. Want some?"

"I'm good." He watched her head back to the counter, and checked his watch. It wasn't even 7 p.m. yet. Gonna be a boring shift.

Famous last words.

His hands were shaking. Delayed shock, or adrenaline dump, or whatever. It had just been a pub fight. Nothing Gio hadn't dealt with before, except this time he'd been on his own. He'd taken an elbow to the jaw before he'd managed to spray the guy—and copped a secondary exposure himself—and he'd barely managed to blurt into the radio that he needed help before he'd been on the ground.

What a fucking mess.

Gio sat on the examination table in the hospital. His eyes were still stinging, and his jaw was swollen. Outside, he could hear someone complaining loudly that he didn't need a bloody doctor, thanks very much. It sounded like Gio's new best mate, Barry. Barry was sixty years old if he was a day, and full as a tick, but he'd helped Gio hold his assailant down—while the security guard had yelled at the guy's mates to back the fuck off—until Sergeant Quinn had arrived sixteen minutes later.

Sixteen minutes was a long fucking time to be rolling around on the floor, eyes burning, while some asshole tried to grab for his gun.

The curtain rattled on the rail as it was pulled back.

"How are you feeling?" Vicki asked for what must've been the hundredth time. "Put your head back."

Gio held a towel around his neck as she began to flush his eyes out for the third time since arriving at the hospital. "Is Barry okay?"

Vicki snorted, and squirted more water into his eyes. "He'll be getting free drinks out of this story for months. You've made his year."

Gio smiled despite himself.

"Wait here. I'll go and track down the doc. See if he's ready to give you the okay to get the hell out of here." The curtain rattled again as she left him.

Gio's hands were still shaking. He curled his fingers into loose fists to try to control it. In his pocket, his phone started to buzz. He pulled it out, struggling not to drop it, and squinted blearily at the screen. A private number. "Hello?"

"Giovanni?" a gruff voice asked.

A stranger's voice. Gio tensed, damp fingers slipping as he gripped the phone tighter. "Who's this?"

"This is Senior Sergeant Gordon," the man growled. "District duty officer."

Gio winced. Fuck. Fuck his life. "Sorry, sir."

"That's alright." His voice was still a growl. "You've had a rough night. I'm calling to check how you're travelling. You still at the hospital?"

"Yes, sir." He'd been injured on a job. The DDO in Townsville had to contact him. He'd probably have a call from the inspector tomorrow, and the HSO, and whoever the hell else needed to climb on the officer welfare bandwagon and pretend they gave a fuck. Just so Gio couldn't sue them later down the track.

"Well, you're talking, so I'm guessing your jaw's not broken."

"Just bruised."

"Take the rest of the night off, and as long as the doctor says."

"Yes, sir."

"Righto, then. Welcome to the district, and try not to get flogged again."

"I'll try, sir."

The DDO grunted and ended the call.

It was almost 5 a.m. by the time Gio made it back to the station. He was tired, and his whole body ached from his impromptu wrestling match. He headed straight to the armoury, to get rid of his Glock and taser. Sergeant Quinn had already seized his empty canister of spray, because of course there'd be an investigation. Just what Gio needed. Fuck. He'd barely made it through the last one. How many people would use this as an opportunity to fuck him up completely? To get rid of him, even though he hadn't done anything wrong. Not back then, and not tonight, but he was a troublemaker, wasn't he? A whistle-blower. And despite the lip service all the bosses paid to being fair and ethical and transparent, Gio knew they wanted him gone.

He locked his weapons up, and then headed for the shower room. His locker was beside Sergeant Quinn's. Gio couldn't get the key in the lock. His hands were still shaking. He closed his eyes and leaned his forehead against the cool metal surface of his locker door.

Fuck.

Fuck fuck fuck.

What was it Sergeant Quinn had said that time?

"This isn't the Coast. You don't have twenty other coppers right behind you ready to back you up."

Tonight wasn't the fucking issue. Not the fucking issue at all. The issue was that two months ago, Gio had waded into a brawl on Orchid Avenue, and there should have been at least three other coppers behind him. Coop, his partner for the shift, and Carlos and Sarah, who'd turned up at the incident at the same time. By the time Gio had realised they weren't backing him up, it had been too late to turn around.

"What are you bitching for?" Coop had said later, flashing his wide, easygoing smile. It didn't reach his eyes. *"You had it under control, mate. Don't be such a drama queen."*

That was the trick with those arseholes, wasn't it? They never did anything, said anything, that they couldn't later argue that Gio had misinterpreted. They'd swear blind that Gio had never been in danger—and maybe he hadn't, but who knew better than coppers how quickly a situation could turn to shit?—and that if he was offended by being called a drama queen, well, he was just being oversensitive. Coop said stuff like that to everyone. It was only a joke. What was Gio's problem that he couldn't take a joke?

"Gio?"

Gio spun around quickly, his heart thumping, to see Sergeant Quinn standing beside him. He hadn't even heard him approach.

"Are you okay?" The sergeant's gaze tracked over him, lingering on his bruised cheek.

Gio curled his trembling fingers around his keys. "Yeah, Sarge. Just tired."

Sergeant Quinn held his hand out. "The key sticks sometimes."

It probably fucking didn't, but Gio lifted his arm and dropped his bundle of keys into Sergeant Quinn's hand anyway. He shuffled aside, leaning back against the sergeant's locker as the sergeant slid the key into the lock and turned it. The door grated and squealed as Sergeant Quinn tugged it open.

"That's got it." Sergeant Quinn's mouth quirked in a slight smile, and the skin at the corners of his eyes crinkled. "Finish up here and head on home."

Gio fumbled with his utility belt. "Do you want help with the paperwork, Sarge?"

"Go home, Gio." Sergeant Quinn put a hand on Gio's shoulder. Squeezed gently. "It's been a rough night."

It had just been a couple of punches, Gio wanted to tell him, and a secondary exposure to the spray. Except he wasn't sure he'd be able to say it without his voice shaking, and he didn't want the sergeant to think he couldn't handle himself in a pub fight. Didn't want him to think he was so easily shaken up.

A drama queen.

"Go on," Sergeant Quinn said, and dropped his hand.

It wasn't until Gio was halfway across the scrubby paddock that separated the station from the houses, the stars wheeling in the vast field above him, that he did the maths.

Sixteen minutes it had taken Jason Quinn to get from his house to the pub in the middle of the night, and get kitted up on the way. Sixteen minutes where time had lost all meaning for Gio. The wait had been interminable, but at the same time somehow over in the blink of an eye as he and Barry struggled with the guy on the floor of the pub. Even with the cuffs on, the arsehole hadn't stopped fighting. Sixteen minutes for the sergeant to be there, from bed to boots on. It hadn't been much time at all.

It certainly hadn't been enough time to get a babysitter for Taylor.

Gio didn't sleep well, despite his painkillers. He tossed and turned until dawn, and then gave up and climbed out of bed.

Got assaulted last night, he texted Sophie.

His phone started to ring almost immediately.

"What happened, bambino?" Her voice was pitched high with concern. "Are you okay?"

Jesus. Now he felt like a total arsehole for not having spoken to her in so long.

"I'm okay. I just have a bruised jaw. And I'm not your bambino." This was a fight they'd been having for years. If Sofia Giulia Valeri had decided when she was twelve that she wanted to be called

Sophie instead—and later completed her disguise by marrying Ian Cartwright—then she didn't get to come over all Italian when it suited her and call him bambino.

She'd never had a counterargument so much as she'd always had a *fuck off, Gio.*

"Oh, Gio." She sighed down the phone. "Why'd you have to move so far away?"

For once, the words didn't come with a sharp edge of blame.

"I just needed a change, Soph," he said, and closed his eyes.

"Is it because you and Pete broke up?"

"Yeah." Because he and Pete broke up. Because Gio had ruined Pete's career, his future, and at the same time had destroyed every friendship and professional relationship he'd ever built.

"Gio." She sighed again. "Does it totally suck out there?"

He managed a slight laugh at that. "It does this morning."

Sophie made a sympathetic sound.

Gio leaned against the back doorway, catching the slight breeze that whispered through the screen door. A flock of cockatoos, silhouetted by the pink and orange sky, settled in the rain tree at the back of the block, dangling from the branches as they screamed at one another. He could see the back of the Quinns' house from here. Taylor's bike was dumped at the bottom of the back steps. A cat, too skinny and furtive to be anyone's pet, slunk out from underneath the house as Gio watched, and then darted away.

Gio closed his stinging eyes. "How's the family?"

"You mean, 'How's Dad?'"

He rubbed a hand over his forehead. "Yeah. How's Dad?"

"We went to visit him on the weekend. He kept calling me Lucia."

Their mother's name. "Shit," he murmured.

"It's hard, Gio," she said. "I wish you hadn't left. Maybe he'd be better if you were here . . ."

Gio knew his father wouldn't be any better if he were there. But Sophie might. For things like that, family was supposed to step up. They were supposed to lean on one another. Gio was supposed to be there for her.

"I'll visit as often as I can," he said, even if the thought of the drive made him want to cringe. He could drive as far as Townsville, maybe, and fly down. "This is just . . ." He drew a breath. "This is something I had to do, Soph."

She was silent for a long moment.

"I know," she said at last. "I know. For the record though, your timing sucks."

"Yeah," he said, his throat aching. "I know."

At a little past eight thirty in the morning, Gio heard the screen door at the Quinns' house slam in the frame. He opened his back door and looked across to the house, in time to see Taylor heading down the stairs in his school shirt, shorts, hat, and backpack. He jumped off the last step onto the ground, raising a cloud of dust, then set off towards the road.

Maybe it was just the oversized backpack, but he suddenly seemed very small.

CHAPTER SIX

Jason would have preferred not to use his day off to drive a prisoner to Charters Towers, but Gio had to go and get himself assaulted, didn't he? Not that it had been his fault. Kev Lindeman hated coppers. He'd had a go at Jason one night, high on ice and armed with a knife to boot—Dan had tasered him. Lit him up like a Christmas tree. Apparently Kev's previous experience with Richmond's finest, and his six months in prison for waving the knife around in public, hadn't taught him how to pull his head in. Gio had been lucky that Barry had been happy to dive in and help.

Jason did some paperwork at the station until he saw that Taylor had headed off for school okay, and then got Kev Lindeman out of his cell.

The three hours to Charters Towers was painful. Kev was still sobering up, or coming down, or both, and wasn't happy to find himself in the pod in the back of the LandCruiser. He spent most of the drive yelling and kicking at the sides of the pod. Jason made sure he hit every pothole he could find.

He radioed the guys in Charters Towers when he was about fifteen minutes away, and they met him at the back of their station and hauled Kev out. He could cool his heels in their holding cell for a while, until they were ready to take him halfway to Townsville. They were waiting on the call from the Townsville crew before proceeding.

Sometimes police work was police work. Sometimes it was a fucking taxi service.

"How's your new senior connie going, Sarge?" one of the guys asked him.

Jason shrugged and made a noncommittal sound.

"I've got a mate on the Coast," the second guy said, and they fell into silence. Probably because Jason hadn't given them enough to read the situation yet. Did they shit on Gio or not? Jason wasn't in the mood to encourage them.

"Thanks, fellas," he said.

"You heading back already?"

"Yeah," Jason said, and flashed them a grin. "Day off. Can't you tell?"

Jason didn't go straight back. Taylor would never forgive him if he found out Jason had been all the way to the Towers and hadn't got him Maccas. Jason went through the drive-through and loaded up on cheeseburgers. They microwaved *reasonably* well out of the freezer. For certain values of reasonable. Taylor liked them anyway.

On the drive back, unwrapping a cheeseburger awkwardly against the steering wheel, Jason thought of Gio. He'd looked spooked last night. Not when Jason had raced into the pub to back him up after getting the call from Comms, but in the locker room at the station when it had all been over.

Shit.

Jason wanted to like the guy, wanted to work well with him—he wanted to reassure him and be on his side when he got hurt on the job—but how the hell could he do that when everyone knew Gio couldn't be trusted?

Red dust billowed behind him as he headed west again.

The familiar conversational tones of the ABC's morning presenter carried Jason back to Richmond, interrupted here and there by blasts of chatter from the CB radio that was set up to listen to the truckies, and the back and forth of job details between Comms and Charters Towers on the police radio. The blast of static had been part of the soundtrack of Jason's life for years now.

When Jason got back, it was just past midday. He parked the LandCruiser behind the station, checked in with Sandra to let her know he was back and make sure there was nothing that needed his attention, then headed home. The sun beat down as he walked, and the thick soles of his boots crunched against the clumps of dry grass. Flies buzzed around him, attracted to his bag of cheeseburgers.

Jason waved them away, clamping his mouth shut to avoid inhaling one of the little bastards. They were getting bad again, but they were preferable to the mosquitoes that would come once the rain did. Anything was preferable to the mosquitoes.

Jason climbed the front steps and unlocked the door.

The air inside the house was still and warm. Jason turned on the ceiling fan in the lounge room as he made his way inside. It clicked and whirred as the blades began to spin. Jason went through to the kitchen and stashed the bag of cheeseburgers in the freezer. Taylor would never look behind the frozen broccoli, not in a million years.

There was a bad smell coming from the rubbish bin in the corner of the kitchen. Jason poked the lid warily, dislodging a lazy couple of stench-drunk blowflies and a wave of something rancid.

"Jesus." Jason grabbed the spray from under the sink and blasted the flies. Then he carefully lifted the lid off the bin and pulled the edges of the bag shut, shutting in the offending tuna tin.

That bloody cat.

That bloody *kid*.

Jason had told Taylor not to feed the stray that had been hanging around, and he'd promised he wouldn't, but Jason had noticed tins of tuna were finding their way into the trolley at the weekly grocery shop. And he didn't need to be a cop to figure out why.

Jason snorted as he let himself out the back door and went downstairs to dump the bag in the wheelie bin. Taylor might be constantly gobsmacked at the way Dad saw through all his schemes, but he was ten. He wasn't anywhere near as sneaky as he thought he was.

Jason disposed of the bag, and then picked up Taylor's bike from where he'd left it lying at the bottom of the steps and leaned it against the back of the house. Then, glancing over at Gio's house, he sighed and set off across the yard.

A bronze skink scuttled out of his way.

Gio's car was parked under the house. The back steps creaked as Jason climbed them, and he could hear a movie or a video game with explosions playing in the background. He rapped on the screen door. "You home, Gio?"

The sound cut out, and a moment later, Gio appeared at the back door.

"Sarge." Something almost like panic flashed over his face before his expression shuttered.

"Can I come in?"

"Sorry, Sarge. Of course." Gio fumbled with the door, pushing it open. He stood by the door as Jason stepped inside.

Jason glanced around. The back door opened up into the kitchen. Beyond that was the open-plan living and dining area, and the seldom-used front door. When Dan and Gabby had lived here, there had been shit, as Dan said, from arsehole to breakfast. A couch that had always been half-covered by an overflowing basket of ironing. The baby's playpen. Toys strewn over the floor. Shelves stacked with books and DVDs. The house had been messy, lived-in, and somehow welcoming at the same time. Now the living room seemed almost bare. Just a couch and a TV. The table in the dining area had two chairs and had clearly been made for a small kitchen nook. There was nothing hanging from the hooks on the walls.

Jason pulled his gaze back from the empty living area, to Gio. He was wearing track pants and a T-shirt. He looked sleep-rumpled. His hair stuck up a little at the back. There were dark circles under his eyes, and a hint of stubble along his bruised, swollen jaw.

"You slept at all?" Jason asked him.

"I got in a couple of hours." Gio raked his fingers through his hair, and then nodded towards the unnecessarily complicated coffee maker sitting on the kitchen bench. "Coffee?"

"Thanks."

Gio stared blankly at the machine for a few moments—he'd probably been lying about getting sleep—and then he hit a button and started it up.

"How's the jaw?" Jason asked him.

"The painkillers are pretty good." Gio raised a hand and touched his jaw. His gaze slid to Jason. "Did you just get back, Sarge?"

"Yeah." Jason glanced around the kitchen. There was a toaster on the bench, with a loaf of bread sitting out beside it. A fridge with a surface entirely unpolluted by magnets and photographs and to-do lists. "I left him at the Towers."

Gio nodded. "What happens next?"

"What do you mean?"

"The cap spray." Gio's brows tugged together. "The use of force."

"It's nothing," Jason said. "You did everything by the book."

Gio jerked his head in a nod, and turned to fiddle with the coffee machine. "I've got, um, I've got a lot of people waiting for the chance to dog me."

Jason studied the tense line of his shoulders. "Because of the Coast?"

"Yeah." Gio didn't turn around. "It'd be good to know you've got my back here."

Yeah, Gio hadn't slept at all today, had he? A punch to the face, a closer call than he wanted to admit even to himself, and he'd been too wired to sleep afterwards. Too hyperaware of not what had gone right, but what could have so easily gone wrong. Jason had been there.

Jason stepped forward and nudged Gio out of the way of the coffee machine with his shoulder. "Do the cups go here?"

Gio nodded.

Jason put the cups in place a fraction of a second before the coffee began to dribble out. Gio was still standing close. He smelled faintly of some bodywash or deodorant Jason didn't recognise. His warmth leached into Jason's space.

"I've got your back on this, Gio," he said, as the rich scent of coffee rose in the air. "I don't care about what happened down on the Coast." A lie, but what else could he say? "I judge you by your actions here, okay? And from what I saw last night, and from what all the witnesses say, you did everything by the book."

Gio's shoulders sagged, and he gave Jason an almost furtive look. He reached for one of the coffee cups, curled his fingers around it, and then put space between them. "Thanks, Sarge."

Jason took his own cup. "Have you got any sugar?"

"No." Gio gave a slight shrug. "Sorry."

"That's okay. It's better for me like this, right?"

"Right," Gio agreed.

"You should get some sleep," Jason told him, leaning back against the bench and sipping his coffee. It was good and strong. "Listen, I'm firing up the barbeque tonight. Nothing special. Just some snags. But you're welcome to join me and Taylor for dinner."

There was something about Gio's kitchen—probably how clean it was—that made Jason wonder if the guy was living on sandwiches and coffee when he wasn't on shift. That might have worked down on the Coast, but the options for takeaway in Richmond were sadly limited.

Still, he half expected Gio to say no, and was surprised instead when Gio hesitated and then nodded.

"Thanks, Sarge," he said at last. "That'd be good."

Taylor's face scrunched up as he carefully positioned the tomatoes into a line on the chopping board and reached for the big knife. Jason watched closely, worried Taylor was still too little for this, too clumsy and uncoordinated, and it would all end in tears and bloodshed. But he was ten. Jason had been handling knives when he'd been ten. A part of him knew Taylor was easily old enough to do this. Another part of him wondered what the hell his parents had been thinking.

"Watch your fingers," Jason reminded him.

Taylor nodded seriously, and began to slice the tomatoes. "Hey, Dad, you know on TV when the chefs just go *chop-chop-chop* like Fruit Ninja?"

"Don't even think about it," Jason cautioned, and Taylor grinned at him. "Pay attention, mate."

"Can I do the onions too?"

"If you don't cut your fingers off doing the tomatoes."

Taylor snorted, but squinted with concentration as he worked. Jason watched him, warmth creeping through him. This kid. This exasperating kid. God. Alana wouldn't believe how tall he was now. What a little smart-arse he'd grown into. Okay, well, maybe she would have believed that. Taylor had been talking back since before he could make proper words.

The blade of the knife slid through the last of the tomatoes and landed with a dull *thock* on the chopping board. Taylor looked around for Jason.

"Can I?"

"Go on, then," Jason said, and Taylor whooped and scurried to get an onion from the fridge.

Jason supervised the onion chopping, and then headed downstairs to put the onions and sausages on the barbeque.

He figured it was the smell of the cooking sausages that drew Gio over. And Gio wasn't the only one who noticed. The smell certainly got the attention of every fucking blowfly in the entire region too. Gio was waving a few of them away from his face as he crossed the yard between the houses.

"Come on upstairs," Jason said, transferring the sausages and fried onion onto a plate. "Not as many flies."

Gio followed him up the back steps.

"Hi, Gio!" Taylor exclaimed, his eyes widening. "Wow. Look at your *face*."

Jason winced internally. "Mate."

Gio smiled slightly. "It's pretty bad, right?"

"This one time, I crashed my bike and I landed on the handlebars, and the bruise was purple for *weeks*," Taylor said. "Yours is cool but."

Gio's smile widened, and he let out a small laugh. "Thanks."

Jason should have done this earlier. Invited Gio over for dinner, and at least made half an attempt to be a bit more sociable. Because there was a difference between being friendly and trusting the guy, and Jason should have remembered he could do one without the other. Inviting the guy over every couple of days didn't mean he was setting himself up to be shit on. He'd told Gio earlier that he was only going to judge him by what happened here, not on the Coast. It was about time he actually gave that a try, right?

He carried the sausages and onion through to the dining table.

Dinner was surprisingly okay. Gio ate slowly thanks to his jaw, but he seemed relaxed, and he joined in the conversation. The conversation itself was awkward at first. Jason would have been happy to fall back on talking about work, but Taylor's presence stymied much of that. No way in hell did Jason want Taylor spilling all the gossip on the school playground.

"Do you know how to surf?" Taylor asked, picking apart his lettuce. "Everyone from the Gold Coast knows how to surf."

"Not me," Gio said. "I used to go swimming a lot, and sometimes boogie boarding, but I can't surf."

"Sometimes when we go out to the lake, we tie a boogie board to the back of my friend Kane's dad's tinny, and that's almost like surfing!" Taylor beamed. "You should come with us!"

Gio glanced at Jason.

"Maybe we should let Gio recover from his current injuries before we try and give him some new ones, hey?" Jason poured himself another glass of water.

"Okay!" Taylor was silent for about half a second. "You can just swim at the lake too. It's awesome."

"I'll keep it in mind," Gio promised him.

There was an odd sort of furtiveness to Gio. He was guarded, and it didn't seem to stem from last night's assault. He unfurled a little in Taylor's presence though, the stiff line of his shoulders relaxing as they ate, his mouth curving into a smile. Jason liked Gio's smile. It made him look brighter, even with the swollen jaw.

"I like Gio, Dad," Taylor said much later, squinting into the bathroom mirror as he tugged his damp hair up into spikes.

"Good," Jason said. "Now brush your teeth."

He left Taylor to it.

It was later still when Taylor was finally in bed and Jason was packing his lunchbox for tomorrow. He gazed out the kitchen window. There was a light on at Gio's place, and Jason wondered what he was doing. It seemed dumb for Gio to be over in his own house watching a movie, when Jason was probably just going to do the same thing. But there was a difference between being friendly and actual friendship, wasn't there? And everyone in the Service knew what Gio Valeri did with actual friendships.

Jason put Taylor's lunchbox in the fridge, checked the back door was locked, and went to bed. He lay awake for a long time before drifting off to sleep.

CHAPTER SEVEN

Gio wasn't sure when his texts with Richard from Baxter Mine had turned from friendly into flirtatious. Maybe they'd been that way from the start, because blokes didn't just text one another randomly through the day, did they? Not if they were only acquaintances. Not unless they were both trying to be something more.

Thinking of you, Richard sent one day, and the accompanying dick pic filled Gio with relief and arousal all at once. Relief that he hadn't been misreading this whole situation and that Richard had actually made an unequivocal move, and arousal because that was a nice dick.

That was what he sent back: *Nice.*

And then he jerked off, imagining Richard doing the same thing two hundred kilometres away.

"You're looking chirpy," Sandra said, eyes narrow with suspicion when Gio let himself in the back door of the station in time to start his 2 p.m. shift.

"It's a beautiful day," Gio replied.

"No, it isn't," she said. "It's a *Monday*."

"Right." Gio frowned. "Speaking of, why are me and the sergeant both rostered an afternoon shift on a Monday? Is there something on in town tonight?"

"Mmm." Sandra picked up a folder of court briefs and smirked. "It's *bingo* night. Jason isn't going to let you handle your first bingo night on your own."

"Why?" he asked.

Sandra laughed and whisked the court briefs away.

Gio figured maybe she was just winding him up.

Bingo started at six, but their first patrol of the hall beside Saint Patrick's Church was at four, when the volunteers were still setting up the tables and unstacking all the chairs. The ceiling fans spun slowly. A corner of the hall was decorated with finger-painted pictures courtesy of St. Paddy's Playgroup, according to the banner tacked up above the makeshift gallery. There was a small stage at one end of the hall. A middle-aged man in thick glasses huffed and puffed as he fiddled with an uncooperative microphone system. A large trestle table sat underneath the windows on the east side of the hall. One end of the table was stacked with coffee mugs. The other was crammed with plates full of biscuits, scones, and cakes, every one plastic-wrapped against the flies.

"Hello, Jason, dear!" one of the ladies by the table called, and Sergeant Quinn waved and moved towards her.

Gio followed, fixing a polite smile on his face as he prepared to get sucked into yet another round of small-town introductions and pleasantries. Hell if he knew why both he and the sergeant needed to be rostered on for this. It wasn't exactly Cavill Avenue on a Friday night in Schoolies Week, and the Richmond Catholic Ladies' Auxiliary wasn't exactly a horde of rampaging teenagers hopped up on booze and testosterone. Gio shook hands with all of them, trying—and immediately failing—to commit their names to memory.

"Do you play bingo, Gio?" one of the ladies asked him. Anthea? Andrea? She was wearing a brooch on the bosom of her purple blouse. It was a cat made out of pink diamantes, and Gio didn't think it was supposed to be vintage, retro, or ironic.

"No," he told her. "I wouldn't even know how."

She brightened. "Oh, well, it's easy enough. You—"

Sergeant Quinn saved him from what was probably going to be a lengthy explanation. "No gambling on duty, Gio," he said with a broad smile and a wink that made the ladies laugh.

"No, Sarge," Gio agreed gratefully, and drifted away from the table while he could. The place his dad was living had bingo nights. Gio remembered that from one of the pamphlets Sophie had given him. Bingo nights, and talent shows, and arts and crafts. Like Dad was embarking on a holiday, and not a slow, pitiful decline into infirmity, a race between his body and his mind as to which one could reach rock bottom first.

Gio had stared at those pamphlets until every word and every bright, glossy picture had bled together.

Warm hands on his shoulders, thumbs digging into the knots in his neck. *"Come to bed, Gio."*

"Soon."

"Come on, babe, I'll tire you out."

He'd laughed at that, despite everything, and let himself be distracted by Pete's hands tugging at his shirt, Pete's teeth biting down on his earlobe. Pete's warm breath on the back of his neck, sending a shiver down his spine and a lick of heat curling through his gut.

Gio jolted at the memory, ignoring the goose bumps that had broken out on his skin. The last thing he needed to do was get an erection in a room full of old Catholic ladies. One little text exchange with Richard this morning and he couldn't stop thinking about getting laid. Still, apart from the risk of inappropriate erections, maybe that was a good sign, wasn't it? Maybe he was finally finished just going through the motions every day. Maybe he was actually ready to claw a semblance of a life back.

Maybe.

They bought dinner from the servo, and returned to the station to eat it. Gio unwrapped his steak burger and ate it at his desk, yesterday's local newspaper underneath it to catch the onions and beetroot that abandoned ship while he ate. Sergeant Quinn ate at the spare desk in the dayroom; the one usually used by Taylor after school. There was a *Rogue One* pencil case lying there, and a crinkled-up ball of foil that had possibly once been a Yowie wrapper.

Gio's radio crackled, and a few times he paused to listen and make sure Comms wasn't calling them. There was a violent DV occurring in Charters Towers that had both their general duties crew and their one-up traffic unit attending, and the copper from Hughenden was doing a few traffic stops, but nothing for Richmond. Back on the Coast, meal breaks had been a time to kick back and joke around, and maybe get a head start on some paperwork since it had never been a case of *if* the shift would turn to shit later, but *when*. Here though . . . here there was nothing to do but check his emails, check his text messages, and count down the minutes until it was time to head out on yet another patrol of town.

"Hey, Taylor."

Gio looked over at Sergeant Quinn, then turned away again. It was one thing to listen in to a private phone call. It was another thing to do it openly.

"Did you finish your homework?" The sergeant snorted at whatever response Taylor gave him. "No, you eat whatever Sandra puts on your plate. Yes, mate, even if it is cauliflower."

Gio hid a grin.

"Of course that goes for broccoli too."

The buzzer from the front door sounded. Gio rose to his feet, wrapping the remains of his burger back into the bag, and waved at the sergeant not to get up. He walked through to the foyer, and unlocked the front doors. There was a woman standing there, her arms folded across her chest despite the heat. She looked to be in her sixties, maybe older. One of the bingo crowd.

"Can I help you?" Gio asked her.

"Is—is Jason here?"

"He's tied up on a call right now," Gio said. "I'm Senior Constable Valeri. Gio. Can I help you?"

"I . . ." For a moment it appeared the woman would refuse, but then she seemed to steel herself. She dropped her arms to her side, nodded, and stepped into the station.

There was something about her, something about the way she held herself that Gio recognised. He knew, even before she opened her mouth and began to speak haltingly, just what she was going to say.

There was no such thing as a typical domestic violence victim. Patricia Howe was sixty-eight years old. She was the head of the CWA—an organisation Gio hadn't known existed anymore—and lived on a property about twenty minutes from town. Her husband thought she was at bingo.

Gio took her into Sergeant Quinn's office—the sergeant was still on the phone to Taylor—and sat her down at the desk.

The story she told him was unremarkable. He'd heard a thousand variations of it before. He watched her face as the words spilled out in fits and starts, and could predict the exact moment she started to make excuses.

"It's not that bad," she said, as if she were trying to convince herself instead of Gio. And she was, he knew. Because if it *was* that bad, then why hadn't she done anything before? How had she let it go on so long? To deny the severity of the abuse wasn't just about protecting her husband. It was about protecting her self-image as well. Because what had happened that she'd let it continue? What had happened to the person she was inside that he'd been able to twist her so easily? That he'd made her an accomplice in her own abuse? The most insidious victim blaming didn't come from the outside.

"Small steps." Gio shrugged when she lifted her gaze and met his eyes. "He started with small steps, didn't he? Things that didn't seem worth fighting about."

Patricia pursed her lips and nodded. "He won't go to the doctor."

Gio waited.

"My sister-in-law Anne," Patricia said. She smoothed a hand over her knees, straightening the fall of her floral skirt. "Her husband had these awful mood swings, and it was his diabetes. I think that Brian might have it too, but he won't go to the doctor."

"It could be that. But, even if it is, you don't have to put up with the way he's been treating you in the meantime." There was a box of tissues on the sergeant's desk. Gio pushed them towards her. "Has he hit you?"

For a moment she wavered on the edge of a denial and then, at last, gave another short, sharp nod. "Only once."

"Once is enough though."

"We've been married for forty-one years!"

"Once is enough," Gio repeated carefully. "And domestic violence isn't just physical violence. It can be about emotional or psychological abuse. It can be about him not letting you have control of your money, or threatening to damage your property, or hurt your pets. It's not just about if he hits you. There are other things too, even if they're not so obvious."

Gio saw a flash of movement from beyond the open door, and looked up to see Sergeant Quinn standing there, listening. The sergeant nodded at him.

Patricia tugged a tissue out of the box. She blew her nose; a lengthy wet honk that made Gio fight not to flinch. "I don't know how this happened!"

Gio nodded, although he knew the answer. Because it had started slowly, in creeping little increments that could be excused or ignored, and by the time Patricia had realised how deep in she was, she'd already been drowning.

"It's like I don't know who he is anymore!"

"Okay," Gio said. "Do you have somewhere to stay tonight, Patricia?"

She looked at him, clearly startled, and balled the tissue up in her trembling fist. "I'm going *home*."

"Do you think that's a good idea?" It wasn't, and Gio would argue the point if necessary, but he started off soft, conciliatory.

"I'm not going to *leave* my husband," she said, eyes widening.

Gio felt a rush of anger that he knew was unfair, and only borne out of frustration. He was careful to keep his voice calm. "Okay, Patricia, what I want to do tonight is take out what's called a Temporary Domestic Violence Order. That means that until it goes to court, Brian is going to be prohibited from coming near you. It's for your protection and his that I don't want you to go home tonight. It keeps you safe, and it keeps him from getting in trouble."

But she'd only seized on one word. "*Court*?" Tears slid down her face. "I came to you for help, and—"

Suddenly Sergeant Quinn was standing beside Gio. "This is how we help you, Patricia. We put safeguards in place for you."

Safeguards. As though a piece of paper had ever stopped anyone from hurting their partner. Or maybe it had; fucked if Gio knew. He'd been to plenty of violent assaults, and a few homicides, that said otherwise though.

She wavered. "I don't know . . ."

"Stay in town tonight," Sergeant Quinn said. "We'll take the order out, serve it on him tomorrow morning, and you can get the support you need. Just because it goes to court doesn't mean that Brian goes to jail. It only means that with an order in place, he has to be of good behaviour. If he breaches the order, he might be looking at jail time, but just putting the order in place? It doesn't even go on his criminal record unless he breaches it."

Patricia looked between them worriedly.

Gio leaned forward. "This might be the wake-up call he needs, Patricia. To see a doctor. To change his behaviour."

It felt like a cheap shot, like playing on her hopes, because Gio was too much of a cynic to believe it was true.

"Yes," she said at last, nodding. "Yes, I'll do it."

Sergeant Quinn dropped Patricia off at her friend's house in town while Gio worked away at the Temporary Domestic Violence Order.

"Any reason we're not serving this on the respondent tonight?" he asked when the sergeant got back.

"Bingo night." Sergeant Quinn shrugged. "We're about to get busy."

Gio huffed. "What does that even—"

His radio burst into life. "VKR Townsville calling Richmond two-eight-nine."

Gio turned his head towards where the microphone was hanging off his epaulette. "Two-eight-nine, VKR. Go ahead."

"Job details when you're ready."

Gio scrabbled for a pen and looked up at the sergeant.

"Bingo night," Sergeant Quinn repeated, and tapped the side of his nose.

Andrea was no longer wearing her glittery pink cat brooch. She was no longer wearing anything at all by the time they escorted her through the back door of the station and into the holding cell.

Her clothes had made a trail all down Church Street from the hall at Saint Patrick's to the school on the next corner. They'd located her on top of the monkey bars.

"Who called the cops?" she'd demanded.

"Come on, Andrea," Sergeant Quinn had said with a sigh. *"Time to come down."*

Bingo night.

Gio ate the rest of his cold burger, hours old now, while he finished up the paperwork from the DV, and listened to Andrea singing off-key from the holding cell. He looked up as Sergeant Quinn crossed through the small dayroom, a bottle of water in his hand.

"So that's bingo night," Sergeant Quinn said, as Andrea failed to hit a high note but kept trying anyway.

"*Every* bingo night?"

The sergeant transferred the bottle of water to his other hand. Condensation slid down the sides. "The thing with Andrea is that for thirty days out of every month she's a saint. She wouldn't even dream of jaywalking. But when she has a few sherries at bingo . . ." He shrugged, as though that was all Gio needed to know.

Gio was silent for a moment. Bingo night was obviously a running joke, but it had also been part of his induction into policing in Richmond, just like visiting Janey Ferguson's house, and doing a run out to the mine and the cattle stations. It was Sergeant Quinn showing him the ropes still. And it rankled.

"Any reason we both needed to be rostered on to deal with her?" Gio asked.

The sergeant didn't even try to sugarcoat it. "I wanted to make sure you knew how to handle it the right way."

His way being the right way, of course, like Gio was some dumb-as-shit first-year constable who had no idea how to do the job.

Bingo night was a joke. It was also a test.

And Gio was tired of being tested.

He raised his eyebrows. "Are we charging her?"

The sergeant met his gaze squarely. "Nope."

"Why not?" Gio set his burger down. "You keep reminding me the rules are different out here, Sarge, and I know we've got discretionary powers. I know we don't have to charge her, but if there's a reason you're not charging someone who habitually gets drunk and runs naked down the street, then—"

"Andrea was a nurse," the sergeant said, his expression hardening. "Before she retired. She was my wife's nurse."

Great. So Gio had waded straight into a shit fight here, hadn't he? But that didn't mean he was wrong. "Does that give her a free pass, Sarge?"

The water bottle made a *crack* as the sergeant tightened his grip on it. "If you want to charge her . . ." He shook his head. "If you really think there's a benefit to the community in charging some woman who wouldn't hurt a fly just because she had too much to drink tonight and did something silly . . . if you want to humiliate her by putting her up in front of a magistrate, then you go right fucking ahead, Gio. That's what you do, isn't it? You fuck up people's lives."

Gio froze, a wave of hot, sick shame breaking over him.

"If you want to charge her, you be my guest," Sergeant Quinn said, his voice dropping to a warning tone that made Gio fight not to flinch away. "And if you want to complain that I'm not doing my job properly, well, you've got Ethical Standards on speed dial, don't you?"

He didn't wait for Gio to reply, and Gio wasn't sure he could have found the words in any case. The sergeant headed down the short corridor to his office, and slammed the door shut behind him.

Gio sat there, numb, the blood roaring in his skull and the silence only broken by Andrea's off-key singing from the cell.

CHAPTER EIGHT

The entrance to Windermere Station was marked on the highway by a tyre hanging from a post. The tyre was painted bone-white. If it had ever had the station name on it, the weather had long ago worn it away. A baked dirt road crazed with heat cracks led up to the house. It churned into red dust under the tyres of the police LandCruiser. The drive out from town had been quiet, the tension tugging at the ends of Jason's frayed nerves. He wished this was the sort of job he could knock over by himself, but better to spend an uncomfortable few hours in Gio's company than head on out to Windermere on his own to serve Brian Howe with his DV paperwork and seize his firearms. The serving of the paperwork should be fine. It was the firearms that Jason was cautious about. There was never any telling how someone would take the news that they were being divested of their weapons. Most of the property owners in the division had firearms for taking care of pigs and roos. Of course Brian Howe would be pissed off they were getting taken off him.

The LandCruiser bounced over the potholed dirt road.

Jason risked a glimpse at Gio. Gio was tight jawed. He was wearing sunglasses. His face was a tense mask.

Yeah.

Okay, so the dig about Ethical Standards had probably been uncalled for, but Gio needed to wrap his head around the fact that things out here were *different*. They had to be. A country copper didn't get to put a divider up between on duty and off duty, between work and home. The lines bled together. The edges blurred. Jason had to live in the community he policed, which meant that he had to use his discretion when it came to arresting or charging people. Jesus. It meant that he thought twice about giving out speeding tickets rather than warnings. Jury fuckers, he'd heard tickets called before; all it took to sink a prosecution was one juror with an entirely unrelated grudge about that time the coppers had cost them a few hundred dollars. And take that attitude and multiply it by a hundred in a small town. Nothing would put an entire community offside faster than some uptight arsehole who refused to give anyone any slack. Nothing would shut down cooperation faster than charging someone like Andrea with wilful exposure and being drunk in a public place, instead of just letting her sleep it off in a cell and then driving her home. Successful policing in country towns wasn't measured in arrest stats. It couldn't be.

Still, his dig about Ethical Standards had been pretty bloody low.

But then Gio's behaviour on the Coast had been low as well, hadn't it? It had been a dog act. Everyone knew that.

There was still a shadow of a bruise on Gio's jaw courtesy of Kev Lindeman, and Jason tried not to think of how vulnerable Gio had seemed in the aftermath of the assault.

"It'd be good to know you've got my back here, Sarge."

And Jason wanted to promise that he did, but trust was a two-way street. Jason would have liked to believe the reverse was true as well, but he knew better.

They continued the drive in silence as Windermere Station slowly resolved itself from the haze of heat and dust. A homestead and outbuildings. Sun-bleached fence posts and rusted tin roofs. The house yard was a riot of colour. Shrubs of bougainvilleas dotted what must have been a hard-won patch of lawn, bursts of bright petals waving in the breeze.

Jason parked the LandCruiser in front of the house, grabbed the paperwork, and stepped out into the heavy heat of the day. Gio walked around the LandCruiser and fell into step beside him as Brian Howe approached them. A blue cattle dog slunk along behind Brian, furtively. A red one, tail wagging, pushed ahead.

Brian Howe had the look of every other man from this sort of country. Deep lines cut through the tanned skin around his eyes. His nose was scarred where old skin cancers had been cut out, and his thick greying hair held the imprint of his hat even when his battered Akubra was wedged under his arm. He wore elastic-sided boots, faded jeans, and a worn plaid shirt in three different shades of dust.

"G'day, Brian," Jason said. "We're here about Patricia."

"What about her?" the man asked warily, and that just confirmed it, didn't it? His wife hadn't come home last night and now the police had turned up, but he wasn't panicking that she'd driven off the highway into a ditch. He knew exactly what this was about.

Gio stood beside him, a solid presence. Jason glanced at him and saw that his hand was resting on his utility belt. It was a casual pose, but it also put him in easy reach of his taser if he needed it. Which Jason didn't think would be necessary, but he'd been a copper long enough to know that things could turn to shit in a heartbeat. And whatever differences he and Gio had, when it came to the job they both wore the same uniform.

"She came to see us at the station last night," Jason said. "She made a statement about domestic violence."

Jason kept his expression impassive as Brian's ran the gamut between anger and denial. He settled on denial in the end. "I don't know what you're bloody talking about!"

"I'm here to serve some paperwork on you," Jason said. "It's called a Temporary Domestic Violence Order, and there are conditions that I need to explain to you and—"

"I didn't bloody touch her!" Brian exclaimed, face going red.

Gio took a step forward. The red cattle dog snuffled around his boots. The blue one slunk away.

"There are conditions I need to explain to you," Jason repeated, "and you'll need to appear in court."

"I didn't!" Brian huffed, squinting at him.

"I'm not the one you need to argue with, Brian." Jason held out the order. "You get to go to court and tell the magistrate your side. But until then, Patricia's not coming home, and this order says that you're not to try and approach her in the meantime, or phone her, or get anyone else to do it for you, okay?"

"I'm not signing anything!"

"You don't need to sign anything," Jason said, his voice level. "You don't even need to read the order, but I'm going to verbally advise you of the conditions, and I'm not leaving until you confirm that you've understood them."

Brian snatched the papers out of his hands, and for a moment Jason thought he was going to tear them up. Then, hands shaking, he folded the papers up and jammed them into his shirt pocket. "This is rubbish!"

"If you breach any of the conditions on the order, you *will* be arrested."

Brian sagged then, mouth opening and closing like a guppy's, and Jason felt a flash of contempt for him. A blustering bully when it came to dealing with his wife, but nowhere near as bloody tough when it came to Jason and Gio. Brian stood there like a lump while Jason recited the conditions on the order.

Gio was a silent presence at his side.

"Do you understand these conditions?" Jason asked when he'd gone through them.

"Yeah," Brian mumbled, and spat in the dirt.

"Your court date's on the twenty-fourth," Jason said. "Nine a.m."

Brian huffed.

And now for the fun part.

Jason exchanged a look with Gio. "And Brian? We're gonna need you to turn over all your guns."

"Who pissed in his Cornflakes?" Sandra muttered as Gio shouldered his way through the back door of the station with Brian Howe's .222 Remington Bolt-Action in one hand, and a .303 Lee-Enfield that dated back to the Second World War—and definitely wasn't registered—in the other. Gio either didn't hear her or ignored her as he headed to the armoury to lodge the firearms.

"We had a run in last night," Jason muttered, and shot her a warning look. "I'll fill you in later."

"I'll hold you to that," she said, and adjusted her glasses. "We're almost out of toner so I'm putting an order in. There's only so many times we can pull it out, shake it, and expect it to keep working, and I think we're fast approaching that point. Do you need anything?"

"Yeah. How do we keep losing staplers?"

She fixed him with a stare. "I'm stealing them to sell on the black market to fund my retirement."

"Huh." Jason rolled his shoulders. "And how is the stapler black market business?"

"Booming," she shot back. "I'm sending this order off and then I'm going out for lunch. Want me to get anything?"

"The bakery?" He waited for her nod, and dug his wallet out of his pocket. "Steak pie, no sauce."

"You're an odd duck, Jason."

"At least I'm not an old duck."

That earned him a snort of laughter as she took his money. She raised her eyebrows and nodded towards the armoury. "I'll go and see what Petal wants too, shall I?"

Well, with an attitude like hers, at least Jason wasn't going to be the only one of them that Gio reported to Ethical Standards. "Sandra, you—"

Gio stepped back out into the dayroom, holding an opened envelope. Internal mail, by the look of it. "When did this come?"

Sandra frowned. "This morning. Why?"

Gio shook his head. "Doesn't matter."

"What is it?" Jason asked.

Gio clenched the envelope tight in his fist. "It's nothing. It's personal."

"Hey, I'm going for lunch. Do you want anything at the . . ." Sandra trailed off as Gio headed for the back door. It slammed shut behind him. "At the bakery, you arrogant little dickhead?"

Jason sighed. "Sandra . . ."

"What?" she asked. "Don't talk about him like that?"

"No." Jason rubbed his forehead. "Just be careful he doesn't hear you."

Sometimes Jason looked at Taylor and felt a sudden rush of some emotion so deep, so all-encompassing that even the word *love* couldn't do it justice. He'd felt it first the moment he'd held Taylor after he was born; this weird, wrinkled little thing that somehow he and Alana had made. It had been impossible to wrap his brain around it, because suddenly there had been this entirely new person where there hadn't been one before. And Alana had been utterly wrung out, her hair a sweaty, tangled mess on the pillow behind her, but she'd had just enough energy left to laugh at the stunned expression on Jason's face. Sometimes Jason looked at Taylor and still felt the shock of that miracle, a decade later.

And other times Taylor helped himself to Jason's razor and tried to teach himself how to shave.

"You are *ten*," Jason told him as he held a wadded-up paper towel to Taylor's chin. "You don't have any facial hair."

"Not anymore," Taylor mumbled.

"No, now you don't have any skin," Jason corrected him. He took Taylor's hand and pressed it against the paper towel. "Hold that there while I find a Band-Aid."

Taylor nodded grimly.

Jason dug around in the top drawer in the bathroom cabinet for a Band-Aid. Alana would have been better at this than he was, or at least that was the position he defaulted to whenever Taylor got hurt. It was his guilt talking. He liked to tell himself it was impossible to imagine her struggling how he still did sometimes, impossible to imagine her falling apart the way he had in the aftermath of her death, but he couldn't know for sure. Maybe the truth wasn't that he really thought she'd be better at raising Taylor alone than he was, but simply that if one of them had to die, he wished it had been him. It wasn't fair that she never got to see her son grow up.

He found a Band-Aid at last, and some antiseptic cream, and shifted back to where Taylor was sitting on the edge of the bathtub. "Okay. Show me."

Taylor peeled the paper towel away carefully.

It was only a shallow cut, right on the end of his chin, but it had bled freely. Jason dabbed a little of the antiseptic cream on his finger, and then onto the cut, and Taylor hissed. Jason stuck the Band-Aid on, tamping the ends down.

"That feels weird," Taylor complained.

"Don't touch it," Jason said. "It can stay on until you have your shower tonight." He scrubbed his knuckles over Taylor's head, through his hair. "Now, do you want to tell me why you were shaving?"

"Kane's brother Alex shaves."

"Kane's brother Alex is nineteen!" Jason shook his head. "When your chin heals, I'll show you how to shave. Without a blade."

Taylor brightened. "Okay!"

"Now go and do your homework like you were supposed to be doing."

Taylor scurried away.

Jason disposed of the Band-Aid wrapper and the paper towel, and then turned the tap on and washed the blood out of the sink and down the drain. He caught a glimpse of his reflection in the mirror, and grimaced at the bags under his eyes. Hopefully he'd get an early night tonight and not get called out in the middle of it.

Homework. School lunches. Ironing. Dinner. Sometimes, with his shift work, it was hard to stick to routine. Jason relished it when he was working a few day shifts in a row. It was a hell of a lot easier on both him and Taylor. He got the chance to actually get organised for the next morning, and Taylor got to go to bed in his own room instead of falling asleep in Sandra's spare room and getting woken up again when Jason picked him up after ten.

Jason made Taylor's lunch for tomorrow, and glanced through the kitchen window over towards Gio's house.

He probably owed Gio an apology over the whole Andrea incident. He could have taken the time to explain how things were necessarily different here, and how using their discretionary powers in Andrea's case bought more goodwill around town than charging her would, but instead he'd gone right for the low blow. It had been uncalled for. And, if Gio really did have Ethical Standards on speed dial, pretty fucking stupid too.

Taylor padded into the kitchen. "Are you making me a Vegemite sandwich?"

"Yep." Jason turned his head to look at him. "Problem?"

"No. I was just making sure." Taylor perused the lunch makings critically and then helped himself to a rice cracker. "What are we having for dinner?"

"Plain broccoli." It was an old joke, or an empty threat, and it always made Taylor snort.

"Dad, listen." Taylor's eyes were bright and he was grinning. "Broccoli, E. coli. Coincidence? I think not!"

Jason laughed. Taylor looked ridiculously proud of himself. He'd obviously been sitting on that one for a while, just waiting for the right moment to bust it out. "Smart-arse."

Taylor beamed, the Band-Aid on his chin shifting, and rewarded himself with another rice cracker. "So, what is for dinner?"

"How about spaghetti?"

"Okay." Taylor grabbed a juice from the fridge and wandered away again.

Jason's bolognaise sauce was his mum's recipe. Mince, a can of tomato soup, an onion, and a dash of dried spices. It was a quick, bland knockoff of the real thing. Actual Italians would probably scale walls to avoid it, but Taylor liked it. Alana had too. The first night Jason had invited her back to his share house to study, he'd made it for her. It didn't say a lot for their peers that Alana had been so impressed. Okay, so it was a step up from two-minute noodles, but only a short one.

Jason finished making Taylor's lunch and then started on the spaghetti. The late afternoon softened into dusk while he worked, and the light turned golden before it faded into a pink-orange sky dusted with streaks of clouds. The screeching cockatoos flocked back to the rain tree, the branches shifting under their weight, and the stray cat streaked from the tree towards the house, vanishing from Jason's line of sight once it got close. Insects pinged against the screens. A gecko scuttled onto the windowsill to feed on them.

The mince and onion sizzled in the pan, and Jason's stomach growled.

He and Taylor ate at the table. One end of it was still given over to Taylor's homework. Taylor shovelled his spaghetti in quickly, and filled Jason in on his progress in some game he and Kane were currently obsessed with. He waved his fork around enthusiastically while he talked, ending up with a glob of sauce down the front of his shirt.

On nights like these, Jason missed Alana.

Stupid.

He would always miss Alana. But on nights like this, or when Taylor was asleep, and Jason would sit on the couch and watch a movie, or lie in bed and read a book, he missed having someone to talk to. Sometimes he just craved the company of another adult. He'd considered dating again—he was ready, he thought—but it didn't seem fair to expect someone else to be always in third place, behind Taylor and the job.

He watched as Taylor made another wild arc with the fork and left a splat of sauce on the table.

"And, Dad, if I got an iTunes gift card, I could use that to upgrade my dinosaurs."

"Upgrade them how? Opposable thumbs?"

Taylor scoffed. "No, with armour!"

"Oh, well that makes perfect sense."

Taylor was still chattering on about dinosaurs with armour when it was his bedtime, still not at all subtly angling for an iTunes card. He climbed into bed, his hair damp from his shower, lugging a few books with him.

"Good night, mate."

"Good night, Dad."

Jason sat on the couch and flicked through the channels on the TV. It felt selfish to want something more than this. Worse, it felt almost dangerous, as though he were somehow tempting fate. Jason knew how fucked up the universe could be, after all. He didn't need another demonstration. Not in this lifetime.

The quiet was fine.

He must have fallen asleep on the couch, and only woke up when he heard a car door slamming. It took a moment for him to get his bearings and realise he was on the couch and not in bed, and then he stood up, stretching, and made his way to the front door. He stepped outside onto the veranda.

The car was at Gio's place. It was a new model crewman ute. In the bright moonlight, Jason made out the familiar logo on the side.

Baxter Mine.

Jason watched as Richard Hanna headed up Gio's front steps. Gio was standing at the top of the steps, wearing jeans and a T-shirt. It was too far away to make out his expression, but he had his thumbs hooked in the pockets of his jeans. He looked loose-limbed and more relaxed than Jason had ever seen him.

As Jason watched, his stomach twisting with some emotion he wasn't anywhere near ready to name, Gio retreated to his front door.

Richard followed him inside.

CHAPTER NINE

It was Sophie's idea.

You need to get a hobby, she'd texted a few days earlier when Gio had been bitching about having nothing to do in his time off. *Or a friend.*

That had cut close, and Gio hoped that hadn't been her intention, but she had a point. Sitting around the house after every shift playing video games and killing time until he was due at work again wasn't good for his health, either mental or otherwise.

After the shit day he'd had, it had been easy to text Richard. He'd intended to flirt for a while, maybe get each other off with some sexting and some pics, but somehow that had turned into an invitation. Now, four hours after Gio had sent the first text, Richard was walking inside his house. Gio wasn't sure where his unease was coming from. He'd had plenty of hookups before. He'd been spontaneous.

Before Pete.

Before Richmond, where there was no such thing as anonymity, and where he was living in the house next door to his boss.

Before his whole life had gone to shit.

"You need more furniture," Richard said with a half smile as he looked around the place.

"Yeah." Gio nodded towards the kitchen. "You want a beer?"

"Depends," Richard said. "Am I driving back tonight?"

It was a fair question. Gio had been exchanging dick pics with the guy for over a week, and now Richard had driven three hours to town. Gio appreciated that Richard was asking, but he'd also figured it was a foregone conclusion that Richard would be staying over. The sudden thought that maybe it wasn't foregone, that maybe he could still call the whole thing off, made him feel oddly unsettled. He didn't like leaving room for his doubts to creep in.

"Are you working tomorrow?" he asked instead.

"I can start late."

"Then you might as well stay here the night," Gio said, ignoring the knot in his gut that reminded him how long it had been since he'd gotten laid. That the last guy who'd touched him, who'd kissed him, had been Pete. And that he'd been in love with Pete.

Gio went to the kitchen to grab a couple of beers. When he came back into the living room, Richard was standing by the small table, holding up the pack of dog treats that had come in the internal mail to the station that day. Gio's heart skipped a beat.

"You've got a dog?"

"No. That a . . . um, that's a joke," Gio said, shrugging it off with a smile that he knew didn't reach his eyes.

Dog.

A can of Pal had been traditional back in the bad old days, apparently, when corruption had been rife and before the Queensland Police Force had been shaken up, cleaned out and rebranded as the Queensland Police Service, but trying to send a can of dog food through the internal mail would have raised some questions that his former colleagues on the Coast—because who else would it be?—clearly wouldn't want to answer. They hadn't forgotten about him, then, and they wanted him to know that. Half the bloody state away, and they were still fucking with him.

Richard raised his eyebrows and set the Schmackos back down. He was probably wondering what sort of dumb joke a pack of dog treats was. He took the beer that Gio offered him, and twisted the top off. "Thanks."

"Couch?" Gio asked.

They sat together, the TV on for noise mainly, and for something to fill the suddenly awkward silence between them. Gio drank his beer too fast.

"I wasn't sure you'd want to come all this way," he said at last, picking at the label on the bottle with his thumbnail.

Richard smiled. "It's not like I have a reason, usually."

Gio studied the fine smattering of freckles across his nose before he glanced away again briefly. When he looked back, Richard was still staring at him. "Right."

Richard's forehead creased. "Are you into this? Because you seemed like you were when we were texting."

"It's been a while." Gio went with a version of the truth he could live with. "I went through a breakup before I got transferred here."

"Messy?"

"Yeah."

Richard leaned back. "So, my boyfriend and I have been together for three years. We're not exclusive though."

Gio met his gaze. "Does he know that?"

"Yeah." Richard set his beer down on the coffee table. "Is that a deal breaker?"

Was it? Gio wasn't chasing a boyfriend. He wanted a no-strings hookup, and Richard fit the bill. He wondered if Richard was playing him, though, by telling him like this. Telling him here. Like maybe he figured that if he drove the three hours to town before dropping the boyfriend bombshell, Gio would be less likely to tell him to fuck off than if he'd mentioned it by text. Or maybe that was Gio reading too much into it. "No. It's cool."

Richard's motivations didn't matter, did they? Gio was looking for a hookup, for some stress relief, not a lifetime commitment.

He set his beer on the table and leaned back again. Richard followed his movement, and for a second Gio thought of dancers moving together, the space between them melting away, or of planets in a synchronised orbit. Then Richard's breath was hot against his mouth, and then his lips were, and Gio curled his fingers into his hair and tried not to think about Pete.

Gio's phone woke him sometime in the middle of the night, and he fumbled with it for a moment, his fingers clumsy with sleep, before managing to answer it. "H'lo?"

"Gio. It's Jason. We've got an MVC. Meet me at the station in five."

"Yep." Gio scrubbed a hand through his hair, and waited for awareness to filter back into the blank spaces of his consciousness. "Yep."

There was silence for a moment, and then: "Are you awake?"

"Yep." Gio shook his head to clear it. "I'm awake. Got it, Sarge. I'll be there in five."

He rolled out of bed and stumbled towards the door, hitting the light switch. Richard peered at him blearily.

"I gotta go," Gio said. "I don't know how long I'll be."

"Yeah." Richard closed his eyes.

Gio dressed quickly, laced his boots on, and was at the back of the station four minutes later. He was inside and kitting up by the time Sergeant Quinn arrived, with a pyjama-clad Taylor in tow.

The sergeant didn't say anything about the Baxter Mine vehicle parked in front of Gio's house, and Gio didn't say anything about the five-minute detour to Sandra's place to drop a yawning Taylor off.

As they approached the accident, Gio saw the flashing strobes of the ambulance lighting up the scene from hundreds of metres away. It was a straight, flat stretch of the highway, and at first Gio wondered if the driver had fallen asleep at the wheel and ended up off the road. Then their headlights caught the shape of the injured steer lying on the road. Gio climbed out of the LandCruiser, and heard the low, pained bellow of the animal. It sounded almost mournful, like it knew exactly what was coming.

Gio's boots skidded in loose dirt as he followed the sergeant down into the shallow ditch at the side of the highway.

"Vicki?" Sergeant Quinn called out as they walked towards the damaged car. "What've we got?"

Vicki was standing by the car with a young woman who must have been the driver. In the light from Vicki's torch, Gio could see the girl's pale, shocked face.

"Boys," Vicki said. "I was just telling Marnie here that tonight is her lucky night. Not only is she okay, but she's about to meet two of the hottest coppers in the state."

The driver gave a weak laugh. She was young, hardly more than a teenager. Her hands were shaking badly as she twisted the fabric of her shirt in her fingers.

"I mean, there are some unattractive coppers in this world, Marnie," Vicki said. "Some real uggos. But these two here? These are definitely some eye candy, right?"

"My dad is gonna kill me!" Marnie exclaimed. "I only bought this car last month."

"No, he's not," Sergeant Quinn said. "Your dad's going to be happy you're okay."

"I didn't even see it! It was just *there* all of a sudden!"

"It's not your fault," Sergeant Quinn said. "Vicki, are you good here?"

"I'm good," Vicki said. "I'll take Marnie into the hospital to get checked out."

"We'll come and see you there later, Marnie."

"Okay," the girl said, and let Vicki usher her towards the road where the ambulance was parked. Gio walked with them. He stepped out of the way while Vicki got Marnie situated in the back of the ambulance.

"Thanks, Gio," Vicki said, slamming the doors of the ambulance shut.

"She okay?"

"Yeah. Shaken up, but she was already out and walking around by the time I got to her. They'll check her out at the hospital, but I think it's her lucky night." Vicki flashed him a tired smile. "See you fellas back in town."

The ambulance rumbled off towards Richmond.

Gio watched as the sergeant strode over to the police LandCruiser. He opened the back and took out the rifle. He walked toward the injured steer, his shadow lengthening in the headlights.

Gio looked away.

The steer bellowed again.

A shot rang out, sharp and clear.

Moments later, the sergeant returned to stow the rifle.

There was a winch on the front bull bar of the LandCruiser. Sergeant Quinn fed the cable out and fastened the end around the back legs of the dead steer. Then he reeled it in, and reversed the LandCruiser off to the side of the road, dragging the steer with it. It was the work of minutes.

"We'll call the council in the morning to get rid of the carcass," he said.

Gio nodded. "What about Marnie's car?"

"It's off the road. No hazard. She can arrange to get it towed in the morning."

"Let me check there's nothing in it that'll get nicked," Gio said, and headed back down to Marnie's crumpled little hatchback. She might have just bought it, but it wasn't a new car. It was second-hand, at least five years old, though clearly her pride and joy with its matching seat covers and floor mats, and the sparkly crystal hanging off the rearview mirror. Her phone was still plugged into the stereo, and Gio unplugged it. He found her handbag half wedged under the front passenger seat, and wrenched it out with some difficulty. The bag was pink and glittery and made Gio think of princesses and tea parties and how Chloe would be getting into that stuff soon and he wouldn't be there to see it. The familiar ache of homesickness rose up in him, and he pushed it down again. He slipped the phone inside the bag, checked the back seats, and then removed the keys from the ignition and put them in the bag as well.

He didn't bother to close the driver's door. The chassis was so buckled it would have been pointless. He walked back to the police LandCruiser, taking a moment to look up at the stars. They were bright here, and low.

Gio climbed into the passenger seat.

"I'm sorry about this," Sergeant Quinn said as they headed towards town.

"About what?" Gio asked.

"About calling you out for a job I could have handled on my own," the sergeant said. "Comms didn't have much info on it. I thought it might have been a bad one."

"It's not a problem, Sarge." Gio held Marnie's handbag on his lap.

"Yeah, well . . ." Sergeant Quinn shrugged. "You had company."

Gio stilled, his mind working frantically. It took him a long moment to find any words, because the sergeant wasn't dumb. He had to know exactly who Gio's company was. They hadn't met any women out at Baxter that day. "Is that a problem?"

"No." Sergeant Quinn glanced at him and then looked back at the highway. "It's not a problem."

Which didn't explain the strange tension in his voice. Gio had dealt with plenty of people before who paid lip service to diversity but then carefully froze him out of their social circles. It was an insidious sort of homophobia he'd dealt with his entire career, an experience that he and Pete had in common, and had laughed about more often than not. Who gave a fuck how uncomfortable they made some fucking arseholes? It had been easy to laugh at when he'd been with Pete, and when he'd been part of a team that liked him. It wasn't now that he was facing it alone.

He nodded and hoped that the sergeant was done talking to him.

He wasn't.

"What I said yesterday . . ." Sergeant Quinn gripped the steering wheel tightly. "About having Ethical Standards on speed dial."

Gio's stomach clenched.

"It was out of line. I'm sorry."

"It's okay." The words tasted like ash, but what the hell else could he say?

Fuck you. Fuck you, Sarge, for giving me that whole speech about judging me on the quality of my work, for making me believe it, and then saying that. Fuck you, and fuck the QPS, and fuck everyone in this two-headed one-horse town.

There was a time and a place for speaking the truth, but it sure as hell wasn't now and it sure as hell wasn't here. Gio turned his head and looked out the window, and counted down the kilometres back to Richmond.

Gio had joked once about being able to do his job in his sleep. It wasn't far from the truth tonight. It was almost 4 a.m. by the time they reached the hospital and caught up with Marnie again. She was a wreck.

"My dad's going to kill me," she said again, her lower lip trembling.

"He's not," Gio promised her, and the man proved it when Gio called him a few minutes later to let him know what had happened.

"Ah, it's just a bloody car," he said, his tone light with relief. "Hell of a lot easier to replace one of those than a daughter."

There was no other traffic on the road when they left the hospital. The world was quiet and empty.

Sandra's house was in darkness when they reached it. Sergeant Quinn pulled up out the front. Gio stayed in his seat and checked his phone while the sergeant went inside. Half past four, and he was supposed to start work at eight. He could get a couple of hours' sleep in before then, hopefully.

A light flickered on in a front room of Sandra's house. A few moments after that Sergeant Quinn reappeared, carrying Taylor. The kid was too big to carry, probably. He was all long skinny limbs.

Gio climbed out and opened the back door. No way would Sergeant Quinn manage it with his arms full of Taylor.

Taylor mumbled something as the sergeant bundled him carefully into the back seat.

"Seat belt, mate," Sergeant Quinn said.

Taylor yawned, and straightened up to let his father get the seat belt clipped around him. "Dad?"

"Yeah, mate. It's me."

Taylor blinked his eyes open, still yawning. "Can you put the siren on?"

"Not tonight." Sergeant Quinn scrubbed his knuckles gently over Taylor's hair, and then stepped back and closed the door carefully.

Taylor was dozing again by the time they reached the back of the station. The arc of the headlights cut across the scrubby yard between the station and the houses. Richard's car was gone. Gio was unsurprised. Richard had had no way of knowing how long he'd be gone. Also, it was hard to regret when his top priority right now was sleep.

"Sorry," Sergeant Quinn said, his gaze following Gio's.

"It's fine, Sarge."

At least being called out had saved him an awkward farewell. He wasn't sure he and Richard had really clicked. It had been okay, but not exactly mind-blowing, and the feeling was probably mutual. There didn't seem to be enough of a spark between them for Richard to bother driving three hours each way for what had been fairly mediocre sex.

Then again, loneliness was a hell of a motivator, wasn't it?

Sergeant Quinn carried Taylor inside the station. Gio followed him to the armoury.

"Come on, Taylor," Sergeant Quinn said softly. "Come on. I have to put you down."

Taylor grumbled and wrapped his arms around Sergeant Quinn's neck more tightly.

"He gets clingy when he's tired," Sergeant Quinn said.

Gio divested himself of his firearm, his spare clip, his taser, and his spray, and set them in the safe beside Brian Howe's rifles. "I got it."

Sergeant Quinn turned, angling his hip towards Gio, and hitching Taylor's legs out of the way. Gio unclipped Sergeant Quinn's holster and drew his Glock out. He did the same with the taser on his other hip, and then his spray and spare clip. He couldn't help but notice how the sergeant's forearms were corded with the effort of holding Taylor. Taylor's face was buried in the crook of his neck, and he was still holding on tight like a possum.

"Done," Gio said, and closed the door to the weapons' safe.

"Thanks."

They locked up the station behind them, and set out across the grass towards their houses. The moonlight was bright enough that Gio didn't bother with his torch. The stars in the zenith of the sky were still vivid, although dawn was beginning to soften the edges of the sky. The moon hung huge and low, almost brilliant orange. Gio didn't think he'd ever seen a sky so radiant.

Their boots crunched through the grass.

"Gio? Can you help me out with my keys?"

"Um, yeah." This dance was even more awkward than the one in the armoury. Gio slid his hand inside the sergeant's pocket, and tried not to dig too deep. He hooked the keys out easily enough, and flicked through them until he found what looked like a house key, and then preceded Sergeant Quinn up the front stairs and unlocked the door for him.

"Thanks, Gio." Sergeant Quinn leaned against the doorjamb, still holding a sleeping Taylor in his arms. "I appreciate it. And I am sorry for wrecking your night."

"You didn't." Gio was glad the darkness of the veranda hid his flush. "It was just a hookup, you know?"

He was surprised to hear the sergeant's huff of laughter.

"Nah. It's been a bloody long time since I had one of those."

A weight Gio hadn't even realised he was carrying lifted. A joke, but it wasn't on him. Wasn't on his sexuality. "Yeah, well, it didn't exactly rate."

Another huff. "You're only saying that to make me feel better."

If he'd been on first name terms with the sergeant, if they'd been friends, Gio might have made a joke about how surely it was impossible he wasn't getting something on the side. A good-looking guy like Jason Quinn? That had to be a crime. But Gio didn't know him well enough to make that joke.

He smiled slightly instead, and ducked his head. "Maybe."

"Good night, Gio."

"Good night, Sarge."

The sergeant paused, half turned in the doorway. "It's Jason."

"Right." Gio nodded. "Jason."

"Good night," Jason said again, and stepped inside. He closed the door behind himself.

Gio headed for home, with the moon at his back.

CHAPTER TEN

Taylor was tired and bad-tempered at breakfast, and Jason packed him off to school with his backpack, his lunchbox, and a reminder to keep out of trouble that hopefully wasn't a waste of breath. He went back to bed after Taylor left, but couldn't sleep. Guilt, probably. After all, if his son was facing the day sleep-deprived and grumbly, Jason deserved no less. After lying in bed for twenty minutes, he gave up and went downstairs to throw on a load of laundry. The stray cat watched him narrow-eyed from her perch on top of his tool cupboard, and Jason pretended not to notice her. He wasn't caving. He just didn't have the energy to get into a battle of wills with a bloody cat. Not today, when he was pretty sure the cat would win. Jason's ego couldn't take a blow like that, not after Sandra had torn strips off him last night over Taylor.

"This needs to stop, *Jason,"* she'd said, looking terrifying despite her pink fluffy dressing gown. *"I love you, and I love that kid, but you are fast using up what little goodwill I've got over this."*

"I'm working on it."

She'd fixed him with a stare. *"Work* harder."

He'd felt smaller than a chastened child.

With the load of laundry in the machine, Jason headed back upstairs and dug the vacuum cleaner out of the cupboard in the hallway. It had a thin layer of dust covering it, which was a damn good indication of how long it had been since Jason used the thing. He gave the living room a cursory sweep, and then tackled the bedrooms.

"What is dust anyway?" Alana had asked once. *"It's just tiny bits of* stuff."

They'd been high at the time, lounging around in Graham's room in that shitty share house in Aitkenvale he'd been living in. Alana and Graham had laughed themselves stupid because Jason had insisted on locking the door and pulling the curtains closed. He was going to be a *cop*. He couldn't get busted for *drugs*. Except the more he'd tried to emphasise the gravity of the situation, the harder they'd both laughed at him. He'd tried to shush them every time a car had driven past, and they'd just fucking *howled*.

Idiots.

Last Jason had heard from Graham, he'd been going to Laos to do humanitarian work. It sounded like a great fit for the weird pot-smoking Nietzsche-quoting guy who'd been taking everything from Philosophy to Anthropology, to Politics to Human Geography. Jason was sure they'd have nothing in common these days, but back then he, Alana, and Graham had been thick as thieves.

Jason smiled at the memory as he worked, feeling the same ache in his chest that he always did when he thought of Alana. It had been years since his grief had been sharp enough to tear new wounds into him, but the ache remained. He was accustomed to the weight of it. He missed her, and he always would, but lately he'd been thinking it would be nice if there was room in his life for someone else.

The vacuum cleaner made a high-pitched grinding noise, and something that sounded like plastic rattled down the tube. Shit. Of course Taylor had left Lego or another toy on his floor, and now Jason was going to have to dig through a bag full of dust and crap to retrieve it. From existential crises to this. It seemed like a pretty solid metaphor for life, actually, but Jason didn't mind.

He didn't regret for one minute that he wasn't in Laos trying to save the world. He had Taylor and Taylor, despite his inability to keep his Lego pieces off the floor, was Jason's whole world. Everything else—his tiredness, his loneliness, his need for adult conversation and maybe touch as well—got pushed aside for now. For now, Jason always told himself, but it worried him how it had started to sound more and more like *forever* in his head.

He dragged the vacuum cleaner out onto the back stairs, and carried it down to the scrubby grass. The cat slunk out from under the house and watched warily as Jason gutted the strange creature in front of her, sending clumps and chunks of dust and lint rolling like tiny tumbleweeds across the yard. Jason dug around in the bag until he found the culprit: a formerly yellow Lego block that could now use a rinse under the tap.

"Got it," he told the cat, holding it up to show her.

He liked to imagine the cat looked grudgingly impressed.

Jason lugged the vacuum cleaner back upstairs again, glancing over at Gio's house as he did. Gio was managing, wasn't he? Only in town for a few weeks and already hooking up with someone. Richard fucking Hanna. Jason wasn't sure if the low burn in the pit of his stomach was because he was jealous of the pair of them, or just Richard Hanna. The guy was a nobody though. Only a hookup. What was it Gio had said last night?

"Yeah, well, it didn't exactly rate."

Maybe that meant Richard Hanna was already out of the picture. Jesus, and here Jason was again, forcing away some very unprofessional thoughts about Gio who, even if hooking up with a close colleague wasn't the worst idea in the history of the world ever, had to be the worst candidate for that hypothetical position anyway. He'd fucked that bloke on the Coast, and then completely fucked him over. Gio was bad news. Except the more time Jason spent with him, the harder that was to remember. Because, okay, they'd disagreed about a few things, but as far as Jason could tell, Gio wasn't looking to make trouble.

That was probably what his colleagues down on the Coast had thought too.

Jason shoved the vacuum cleaner back in the hallway cupboard, and checked his watch. He didn't start work until two, but he could go in early and get his paperwork out of the way. See if Gio wanted to grab lunch with him or something.

He dug a clean uniform out of the ironing basket, figured the worst creases would wear out in this heat anyway, and then dressed and headed for the station.

Sandra was on a day off today, so the front counter was unattended. Jason wasn't proud of the relief that washed over him at that. He didn't want a repeat of last night's dressing down. He'd put off chasing up childcare for Taylor for too long already though, and they both knew it. Jason needed to get his shit together on that front, and at least put a few feelers out around town.

Jason headed into the dayroom.

He hadn't noticed either of the vehicles missing when he'd come in, so he didn't think Gio was out on a call or on patrol, but he wasn't in the dayroom. Jason walked down the short hallway to his office, and heard voices.

Gio and . . . Patricia Howe. Gio must've taken her into his office for the illusion of privacy, even though the station was otherwise empty. A more comfortable chair and a box of tissues made all the difference sometimes.

"He's not a *bad* man," Patricia was saying.

"Nobody's saying he is." Gio sounded calm, patient. Jason wondered if he really believed what he was saying or if, like Jason, he wanted to punch Brian Howe in the face and make him taste his own medicine for once. "But if you tell the magistrate you don't want to go through with the order, that just shows Brian that he can do what he likes, and you'll let him."

"He doesn't mean to hurt me!"

"Patricia, it doesn't matter if he *means* it or not." A hint of impatience crept into Gio's tone. "He hurts you. Full stop."

"You don't understand!" Patricia began.

"I do." The quiet certainty in Gio's tone sent a chill through Jason. "I *do*."

Jason slipped away.

It was an uneventful shift. Taylor turned up after school and fell asleep halfway through his homework. Gio left at four, flashing Jason a smile as he did. Jason was sure his answering smile was hollow. Jason stayed in the station as long as he could, before packing Taylor into the LandCruiser and doing a few laps of town. He was always a little uneasy taking Taylor around with him, but after last night's run-in with Sandra, he wasn't going to push his luck with her tonight.

"Dad, can we pull some cars over?"

"Nope."

Taylor slumped in his seat, but brightened up again when they went to the truck stop for dinner. Jason thought of Gio as he ate. Thought of the large implications behind those very words: *"I do."*

It unsettled him.

Back at the station, Jason took a call from Senior Sergeant Gordon, the DDO in Townsville.

"Hey, Gordy," he said. "How are things?"

"Living the dream, mate," Gordy drawled. "Living the dream. Listen, I'm calling because I've got the report on Valeri's Use of Force arrest in front of me."

"Oh, yeah." Jason retreated to his office, although Taylor looked to be fairly mesmerised by whatever game he was playing on his iPad. "Is there a problem?"

Kev Lindeman's arrest had been messy as fuck, but Gio hadn't done anything wrong, and he'd had the bruises to prove it. Jason remembered how shaky Gio had been after Kev had assaulted him. He remembered how he'd wanted to reach out and trace the swelling on his jaw.

"That all depends on you," Gordy said.

Jason wondered exactly what he was offering here. A way to fuck Gio over instead of standing by him? A way to get rid of him? If that was what Gordy was implying—a rewriting of Jason's report to screw Gio over instead of backing him—did Gio even know how precarious his position was?

"I've got, um, I've got a lot of people waiting for the chance to dog me."

Yeah. Of course he knew.

"Gio didn't do anything wrong, Gordy," Jason said firmly. "It was a good arrest."

Gordy was silent for a moment. "Good. I just wanted to make sure you thought so."

"Do you know what happened down on the Coast?" Jason asked.

"I heard he lost a good copper his job."

"You think there's another side to that story, boss?"

Gordy grunted. "I think if you think there's only two sides to any story, you're severely lacking in imagination."

"Yeah," Jason said, thinking again of Gio's words to Patricia Howe. "Yeah, you're probably right."

At 10 p.m. Jason locked up the station and followed a yawning Taylor home.

"Bedtime," he said, smacking Taylor gently on the bum when he didn't move up the stairs to the front door quickly enough.

Taylor squawked in feigned outrage. "Dad!"

Gio's lights were still on.

"I'm just going next door for a bit, okay? Brush your teeth and get into bed and I'll be back in time to turn your light out."

"Okay!" Taylor scurried inside, and Jason moved back down the steps again and headed for Gio's. He crossed towards the back of Gio's place, boots treading the familiar path. He'd walked it often enough when Dan and Gabby had lived in the house. They'd rarely used each other's front doors.

The stairs squeaked as Jason climbed them. From inside he could hear the television. He rapped on the screen door. "Gio?"

Gio appeared within moments, his brow creased in a slight frown. "Sarge?"

Jason raised his eyebrows.

"Jason," Gio corrected, mouth quirking. He flicked the lock on the screen door and opened it. "What's up?"

There was no easy way to ask what he wanted to know. "Your ex, down on the Coast, did he assault you? Is that why you reported him to Ethical Standards?"

Gio's expression froze.

"I heard you talking to Patricia today," Jason said. "Pretty obvious you were talking from experience."

Gio stepped aside, and motioned for Jason to come inside, and then turned and headed for the kitchen. "Beer?"

"Yeah." Jason followed him into the kitchen and leaned against the bench near Gio's ridiculously fancy coffee machine.

Gio rattled around in the fridge, pulling out two beers. He passed one to Jason, and kept the other one, twisting the top off it, and flicking the cap into the sink. "My team down the Coast . . ." He took a sip of beer. "We were really competitive. Better than any fucking GDs crew. We ran our own ops where we'd go in hard and fast. We were all about getting the most pinches. We lived and breathed the fucking job. We were beyond competitive."

Jason watched him carefully.

Gio picked at the label on his beer bottle for a moment, and then took another swig. He fixed his gaze on some point over Jason's shoulder. "This one time, Coop outran Pete chasing down a grub, and didn't let up about it, so Pete started spending more time at the gym. I had other stuff going on at the time, with . . . with my dad, so I didn't notice at first. The little changes. Then one night we're at home, and out of the blue he just lost his shit. It was over something stupid, but he completely . . ." His hands shook. "He completely lost it."

"Hey." Jason set his beer down on the bench. He took a few steps forward, closing the space between them, put a hand on Gio's shoulder, and squeezed gently.

"I didn't even fight back," Gio said. "I was too fucking shocked." His mouth twitched in a brief, bitter smile. "So was he, I think."

Jason rubbed his thumb against the binding of the neckline of Gio's T-shirt.

"It's the old story. He promised it wouldn't happen again." Gio shrugged, his muscles moving under Jason's hand. "It did. I didn't—" He cut himself off, his mouth pressing into a thin line briefly before he spoke. "He'd gotten into steroids through these people he met at the gym. Then, this one arrest, he went in too hard. I thought, if I didn't report him, he was going to hurt someone. Really hurt them."

"Someone apart from you?"

"Told myself I could handle it if it was just me." Gio lifted his dark gaze to meet Jason's. "Probably bullshit. Anyway, I told Pete to clean himself up. He didn't. I called Ethical Standards. He failed a drug test. They had to get the drug squad from another division to search our flat. Couldn't have our mates do it."

"Jesus."

"They didn't find anything." Gio swallowed. "I'd already flushed it. He had . . . he had a lot of stuff at the flat. I didn't want them to think he was dealing; I wanted him to go to rehab, not lose his job.

They can do that. I spoke to the HSO. They'll send you to rehab if you've got a problem. It's like you get that one pass, you know?" His voice rasped. "I never meant for them to fire him. If I'd wanted that, I would have told them about the DV."

"You still could."

Gio flinched. "I already ruined his fucking life."

Jason shrugged. "Sounds like he ruined it himself."

"Right." Gio choked on a laugh. "Nobody else sees it like that though, do they? He said—" He pulled away and lifted the beer bottle to his mouth. Jason tracked the way his throat bobbed as he drank. Gio lowered the bottle and swiped the back of his hand over his lips. "He told everyone he'd met someone else, and I stabbed him in the back because I was jealous."

"And they believed that?"

Gio's snorted. "Turns out they were his friends more than mine."

"Maybe you should have told them the truth."

Gio expression hardened. "That was the *worst* thing I could have done."

"Why?" Jason demanded. He reached out for Gio again, and gripped his shoulder. He wasn't sure which one of them he was trying to keep grounded. "Why?"

"Because I left it too long! Because it would have looked like a fucking lie I couldn't prove!" Gio shook his head. His eyes shone. "Nobody would have believed me!"

"I believe you." Jason dug his fingers into the muscle of Gio's shoulder. "Gio. Look at me. I believe you."

Gio dropped his gaze. When he spoke again, his voice was rough. "I got my car keyed. Tyres slashed. Got calls in the middle of the night telling me they could see me, and that I was a dead man. Telling me the name of the place my fucking *niece* goes to day care. *Fuck*." He twisted away, pushing past Jason. He crossed to the sink, setting his beer down and then gripping the edges of the bench tightly. His shoulders rose and fell as he breathed heavily. His breath rasped.

Jason moved towards him. Gio looked like he was about to shake out of his body. Jason stared at their reflections in the kitchen window, and met Gio's gaze in the glass. He reached out and gave Gio a moment to flinch away. Then he put his hand on Gio's shoulder again. "Just breathe. You're okay. Just breathe."

Gio didn't try to shake him off this time.

Jason's fingers brushed against Gio's neck. He could feel his frantic pulse in his throat. "You're okay."

Gio dropped his head forward. "Fuck. I'm sorry."

"It's okay." Jason figured this, whatever it was, had been a long time coming. "You're gone now. It's over, right?" Gio tensed. "Gio? It's over, right?"

"Yesterday, in the mail . . ." Gio shrugged.

"What?"

"On the table."

Jason released him and then ran a hand down his back before heading into the dining area to Gio's small table. He picked up the envelope. Internal mail. A packet of Schmackos slid out of the envelope and dropped onto the table.

His blood ran cold.

Fuckers.

Jason exhaled heavily and ran a hand through his hair, sudden anger boiling low in his gut. He set the envelope back down, and then picked up the Schmackos and returned to the kitchen. Gio had turned around again. His eyes were red, and he avoided looking at Jason.

"What do you want to do about this?" Jason asked.

Gio shrugged. "Feed it to a dog?"

Jason's mouth quirked. "Yeah, not what I meant."

Gio was silent for a moment, and then he lifted his gaze. "There's no point reporting it. You think they're stupid enough to do anything an investigation can pin on them? A complaint will just make it worse. It doesn't matter if I know who it is. It doesn't matter if the bosses know who it is, or if Ethical Standards does. They can't do a thing without proof." He shook his head, his mouth thinning into a line. "Have you ever been on the wrong side of something like this?"

Jason glanced down at the Schmackos. "Gio, there's no bloody *right* side to this."

"I mean have you ever had this happen to you?"

"No." And Jason didn't have words for how disgusting it was. He'd heard about stuff like this happening before, but only in the vaguest terms. Something that had happened years ago, somewhere else, in a different division. Gossip that was stale long before it got to him, or war stories told by grizzled old coppers that dated back to the Fitzgerald era where shit like this had happened daily to whistle-blowers. Jason had never seen what it looked like close up. "You shouldn't have to put up with something like this."

Gio's brow furrowed. "What other choice do I have?"

Jason had been a copper for fifteen years. He thought he knew the job, thought he knew the sort of people he worked with, who wore the same uniform that he did. He'd seen people dicked around by the Service before, screwed over by management for some reason or another, but he hadn't seen anything this vicious before. Not colleague against colleague. He stepped closer to Gio and set the Schmackos down on the bench. "I don't know."

Gio smiled slightly. "Yeah. Same."

He was close enough that Jason could smell the beer on his breath.

There was silence. A strange tension in the air that Jason suddenly couldn't read. It felt like anticipation. Gio's gaze catching his, and holding it. Gio's expression was raw, naked, and Jason felt the swell of something protective, something almost proprietary, rise up in him.

Jason moved without any conscious thought to do so, his hand settling on Gio's hip, angling his body just right and then leaning in to press their mouths together. He lifted his other hand to Gio's head, and slid his fingers through those curls. Gio made a small, shocked noise that sounded almost like a question, but then his lips parted under Jason's, and their tongues touched. Gio's fingers tugged on the belt loops of Jason's uniform pants, pulling him closer. A jolt of lust ran through Jason, hot as a burst of flame, when their bodies lined up flush.

And then it was over, and Gio was pushing him away.

"Shit," Gio whispered, wide-eyed. "What the *hell*?" He wiped his mouth like he'd taken another swig of beer. "What was that? You're not even . . ."

Jason swallowed, his heart beating fast. Fuck. He'd overstepped the line so far he couldn't even see it from here.

"Fuck," Gio whispered.

"Gio," Jason said. "I—"

"Dad?" The screen door rattled open.

Jason stepped back from Gio. Fuck fuck *fuck*.

"Dad?" Taylor peered into the kitchen. He was in his pyjamas. "You were supposed to come and turn my light out."

"Yeah." Jason glanced at Gio, who had turned away again and was running water in the sink. "Yeah, I'm coming now. Gio, can we talk tomorrow?"

Gio shot him a wild look over his shoulder.

"Dad!" Taylor grabbed his hand and tugged on it. "I waited *forever*!"

"I know, mate. We're going." Jason let his son drag him towards the door. "Good night, Gio."

Gio didn't answer.

CHAPTER ELEVEN

Gio didn't sleep. He lay awake all night in sheets that still smelled of Richard but thought of Sergeant Quinn instead. Richard had sent a text just before midnight: *Thanks for last night.* Gio hadn't replied yet. Not now that Jason Quinn had set up camp in his brain and was refusing to move out. It was a disaster: Gio's confession, and then the kiss. Fuck. Gio couldn't have been more exposed tonight if he'd stripped down naked in front of Jason, which, Jesus, had that even been on the table? Maybe for one crazy, heated moment, before Taylor had turned up.

Gio climbed out of bed before dawn, his gritty eyes stinging, and dug his running shoes out from the bottom of the bedroom cupboard. He used to run all the time back on the Coast—had to keep his fitness up in his team—but running along the Broadwater at dawn and looking out to the Spit as the sun rose over the glittering water had been a hell of a lot nicer prospect than whatever Richmond had to offer.

It was still dark when Gio locked his front door behind himself and headed for the riverbank. There was a bike path that ran for a few kilometres beside the river that Gio had checked out a few times on patrol. He set off at a slow jog to warm up. The soles of his shoes scuffed against the gritty bitumen at the shoulder of the road. There was no traffic to worry about. He heard the descending symphony of a semi's compression brakes in the distance. The dawn was just starting to paint the sky pink when he reached the riverbank. A magpie was warbling in one of the ghost-pale eucalypts. A pair of sulphur-crested cockatoos sat on the back of a park bench, bobbing at one another.

There was nobody around.

Gio began to run.

The cool breeze off the river couldn't quite cut through yesterday's heat rising off the cement bike track. Another stinking hot day lay just underneath the horizon. To Gio's left, the levee rose up and then dropped away steeply to the river. Gio couldn't see the river from the bike track. The trees along the top of the levee leaned towards the water like divining rods.

Gio picked up his pace, losing himself in the familiar rhythm of running. Of muscle memory, of just putting one foot in front of the other, and not having to *think*. The sun was up and he was damp with sweat by the time he finally turned for home. His body ached.

He looked over at Jason's house as he climbed the steps of his own. There was no sign of movement, except for the skinny cat sunning itself on the back steps.

Gio swallowed down the sudden sharp stab of panic that found him again. All the tension that had bled out of him on his run was back again, and rising. He tore his gaze away from Jason's house and then unlocked his screen door and pushed his way inside. He locked the door behind him, and headed for the shower.

His heart was racing, and his stomach was in knots.

This last year had been a disaster. Gio had always been confident, outgoing, willing to admit to the mistakes he made and to learn from them. But this last year had undermined everything. He couldn't remember the last time he'd had a full night's sleep. Couldn't remember the last time he hadn't second-guessed every damn decision he'd made. It might have been easier if he could have kept his personal life and his professional life separate, but that had never been an option. He couldn't compartmentalise like that. Not when it was his entire fucking life. The only thing he'd been able to do at all was keep Dad and Sophie out of the shit fight as best he could, and the only reason he'd managed that much was by letting them both think he'd just decided to up and leave one day, even though they'd needed him there.

Richmond was supposed to be . . . What was it the assistant commissioner had called it?

"It's a fresh start," he'd said with a hollow-sounding affability that had set Gio's nerves on edge. *"It's what you make it."*

Gio had no leverage with the Service anymore. Nobody was going to bend over backwards to help him out given the cloud he was already under. And what could he do anyway? Phone up the HSO and tell them that he needed a transfer out because his sergeant had kissed him? And that Gio had kissed him back for that one stupid moment where it had felt right?

Yeah, that'd be a great career move for the guy already known for screwing over the last bloke he was involved with.

Gio stepped into the shower, making the water a fraction too hot for comfort. The slight burn distracted him from the constant cycle of frenzied thoughts that whirled around in his skull.

The kiss was bad enough. The fact that Gio had told him about Pete? Had *cried* about it?

Gio squeezed his eyes shut and leaned his forehead against the shower wall. The grout between the tiles felt gritty. He curled his right hand into a loose fist and dragged his knuckles down between the tiles. Thought seriously about punching the wall, just to see if he could relieve the tightly coiled tension inside him that way.

He snorted at his own stupidity and flexed his fingers.

What the *hell*, though? What the hell had *happened* last night? Jason had been a solid presence, strong, strangely comforting, and Gio had blurted out the whole sorry story before he'd even had a chance to panic about how it might be received. And then . . . What the hell was the kiss anyway, coming on the heels of that? What the hell was it, and what was Gio supposed to feel about it?

"Gio, can we talk tomorrow?"

Gio really didn't want to have whatever talk was coming, but what choice did he have? He had nowhere left to run.

Gio started at eight. Sandra was already in when he arrived, aggressively stirring sugar into her coffee. Her mouth tightened into a thin line when she glanced up and saw him.

"We're out of biscuits," she said.

"Oh." Gio had no idea what response she was chasing. Was she just stating a fact, was she looking for him to be suitably outraged, or was he somehow expected to do something to rectify the no-biscuit situation?

Sandra gave him an unimpressed stare. "There's money in the petty cash. Can you get some biscuits when you're patrolling?"

"Yeah," Gio said. "No worries."

She swept past him, heading for the front counter. "Get decent ones. None of that Homebrand crap."

Gio wouldn't dare.

His day passed slowly, the plodding progress of the hours broken only with shards of panic that sliced suddenly into his consciousness every time he'd almost managed to forget: *He kissed you. You kissed him back.* And: *"Gio, can we talk tomorrow?"*

Gio patrolled. He bought biscuits that passed muster with Sandra. He found a couple of kids down on the riverbank and drove them back to the school. He took a complaint of wilful damage, one of theft, and attended a dispute between elderly neighbours who were arguing about overhanging tree branches. He ate lunch at the truck stop with Vicki, and checked his phone every few minutes for missed calls or messages. As much as Gio wanted to avoid whatever Jason was going to say to him, he knew he couldn't. And as much as he was dreading it, he wanted it over with. He didn't want to miss the call if Jason came in to work early.

"Lining up a hot date?" Vicki teased him.

"Work stuff," Gio said, and wished to hell it was a lie.

He was back at the station just before 1 p.m., his lunch sitting heavily in his gut. He could hear Sandra at the counter, tapping away on her keyboard. The phone rang once, and she answered it. Gio couldn't hear the conversation, only that she laughed a few times. Gio tried to concentrate on his paperwork, but this was his *job*. This was his job, and after every fucking thing he'd been through down the Coast, he was barely hanging onto it by the skin of his teeth, and he'd fucked up. He'd played right into the hands of everyone who wanted him gone. For months, for fucking *months* he'd weathered the stress and panic of the nonstop shit-storm that had become his life, and now, when he'd actually had a moment to breathe again, he'd fucked up. Because there was no way—no fucking way—that Gio would be allowed to be the victim in this. Not with his history.

And because for a moment, just a breathless, insane moment, Gio had kissed him back. Kissed him back before he'd come to his senses and pushed him back.

"Gio?"

Gio jerked his head up to see Jason standing in the doorway that led out to the car park. He hadn't even heard him come in.

Jason nodded towards the rear door of the station.

Gio followed him outside into the heat of the day.

The door swung shut behind them.

The sun beat down on the nape of Gio's neck as he pressed the toe of his boot down onto a rock, and rolled it back and forth under his foot. He exhaled slowly and watched as Jason leaned against the bull bar of the LandCruiser.

"Okay," Jason said finally. He shoved his hands into his pockets. "I think we need to get some things out into the open."

Gio nodded, bile rising in his throat.

"First of all, what happened was the textbook definition of inappropriate workplace behaviour and, ah . . ." Jason cleared his throat. His forehead was creased with worry. "So I apologise for that, firstly. I'm your boss. I shouldn't have done that."

Gio froze, unsure if he could trust Jason's apology, and unsure that it even mattered. Shouldn't have done it, okay, but he *had*, and Gio didn't know if there was an apology in the world that could make him forget it. And before Gio could think about forgetting it, he wanted to understand it. Gio had lain awake all night wondering what the fuck had happened. Jason didn't get to brush all that aside with an apology.

He forced another nod, pressing harder on the rock underneath his boot. He lifted his gaze, wary. "Why did you?"

Jason chewed his bottom lip for a moment. "I don't . . . I wasn't fucking with you, Gio."

"What?" Gio's heart skipped a beat. "But you're not . . . You were *married*."

Jason tugged his hand out of his pocket and dragged his fingers through his hair. His mouth quirked in an almost bashful smile. "I met Alana at uni because we were both seeing the same guy."

"You're bi." Gio didn't know what to make of the sudden burst inside him of some emotion he couldn't name. It wasn't anything as positive as hope. It was relief, maybe, to discover that whatever it was that had passed between them the night before, however ill-advised, was at least still in the scope of Gio's understanding. That Jason had been acting on attraction, not on something predatory and ugly. That was some consolation, wasn't it?

Jason's smile slowly faded and he nodded.

"Okay," Gio said at last, glad his voice didn't waver.

"Okay?"

Gio held his gaze. "What else do you want me to say?"

Jason exhaled slowly. "Gio, I'm telling you that I fucked up, and that I'd really like to know that it's not going to be an issue."

"You mean you'd like to know that I'm not going to *make* it an issue," Gio said, his stomach clenching. "With my speed dial to Ethical Standards and everything."

"That's not what I said." Jason's tone was suddenly steely. "Don't put words in my mouth. I meant what I said last night. I *believe* you."

"Okay." Gio pressed his mouth into a thin line before forcing himself to relax, or to at least appear relaxed. "Then it's no problem. It was just a lapse in judgement." He caught Jason's look, and wasn't sure how to read it. "From both of us, I mean. And it's nothing that anyone else needs to know about."

"Right," Jason said. The word was bitten off, sounding somehow abrupt and relieved at the same time.

Gio folded his arms over his chest, his heart pounding. "Are we good, Sarge?"

He waited for Jason to correct him like he had before: *"It's Jason."* But today Jason let it go, let Gio insert that space between them again. Because today, Gio figured, they both needed it.

"Yeah, Gio," Jason said at last. He tilted his head forward in a nod, and the sunlight shone in his hair. "We're good."

When his shift ended, Gio went home and changed, and then picked up some groceries from the small supermarket in town.

"Oh," said the lady stacking the dairy case in the supermarket. "You're the new police officer, aren't you?"

"Uh . . . yeah."

It still felt strange to be recognised as a copper, even out of uniform. It had rarely happened on the Coast. He'd had people give him a second glance a few times, frowning slightly as they tried to place him, but Gio had usually been able to slip away before it had clicked that he was the guy who'd given them a Notice to Appear last week when they'd been taking a drunken piss in a public street. Things were very different here.

The woman's gaze fell curiously on his basket of groceries, and Gio was suddenly grateful he hadn't stocked up on condoms and lube. He was pretty sure she was already hard-core judging the fact he was a man in his midtwenties who was buying Munchables snack packs with Jelly Babies.

The woman crooked an ill-kempt eyebrow at him as he escaped to the checkout.

Back at home, Gio sat on the front veranda with his feet on the rail and watched low grey clouds roll in from the horizon. The afternoon shadows gradually darkened. A bead of sweat slid down Gio's spine. He gazed out across the yard over to the station. One of the LandCruisers was missing, which probably meant Jason was on a job, or on patrol.

Gio picked up his phone and took a photo of the back of the station. He sent it to Sophie: *The view from my house. Remember when I used to be able to get away from work?*

He hoped she'd laugh.

He set his phone down and closed his eyes. Drew a deep, slow breath.

Today could have gone worse. The talk with Jason. It was indicative of how shitty his life had become when "could have gone worse" was the best-case scenario.

No. It was okay. He was getting his life back on track. This detour to Richmond was only two years, and then he'd head south again. Not to the Coast. To Brisbane maybe. Somewhere he'd be close enough to Sophie and to Dad to lend a hand. Not that there was a lot to do, practically, but Sophie could use his support. Dad was . . .

Dad was on a downward slide. Tiny memory lapses and moments of confusion for now, but he could still function. The doctors had said it might be a few years until it got bad.

He'd never had the greatest relationship with his dad. His dad had never really come to terms with Gio's sexuality. The old story.

"Gio, he's . . ." Sophie had sighed. *"He's a product of a different time."*

"That's bullshit, Soph. Don't excuse him. Not to me, the finocchio."

"Gio . . ."

He didn't hate his dad. He never had. And he knew his dad didn't hate him either, which made it more frustrating to know that his dad would never come around. But the blazing arguments of Gio's teenage years were long behind them, dead and buried years before his dad's Alzheimer's diagnosis, and Gio had no interest digging them up again. It was what it was. Gio had learned to live with it.

Gio opened his eyes and watched a lizard scuttle along the veranda rail. His gaze was caught by a small figure crossing the yard, his backpack bouncing. Taylor. He was trudging along, dragging a stick and stopping occasionally to poke at things that caught his interest. He reached his front steps, discarded the stick. Then he dropped his backpack on the ground, upended the contents everywhere, and sat on the bottom step while he picked through the mess. He found his key at last, and held it up with a grin, shoving everything back in his backpack—including what had to be a fair few chunks of dirt—and then bounced up the steps to let himself into the house.

Gio flicked through the games on his phone.

Minutes later, the smoke alarm next door began to beep.

The steps shook as Gio hurried down them. He crossed the space between their houses quickly, ignoring the stab of dried stems and bindies under his bare feet. When he reached the Quinns' steps, he gripped the rail and hauled himself up them.

"Taylor?" he called out, pulling the door open.

Taylor appeared, wide-eyed and frantic, from the kitchen doorway. Smoke wafted out behind him.

Gio darted into the kitchen. The microwave door was hanging open, and yes, there was definitely something burning inside on the plate.

Taylor danced from foot to foot anxiously. "I only put it in for a minute and thirty seconds!"

Gio grabbed a tea towel from the bench and reached into the microwave. He dumped the plate in the sink, and ran the tap, and then flapped the tea towel around to clear the smoke. The alarm was still beeping.

It was a cheeseburger, the McDonald's wrapper almost entirely cremated beyond recognition. Gio left the water running over it and grabbed a chair from the dining room. He climbed on it and removed the batteries from the smoke alarm, and then stepped down and set them on the bench.

The microwave timer was flashing. There were four minutes and twelve seconds to go.

"Did you maybe put it on for thirteen minutes instead?"

Taylor chewed his bottom lip worriedly. "Maybe?"

Gio sighed. "Come on. Come over to my place and I'll make you a sandwich, and then we'll call your dad and tell him what happened."

"Okay," Taylor said, clearly downcast. Then he wrinkled his nose and his expression brightened. "Do you have Vegemite?"

When he got a text later that night, Gio thought it might be from Richard. It wasn't. It was from Jason.

Thanks for today. For everything.

It's no problem, Gio sent back.

Yeah. He and Jason could work together.

This could be home for two years.

CHAPTER TWELVE

Court days were a pain in the arse. The magistrate visited Richmond once a month, along with the police prosecutor, and Jason spent the day chasing up paperwork, and coffees, and whatever the hell else they needed to keep the wheels of the justice machine turning smoothly. Gio was on a day off, but he turned up in jeans and a T-shirt to the tiny courthouse in the main street because Patricia Howe would be here today. It wasn't odd exactly, but Jason wouldn't have expected Gio to show up. Maybe he was more of a country copper than he appeared. The potential was certainly there.

The Domestic Violence Protection Order was granted with no fuss, and Jason made sure that Brian Howe didn't kick up a stink about it. He nodded to Gio across the small courthouse foyer as Gio escorted Patricia back outside and Jason ran interference with Brian.

"So this is it, huh?" Brian asked, waving a sheaf of pages in Jason's face. "You take my bloody wife and my bloody guns!"

"And there's nothing keeping you from getting either of them back," Jason told him calmly. "Provided you abide by the conditions of the order."

Brian shot him a narrow-eyed look and stomped outside into the blinding sunlight. Jason followed him.

Gio was standing at the bottom of the steps.

"Did Patricia get out of here okay?" Jason asked in a low voice, watching Brian storm towards his battered ute.

"She's with her friend," Gio said.

"Good. Brian needs to cool off."

Gio nodded.

Jason swung his car keys around his index finger. "Plans for your days off?" he asked as Brian's ute lurched past them, the transmission whining.

Gio flashed him a wry smile. "Does *Overwatch* count?"

"Is that a video game?"

Gio's smile grew. "Yeah. Yeah, it is."

Jason laughed. "And suddenly I feel old. Thanks for that, Gio."

Colour rose in Gio's cheeks.

"Listen," Jason said. "I'm rostered a corro shift tomorrow, and I'm doing a run to Charters Towers. I thought I'd take Taylor, grab some stuff at Target or whatever." He shrugged. "There's not a hell of a lot to do in the Towers either, but you're welcome to come if you want."

Gio's eyes widened. "Yeah. Okay, that sounds good."

"Good." Jason nodded. "We're leaving at about seven."

Gio smiled. "Sounds like a plan."

"Oh, wow! Is that a Captain America shirt?" Taylor's eyes almost bugged out of his head when Gio approached the back of the station early the next morning. "That is so *cool*!"

Gio ducked his head when he laughed.

"Is he your favourite?" Taylor asked. "He's my favourite. Dad, who's your favourite?"

"Loki," Jason said.

"Daaad!" Taylor was clearly outraged. "He's the *bad* guy!"

Gio laughed again, and he looked loose and comfortable. His hair was still damp from his shower, curls springing free. Jason imagined running his fingers through Gio's hair, tugging on those curls. He remembered the feel of Gio's pulse racing under his touch, and the scent of his skin. He tore his gaze away.

"Seat belt, Taylor," he said, opening the back door so Taylor could climb inside.

Gio settled into the passenger seat, and clipped his belt on.

Jason reached for the radio. "Two-eight-nine, VKR. Booking on."

The voice from Comms came through on a burst of static. "VKR, two-eight-nine. Go ahead with shift."

"Working seven to three, VKR."

"Go with payroll."

"User 4010273. Show me heading into the big smoke of Charters Towers."

The dispatcher laughed. "Copy that. Have a good one, Jase."

"You too, Jen." Jason set the handset back in its cradle.

Gio was looking at him with raised brows. "You know their names?"

"Only the ones who've been there awhile." Jason turned the ignition over. "Is your seat belt on, Taylor?"

"Yep!"

"Then let's get this show on the road."

It was a three-hour drive to Charters Towers. Taylor, hyped up at missing a day of school, chattered away for the first hour before his enthusiasm flagged and he fell asleep with his head against the window. Jason rarely got weekends off, so day trips to Charters Towers with Taylor were rare. Jason tried to limit Taylor's absences to one day a term. The last time they'd tried it, a road train had rolled on the highway between Richmond and Hughenden, and they'd had to turn around and head west again. It had been in Hughenden's division, but a big job like that? A crew from Charters Towers had been dispatched as well. The road train had been carrying cattle, and Jason hadn't been able to eat steak for a month without his stomach turning.

Today the drive was uninterrupted. Gio did a few rego checks on the iPad, but nothing that brought up any flags.

Jason had worried there might be some awkwardness between them after the kiss, and maybe they would never have the same easy camaraderie that he'd shared with Dan, but this was okay.

The day was bright and hot. The clouds that had rolled in a few days ago had passed over them. The wet season was still a few weeks away, when the lows would form in the gulf and the monsoonal rain would flood the northwest of the state for weeks. The dry riverbeds would fill with water, and burst their banks, isolating the more remote towns and properties for weeks on end. Gio would get his real introduction to country policing then: hours spent trying to get through floodwaters to stranded motorists, arranging evacuations with the State Emergency Services, and coordinating food drops with the army. That was a level of interagency collaboration that was reserved for ranking officers in the city.

Jason stole a glance at Gio. He was running another rego through QLiTE. Jason snorted.

Gio looked across at him quickly, eyebrows raised. The sunlight made his brown eyes appear almost gold.

"You're on a day off, remember?" Jason tapped his fingers against the steering wheel.

"Right." Gio smiled, and slid the iPad back into the pocket beside his seat. "I'll bet you could do this drive in your sleep, couldn't you?"

"Unfortunately, yeah."

A six-hour round-trip to Charters Towers, and a ten-hour round-trip to Townsville. It didn't matter how many times he did these drives for work, it was always Alana he thought of, and that barrage of frantic specialists' appointments they'd had to deal with at the beginning of her diagnosis. Sometimes Taylor had come with them, strapped into his child seat and grizzling all the way. They'd shared some of their lowest moments on those long trips as the flat countryside slid away on either side of the car. Some of their highest too, laughing and singing.

Jesus.

Jason didn't know how they'd ever managed to laugh, even for a little bit.

"Jason," she'd whispered to him one night, her voice hitching with tears. *"Jason, it's not* fair."

Jason glanced at Taylor in the rearview. Everyone said how much Taylor looked like his dad, but Jason could see Alana in him too. The quick quirk of his mouth when he smiled. The shape of his chin. The untameable cowlick in his hairline.

Jason fixed his gaze on the road again.

Taylor was growing so fast, which was part of the reason for this trip. He'd shot up a few inches in the last few months, and was rapidly outgrowing all his clothes. Jason figured he could get him to pick out at least a few new things before he was completely distracted by the games section in Target.

They arrived in Charters Towers just before ten. The police station was in Gill Street, most of which was filled with heritage-listed buildings that dated back to the gold rush. The station was no exception: a two-storey red brick building with wooden verandas and a steel hipped roof, fronted by a small garden with a white picket fence.

Jason pulled into a parking spot out the front and turned to Gio. "Do you want to come in?"

In the back seat, Taylor was snuffling awake.

Jason watched the indecision cross over Gio's face, and wondered what it felt like to be in his shoes. To be hated the way he was, when nobody this far north had any hope of even knowing the truth.

"I'll come in," Gio said. "I mean, I'm going to meet them at some point, right?"

"Yeah." Jason got out of the LandCruiser and slammed the door shut. He opened the back door and helped a yawning Taylor down, and then reached in for the stacks of paperwork he had to deliver.

Taylor stepped onto the footpath, stretching. "Dad, can we go to McDonald's?"

"Work stuff first, then clothes shopping for you, and then, if you behave, McDonald's."

Taylor grinned.

"Right," Jason said, and met Gio's gaze. "Let's go and make some introductions."

The station, Target, McDonald's, and back in the LandCruiser.

"Anything else you want to check out while we're here?" Jason asked.

Gio dug into his fries. "I'm good, I think. It's, ah . . ."

"Not exactly the Gold Coast," Jason finished for him. His gaze was caught by the way Gio's mouth shone with grease from the fries, and he imagined leaning over and licking Gio's lips clean. Then he remembered they were in the car park at McDonald's and his kid was sitting in the back seat, which put paid to that little fantasy.

He started the engine.

The station visit had been awkward, but nobody had been overtly hostile towards Gio. Speculative, maybe, which might have been just as difficult to bear, but that was probably the best Gio could hope for. It was unfair, but Jason didn't mention it. What good would that do? Gio already knew it was unfair. He didn't need Jason to confirm it.

Gio huffed out a small laugh. "Not exactly. But it's been nice to see someplace different."

"Seeing the World, huh?"

Gio threw him a questioning look.

Jason pulled out of the car park. "They used to call this place the World, back in its heyday. It was the biggest city in Queensland outside of Brisbane."

"Really?" Gio sounded dubious.

"Apparently. More hotels and brothels than you could poke a stick at during the boom."

"I know what a brothel is!" Taylor piped up from the back seat.

"Good for you, mate," Jason told him.

Gio snorted and passed his remaining fries back to Taylor.

"It's probably gonna take more than that to shut him up," Jason commented.

"Daaad!"

Gio laughed.

They headed west.

They made good time returning to Richmond, stopping once for fuel, and once to help a bloke change a blown tyre. Gio seemed more relaxed on the trip home than he had this morning. He was leaning back in his seat, taking in the scenery, and occasionally nodding along to a song on the radio. The reception wasn't always great out here. Sometimes it dropped out for minutes on end and left nothing but the hiss of static, but sooner or later it picked up again.

Gio seemed almost happy. It suited him.

The afternoon sun painted the sky in streaks of orange and gold.

They rolled back into Richmond just past four, and Jason loaded Taylor up with shopping bags and pointed him towards the house.

"Thanks for today," Gio said, stretching. "I was probably going stir-crazy."

"I sometimes forget how it can get a little claustrophobic out here at first." So much empty space, so much open sky, but a small town made its own small spaces and those small spaces could be stifling. That first year, he and Alana had thrown themselves into getting out of the house whenever they got the chance. Fishing. Camping. They'd gone looking for fossils once, even though neither of them had known what the hell they were doing and couldn't tell the difference between a rock and a fossil in the first place. It had been fun. "It's not so bad once you figure out how to entertain yourself."

Shift work and organised activities didn't always work out though. Jason had been on the local footy team a few years back, but it was too hard to make practice, let alone the weekend games.

Gio's mouth quirked. "With something apart from video games, you mean?"

Jason laughed. "Well, it's your choice."

He turned and watched Taylor tramping home, a small, solitary figure, and felt the customary ache he so often did. It was no longer the sharp-edged bite of shock and loss. The years had blunted the edges, but it would always hurt a little. Some days more than others.

Alana had been four months pregnant when she was diagnosed, and together they'd made the choice to terminate so she could start chemo straightaway. Jason tried not to think of it as a baby, so it didn't feel like another thing he'd lost as well. And in moments of cold honesty, he thought it was better the way it had happened. He wouldn't have coped alone with Taylor and a baby.

Asking his parents for help hadn't been an option.

Dan and Gabby had stepped up when Alana had been diagnosed. They'd only been new to town then. Jason had hardly known them, but Dan, quietly earnest, had taken him aside one day and said if there was anything he needed, *anything*, then he only had to ask. And Gabby had visited every day, cooking meals and throwing on the washing, and taking Alana out for coffee. They'd shouldered a lot of the day-to-day burdens. They'd been there to the end, and beyond. When Jason had barely been able to function, Taylor had still been fed and looked after.

He'd felt so lost without Alana.

He turned back to Gio. "Do you want to join us for dinner? I mean, if you haven't had enough of us already."

Gio looked surprised for a moment, and then smiled. "Yeah. That'd be nice. Want me to bring anything?"

"We're good," Jason assured him. "Come over whenever you're ready."

Jason let himself into the station to unkit himself. He checked his desk to see if Sandra had left him any urgent messages on sticky notes before she'd closed up for the day, and then checked the messages on the station phone, but there was nothing that couldn't wait until the morning.

He locked the station behind him and headed home.

Inviting Gio to dinner wasn't a mistake—he hoped. They had to be able to work together, and to an extent, that meant being able to have a friendly relationship outside of work too. It wasn't some city station where they'd never cross paths unless they were rostered together. They were neighbours too. And it was stupid for Gio to go home to an empty house and cook his dinner for one, when Jason and Taylor were cooking right next door. A shared meal every week or so wasn't crossing a line. Jason questioned his motivations though. Was he inviting Gio over because it was the practical and the friendly thing to do? Or was it because he wanted to manoeuvre them both into a situation where another kiss was a possibility?

It wasn't. It couldn't be. He'd shut that down. Gio had shut it down too. But fuck, Jason still *wanted*.

There were a lot of cold showers in his future, probably.

When he got home, it was to find all the Target bags dumped on the living room floor.

"Taylor!" he complained loudly, and Taylor thumped down the hallway.

"What?"

"How is this putting your new clothes away?"

"You didn't tell me to put them away! You just told me to take them home!" Taylor raised his eyebrows. "Anyhow, you're supposed to prewash them!"

Jason rolled his eyes. "Then cut the tags off, and put them in the laundry basket."

Taylor groaned.

"Yeah, yeah," Jason said. "I'm so mean to you. Sort it out, Taylor. Gio's coming over for dinner, and I'd prefer this place didn't look like a bomb hit it."

Taylor's groan turned into a protracted growl, and he stomped forward to collect the bags. Jason crossed his arms over his chest and watched, waiting to see if Taylor dared push it any further than that. He'd find his new video game locked in the gun safe in the station if he did. But Taylor had always had a finely tuned sense of where the line was. He gathered the bags up and tramped off to the kitchen, presumably to get the scissors.

Good. Jason didn't really want to punish him. It had been a long day, and Taylor was overtired.

By the time Gio came over, Taylor's mood had improved, and he greeted Gio with a smile and a wave as he made himself an orange cordial to drink with dinner.

"I thought I said you didn't need to bring anything," Jason said.

Gio shrugged, and set the six-pack of beer down on the kitchen bench. "What can I do to help?"

"I think I've got it under control."

Dinner was leftover curried sausages and rice from the night before. It was nothing special, but Jason hoped the company made up for the menu. Eating alone every night couldn't be much fun for Gio. They talked a little about work—nothing interesting enough for Taylor to fix on—and a little about stuff around town that Gio might be interested in. The conversation flowed easily, and Jason was glad. It felt comfortable with Gio here with him and Taylor. It didn't have to be awkward between them.

"There are a few sports clubs," Jason said, "but you know what that's like with shift work."

"Yeah." Gio nodded. "I'm trying to get back into a routine with running. You know, to make sure I get out of the house. It's a good track by the river."

"It's pretty nice," Jason agreed. "Me and Taylor take our bikes down there sometimes."

"Have you got a bike, Gio?" Taylor asked. "You could come with us!"

"I think my bike is still in the shed at the back of my sister's place in Brisbane," Gio said. "I haven't ridden it in years."

"I wouldn't either, with the bloody traffic on the Coast," Jason said. "Or the hills in Brisbane."

Gio grimaced. "I hated those hills when I lived there."

"I ran over a snake on my bike once," Taylor piped up.

Jason tried not to laugh at the horror on Gio's face.

Gio shot him a wary look. "He's kidding, right?"

"It was a king brown," Taylor said.

"To be fair, we think it was already dead," Jason said.

Gio winced.

"You're having flashbacks to the taipan, aren't you?" Jason asked.

"Every time I close my eyes," Gio deadpanned, and stabbed at a piece of sausage with his fork. "Please tell me this didn't happen on the track by the river? Where I go running?"

Jason hid a smile.

Taylor wrinkled his nose. "Nooo?"

"Very convincing." Gio shook his head. "Great."

"Snakes are more scared of you than you are of them," Taylor said knowledgeably, and then shrugged. "Except that's probably no consolation when they kill you."

"Probably not," Gio agreed, but he was smiling again, his eyes bright, and maybe they'd made another step today away from the awkwardness of the kiss, and towards actual friendship.

That was the goal here.

It had to be.

CHAPTER THIRTEEN

It had been a long time since Gio had looked forward to going to work, a long time since he hadn't had to psych himself up to head in for each shift, but Jason was easy to work with. There were times when they were still a little unsure around one another, a little reserved, but those times were fewer and farther between the more the days stretched out. Even Sandra seemed to be starting to thaw to Gio, once he proved he could get into the station without setting the alarms off, and could actually do his job.

The investigation into Gio's assault and Kev Lindeman's arrest was, surprisingly, ticked and flicked. Senior Sergeant Gordon, the DDO from Townsville, had called Gio to tell him as much, but a part of Gio was still waiting for the other shoe to drop, and probably always would be. There were too many people just waiting for him to fail. And even if he never gave them a reason to fire him, they could throw enough shit at him and tie him up in enough investigations that eventually he wouldn't be able to take it anymore, and he'd quit. And Gio knew that animus directed at him wasn't only restricted to his former teammates. There was at least one superintendent who had told Gio to his face that if he saw him crossing the road, he wouldn't brake.

But it got easier and easier with each passing day to put all of that aside, to relegate it to a different point in geography, to a different point in time. Things weren't like that in Richmond, not with Jason. This was the job as he remembered it at its best. This was someone having his back again.

The pace was so different than what Gio was used to from the Coast—there were no taskings waiting for him, no targeted patrols, no daily briefing from Intel with maps of ever-changing hotspots—but he was growing to almost like it. He knew people now, and not just the town grubs. His small social circle extended beyond Jason and Vicki, to the usual transient population of towns like Richmond: the coppers, the nurses, and the chalkies. It was a younger crowd—a straight crowd as far as Gio could tell—but they were good to get a few drinks in with, either at the nurses' quarters behind the hospital, or the house two of the teachers shared on Victoria Street. Sometimes there were a few backpackers thrown in the mix. Gio was always careful not to drink more than a beer or two. He was learning, slowly, some of those country-copper sensibilities that Jason had tried to explain in the beginning. These people were his friends, but, even if he wasn't working, he was never truly off duty.

The rain arrived in October.

The first drops spattered on the roof of the station, and then the deluge hit with a roar. It didn't relent for hours, and although the worst of the downpour was over by nightfall, it didn't clear. Rain hung over the town in a persistent low grey shroud. By the next morning, a Tuesday, the highway was cut by flooding to the west, and a convoy of road trains and semitrailers pulled up alongside the highway to wait it out. On Wednesday morning, the highway was cut to the east as well, and on Wednesday night the flooding from farther north in the Gulf had made its way through the river system, and the river broke its banks.

The station buzzed with activity on Thursday. The volunteers from the State Emergency Service—bright in their yellow emergency gear—crowded into the dayroom alongside a few shire council workers and local volunteer firefighters. Taylor sat at the front counter playing Bubbles on Sandra's computer, freed from school thanks to the flooding.

Gio stood back and let Jason take charge. He clearly knew exactly what he was doing, and he had an easygoing sort of authority that people responded well to. He was thoughtful and attentive to detail, and if someone asked a question he didn't know the answer to, he was unafraid to admit it. Jason displayed the sort of leadership that Gio had always aspired to, and had the sort of qualities he admired in a colleague and a friend.

The council workers were dispatched to check the signage on the highway hadn't been washed away overnight, and to put barriers up to stop people from attempting to drive through the flooding. Sandra manned the phone, checking in with local property owners. A report came in of people stranded on the road to the Baxter Mine, but they were locals, and had enough provisions to last a few days before they'd be in any serious trouble.

"We've also got tourists stuck somewhere south of here on the Winton road," Jason said, leaning against Gio's desk. "They're definitely in Winton's division, but there's a good chance the crews from there won't be able to get through. So they're probably going to ask us to try before they send out a chopper. We won't know for sure for a few hours, so in the meantime we'll go doorknocking and doing welfare checks." He looked around the room. "Pay particular mind to the oldies. There are sandbags at the council depot, but some of them won't be able to get there. You can strongly encourage them to evacuate either to Saint Pat's or the community hall, but it's not a declared emergency yet, so you can't force them. And remember, Saint Pat's is taking pets, but the community hall isn't." He straightened up. "Okay. Let's get out there."

Gio grabbed his raincoat and left the station.

The rain itself wasn't too heavy. It was more of a persistent drizzle. But with the river system already overloaded from what was being dumped up in the Gulf, there was nowhere for the water to go. The entire town had turned to mud. Residents closest to the river were sandbagging their properties. Gio went from house to house seeing who wanted to evacuate, and who needed help to do it.

Three hours later, working alongside Robbo from the SES, Gio got a call from Jason to meet him back at the station.

"Winton couldn't get through," he said. "We're going south."

Gio left Robbo going door to door on George Street, and drove back to the station. He trudged inside, leaving a trail of mud and water in his wake, and found Jason poring over a map.

"You good to go?" Jason asked, looking him up and down.

Gio was soaked—in rain or sweat, he couldn't tell—but there was no point getting changed. Not when he'd be in exactly the same state the second he walked outside again. He nodded.

They drove through town, heading west on the highway, and passing the lines of semitrailers and road trains on the side of the road. The highway dipped just past the truck stop and the council guys on the roadblock splashed through the water to lift the barrier and let them through. As they hit the flooding, bow waves rippled out behind them. The muddy floodwater made it slow going, and it was impossible to see the state of the road underneath.

Jason grabbed the radio. "Richmond two-eight-nine calling Winton. You there, Emma?"

It took a moment for the woman to answer. When she did, her voice was almost lost in static. "Hey, Jason. You heading down here?"

"As far as we can, yeah. What's it like on your end?"

"The rain hasn't let up in days. I made it as far as Three Mile Creek and couldn't get through. I don't like your chances."

"Me neither. I'll keep you posted."

"Good luck."

A few kilometres west of town, they made the turn south onto the Winton road. The flood markers plotted their route. At first the water was still, but it didn't take long for them to reach the first creek. The flood markers had vanished, and water lapped at the bottom of the guardrails. The water streamed across the road, carrying sticks and brush and circling piles of debris that caught in the rails. Swirling maelstroms rushed around the obstructions.

"Nope," Jason said, peering through the windscreen. "No way we're getting through that."

Gio heard a sudden roar of water. He turned in his seat and saw a crest of sticks and debris being carried down the creek towards them. "Jason!"

"Shit!" Jason threw the LandCruiser into reverse just as the rush of dirty floodwater bulldozed around them.

Gio grabbed for the handle above his door as the water fought against the momentum of the LandCruiser and they were swept onto the bridge. There was a thump on the back of the chassis as something big hit. The knock was enough to push the LandCruiser sideways, and Gio's stomach lurched as they lost all traction.

Metal scraped as they hit the guardrail.

"Hope that holds," Jason said, knuckles white as he gripped the steering wheel. The engine whined.

"Are we moving?" Gio asked, peering through the rain-splattered windscreen.

"Not backwards," Jason muttered. He twisted around in his seat and looked out the back. "Fuck. Okay, so we're going to try this one more time, and then we're going to need to call for someone to winch us out. Cross your fingers."

Gio gripped the handle tightly as the engine whined again and then jolted as the tyres at last found some traction.

They reversed very slowly off the bridge.

Gio's heart pounded wildly.

Jason slumped back in his seat and reached for the radio. "Emma? Tell them they're gonna need to get the chopper out."

It was a week before the floodwaters receded and the highway was reopened. A week of running an incident room out of the station, and keeping tabs on everything. After the first day, Jason and Gio had worked opposite shifts, twelve hours each, so there was always a police officer on scene, in charge. Sometimes the twelve hours bled into fourteen hours. Once, sixteen. By the time the highway was open again, Gio wanted nothing more than a hot shower and an early night, and eight hours of sleep hopefully uninterrupted by a phone call. Fuck the Friday night drunks—was it even Friday? Gio wasn't sure anymore—they could sort themselves out for once.

The call came at seven thirty.

"Giovanni?"

"Yeah?"

"It's Dawn from Comms. We've got a call for a rollover on the highway. Looks like a fatal."

"Right." Gio tugged his fingers through his hair. "I'm heading out now."

He wiped his stinging eyes and called Jason before grabbing a still-damp uniform out of the dryer and pulling it on.

Autopilot.

Gio was tired. So tired that the night came in flashes. The blue and red strobes illuminating the rain-soaked highway. The remains of the caravan strewn across a good hundred-metre stretch of bitumen like matchsticks. The woman, thin grey hair stuck to her scalp with drizzle, shaking fingers holding her oxygen mask onto her bloody face. The *thump-thump-thump* of the blades of the rescue chopper as it came in to land.

The man's body in pieces, ripped apart on impact.

Hours blocking the highway, waiting for a forensic crash investigator to arrive from Charters Towers.

Not being able to move anything until then.

The *tick-tick-tick* of the rain hitting the plastic sheet he'd thrown over the man's arm.

He'd fixed his gaze on Jason, a hundred metres away at the other end of the field of debris, so he didn't have to look at the body parts he'd covered up. Covering them up didn't mean he couldn't see them anymore.

Dozing off leaning against the LandCruiser, and jolting awake with a start. Taking too long to remember where he was. Slipping into a fugue state again, and losing all awareness of his surroundings.

"Come on," Jason said, his face swimming slowly into focus in front of him. "Come on, Gio."

Gio blinked at him, and somehow it was daylight.

The station, and then home, and Jason's hand was on his shoulder, gripping him tightly, and steering him into the bathroom.

"Have a shower," he said. "And get some sleep."

Gio squinted at his watch. How was it 10 a.m.? How had he been on his feet for over twenty-four hours?

"Come on," Jason said again. "Come on, Gio."

"I'm just gonna . . ." Gio blinked. "Just gonna go to bed."

"You've got blood on your uniform."

Fuck.

Gio wrenched his shirt over his head and, breathing heavily, dropped it onto the floor. He looked at Jason. "You too," he said, his skin pebbling. "You've got blood on you too."

He wasn't sure which one of them moved first, only that suddenly his fingers were curled into the belt loops on Jason's uniform pants, and he was reeling him closer. Then he was tugging Jason's shirt out of his pants, and running his hands underneath, up Jason's sides, feeling him shudder underneath his touch. Gio leaned in. Their stubble rasped and their mouths met, open and hungry. And suddenly Gio was awake again, his blood thrumming in his veins as arousal swept through him.

Jason moved away, and for a moment Gio thought that was it, they were done, another fucking mistake, but Jason only pulled his shirt off and dropped it on the floor with Gio's.

Gio raked his gaze over Jason's chest. He was a little more solid than Gio. He didn't have a gym junkie's body. He was strong but not ripped. The fine hairs on his chest were almost gold, darkening where they thickened into a treasure trail below his navel. Gio looked lower, to the obvious bulge in Jason's uniform pants.

"This doesn't have to be a thing," he said. "Just two blokes getting off together."

"Right," Jason said, wide-eyed. He nodded. "Yeah."

Gio sat on the edge of the bath and fumbled with his bootlaces. They were wet, and his numb fingers struggled to unlace them. His breath caught as Jason knelt in front of him to help. Gio withdrew his hands and gripped the edge of the bath tightly.

Jason eased Gio's boots off, and then stood.

"Here," Gio said, and reached down. He drew Jason's foot up, setting the thick tread of the boot against his thigh. He worked the laces loose and drew the boot off, before he did the same with the other foot. Jason's socks were as wet as his own.

Hours standing on that fucking highway . . .

He closed his eyes briefly, and opened them again when Jason cupped his cheek. Jason was staring down at him, looking worried.

"Shower," Gio said, rising to his feet. He unfastened his belt and opened his pants. Hooked his thumbs around the elastic of his underwear, and shoved it all down. His dick was hard already, but he resisted the urge to touch it while Jason was watching him. He stepped free of his tangled clothes, and bent down to tug his socks off. He remembered, out of nowhere, the guy he'd slept with at university years ago who'd left his socks on when they'd fucked, and how Gio hadn't been able to stop laughing about it for weeks afterwards.

He got into the shower and twisted the taps on, hardly waiting until the water was warm before he moved underneath it. His fingers fumbled with the shower gel as he grabbed it from the caddy, and he turned around in time to see Jason stepping in to join him.

A new rush of heat washed over Gio.

It was okay to do this. This was the result of a combination of sleep deprivation and adrenaline, and hookups happened all the time in the job. It was stress relief. It was also more than that. It was a way to feel alive again, to grab on to another living, breathing human being and carve out a moment of pleasure and vitality after spending too many hours surrounded by death and misery. It was pushing back against the horror of blood and body parts strewn across a black highway. It was okay to do this.

They kissed again under the warm spray of the shower, and Gio tilted his head back so that Jason could trace a route from his jaw down his throat. His skin prickled, and he rocked against Jason. Wet skin slid against wet skin, and Gio almost dropped the shower gel. He pushed Jason up against the shower screen and fumbled with the bottle, squeezing a handful of gel into his palm before shoving his hand down between them. He brought their dicks together, and Jason laced his fingers through Gio's.

Fuck.

Yes.

There.

They kissed again, and then Gio leaned away so he could watch. Jason's eyes were closed, his mouth open. Water ran in a rivulet off his lower lip, and Gio leaned in quickly to taste it. Jason huffed a warm breath against his mouth. Heat coiled tightly in Gio's belly, and then lower. His arousal climbed as they worked their dicks together, fingers slippery with shower gel.

Gio groaned and dropped his head forward so that his forehead rested on Jason's shoulder. Jason panted heavily against his ear. Gio turned his head and sucked at the water on the skin of Jason's throat. Licked up to his jaw, chasing the rasp of stubble.

Jason froze, fingers squeezing around their dicks tighter, and then he was coming in hot spurts. Gio rocked against him almost frantically, his own climax chasing on the heels of Jason's, and just like that he was boneless. He sagged against Jason, and then slipped, and Jason caught him before he knocked himself out on the shower screen.

Jason turned them so that Gio's back was against the screen, and angled his body to direct the spray of the shower against Gio's chest and abdomen. He wiped the shower gel and come off Gio's skin with gentle sweeps of his palms.

Gio blinked, and water clumped in his eyelashes like tears.

"You're bloody wrecked," Jason said, the corner of his mouth lifting in a smile.

"Two days ago I was wrecked," Gio told him. "Now I'm totally fucked."

Jason twisted the taps off and pushed the shower door open. "You need to sleep."

Gio followed him out of the shower, placing his feet carefully so he didn't fall over.

Jason wrenched the single towel off the rail.

"There's another one in the linen cupboard, I think."

"We can share," Jason said, his smile growing.

"Yeah." Gio took the towel and gave himself a cursory wipe down before passing the towel back to Jason. He watched Jason dry himself, too tired to be subtle about it. When Jason's gaze fell to their tangled-up uniforms on the bathroom floor, Gio shook his head. "Don't put that back on. You can borrow something."

He led the way down the hall into his bedroom, and gestured at his cupboard. "You can . . ." His bed drew him like a magnet, and he barely managed to haul the covers back before falling in. "Whatever fits."

Jason opened his cupboard. "Thanks."

"Do you want to stay for a while?" Gio asked, already drifting off to sleep. It would be nice, he thought, to fall asleep with Jason here.

"I can't." Jason sounded apologetic. "I have to pick Taylor up."

"Yeah, no problem." Gio closed his eyes.

"Don't come back to work until you've caught up on sleep."

"Okay." He thought about pointing out that he didn't even know what day it was, let alone what shift he was rostered on next, but fuck it. Too many words. He was going to sleep for years now.

As he drifted off to the soft patter of rain against the tin roof, he thought that Jason kissed him again.

Maybe he dreamed it.

CHAPTER FOURTEEN

Taylor seemed happy to be home. He dumped his backpack in his bedroom, leaving Jason to dig through it for dirty clothes, and then headed for the kitchen.

"Did we get any flooding here, Dad?"

Jason followed him into the kitchen, a bundle of Taylor's dirty clothes in his arms. "At the house?"

"Yeah."

"We had some water go through underneath, but not much. Why?"

Taylor inched towards the kitchen cupboard. "Oh, I was just wondering."

Jason turned away just enough to keep Taylor in his periphery. Just enough to see Taylor sneak the cupboard open and smuggle a tin of tuna under his shirt. That damn cat. Taylor was probably worried it had been washed away or something.

"Do you want me to go and put the washing on?" Taylor asked innocently, as though he'd ever been the sort of kid who volunteered to do housework, and wasn't looking for an excuse to hunt down the cat. Jason was almost tempted to let him do it, until he remembered the uniforms soaking in the tub beside the machine. His and Gio's. Maybe he'd crossed a weird line—had he?—but surely it was only practical? Gio would be asleep for hours yet, and blood was a bitch to get out if you didn't soak it in cold water first.

"Nah, I'll get it," Jason said. "I have to throw some uniforms in. I'm sure the cat is *fine*, Taylor."

Taylor gave a guilty jerk and fumbled with his badly concealed tin of tuna, but recovered quickly and followed Jason down the back steps to under the house.

Jason dumped Taylor's dirty clothes in the washing machine. There really weren't enough for the four days he'd stayed with Kane's family, but Kane's mother probably hadn't thought twice about throwing Taylor's clothes in with her own family's when she'd put a load of washing on. That was the thing people did, wasn't it? No line crossing there.

Jason dragged a sopping-wet uniform shirt out of the tub next to the washing machine, and wrung the worst of the water out before dropping it in the machine. He could hear Taylor rattling away somewhere behind him, over near the tool cupboard where the cat liked to perch. He swirled his hands through the tangle of clothes in the tub and pulled out a sock.

His or Gio's?

He thought of Gio's smile, tired and slow but still somehow retaining a hint of brightness, as Jason had knelt in front of him to help him with his boots. He thought of the taste of Gio's skin under the shower, and the way they'd fallen into a rhythm, clumsy at first but very rapidly in sync, their fingers laced together as they jerked themselves off.

"Hey, Dad!" Taylor popped up beside him suddenly. "Those aren't your undies!"

"I'm washing Gio's stuff as well," Jason said, keeping his tone even. *Nothing to see here, move along.* "He's sleeping."

Taylor knocked his shoulder against Jason, and watched as Jason shoved the last of the clothes into the washing machine. "Dad?"

"Mmm?"

"When I was staying at Kane's place for the flood, did you miss me?"

Jason selected the cycle and hit the Start button. The machine lurched to life. "Of course I did."

He'd been run ragged this week. Sleep, eat, work. Sleep, eat, work. More work than the other two, actually, but that was the way things usually went during a major incident. He'd missed Taylor, but not enough to wish he was home. Jason had been too busy to set aside any time for him, and he knew Taylor would have been living it up at Kane's place with video games, and horror movies they weren't supposed to watch—supplied by Kane's big brother Alex, no doubt—and as much junk food as they could sneak in. But yeah, he'd missed him. He'd missed having him close.

Taylor's smile was half-proud, half-embarrassed.

"Why?" Jason slung an arm around Taylor's shoulders. "Did you miss me?"

"No!" Taylor protested, half a second before he relented. "A little bit. *Maybe.*"

Jason laughed. "It's good to have you back, mate."

Taylor beamed.

It took the better part of a week for the town to get back into its usual rhythm after the flooding. It was still raining, a low interminable drizzle that felt like it might set in for years, but the monsoonal rain had eased up in the Gulf, giving the river system a chance to channel the water away to the coastline instead of dumping it across the plains. Life settled slowly back into a normal routine. The school reopened on Monday. The supermarket shelves filled up with bread and milk again. Volunteers helped with the cleanup. The first flood of the wet season was over and done with. It would hopefully be the last, but Jason knew from experience that there would probably be more to come.

The investigation into the fatal accident on the highway had been handed over to the Forensic Crash Unit, which meant less paperwork for Jason and Gio. Not that there were many statements to take anyway. The driver was dead, his wife had been airlifted to Townsville, and the only witnesses had come across the scene after the accident had already happened, and called emergency services.

It had been a bad one though. A messy one. Jason had seen the look in Gio's eyes that night. It had no doubt been reflected in his own. It was such a basic human instinct to shy away from horror like that. It hit on a visceral level, and it was hard to shake. What had happened afterwards with Gio . . . well, that had been basic human instinct too.

They didn't talk about it. Jason couldn't say they ignored it exactly, though. The knowledge of it lay between them in every glance, in every smile or nod in passing, and it felt okay. It didn't feel like a mistake. They could keep it out of the office. Jason was Gio's boss; it was a complication, but it didn't need to be a disaster, did it?

Strange how Jason was trying to rationalise it all now, to turn everything he'd said after the kiss on its head because he *wanted*. But it *could* work. Partners hooked up all the time. The job was fucking notorious for it. More hookups and subsequent breakups than bloody high school. It wasn't all on the down-low either. There had been a married couple working together at Hughenden a few years back, sergeant and senior constable. She'd been his supervisor, but they'd made it work. Hell of a balancing act maybe, when it came to ethics and to public perception, but it was possible. Of course, that relationship had been disclosed. And probably scrutinised by the bosses to make sure there was no collusion. As though a copper would lie for his spouse at work but wouldn't do the same for a mate. Still, public perception mattered. The old *Courier Mail* test that had been knocked into Jason's head at the academy.

"How would it look on the front page of the Courier Mail*?"*

He thought of Gio.

How would it look?

Jason wanted.

He was still awake on Tuesday night past ten when Gio finished his shift. Taylor was asleep, and would sleep like the dead until daylight. Jason watched from his kitchen when the lights went on at Gio's place, and then typed out a text.

Want to come over?

He sent the message. He worried that it was crossing a line though. Worried that it was putting pressure on Gio that he hadn't intended. He worried that Gio would respond badly. And he was worried that Gio wouldn't respond at all.

Jason stood there, his phone in his hand, until he heard the tread of footsteps on the back stairs, and then went and opened the door.

"Hey," Gio said.

"Hey."

There was a strange disconnect in Jason's brain when he showed Gio into his bedroom. The photograph of Alana sat on the bedside table, and there was a tiny voice at the back of his mind reminding him that this was *her* room. But it had been five years. The mattress was new since then, the sheets were. Jason had been replacing Alana's touch by degrees for a long time. A part of him wanted to feel that this was a big step—momentous—but it was no bigger, probably, than the day he'd replaced her old pillow. This had been his room alone for five years.

Gio's gaze slid over Alana's photograph, and he didn't say anything.

He was still in uniform.

"What you said," Jason said. "Just two blokes getting off together. You good with that?"

Gio lifted his chin and looked him in the eye. "I'm here, aren't I?"

"How do you want to do this?"

Gio reached into one of the cargo pockets on his uniform pants and then drew his hand out again. He dropped a handful of condoms onto the end of the bed. "I'm flexible, Sarge. In more ways than one."

"I'm not your sergeant in this room," Jason said, his throat suddenly dry.

"*Jason*." Gio nodded and stepped forward. "How do *you* want to do this, Jason? Do you like to top, or do you like to bottom?"

"It's been a while." All Jason could think of was the feel of Gio's dick in his hand last night, and how much he wanted it inside him.

Gio tapped the bulging pocket on his other leg, like he knew exactly what Jason was thinking. "I brought lube too. Plenty of it."

"You that sure of yourself, huh?" Jason raised his eyebrows.

"Yeah." Gio tugged his mouth up in a grin. "I fucking am."

"Then I want you to top me." Jason pressed the button-lock on the bedroom door. It was the sort that could be easily opened with a butter knife, but if Taylor woke up for some unaccountable reason, they'd have a bit of a warning before he burst in. "If you're up for the challenge."

"Yeah, I reckon I am." The skin at the corner of Gio's eyes crinkled when he smiled. He unfastened his belt. "At least I know this isn't a uniform kink, right? Like, you're not some holster sniffer."

Jason shrugged, warming to the teasing. Maybe it was all bluster and bravado, but it was a side of Gio he hadn't seen before, and he liked it. "Maybe that's why I joined up. To get amongst it."

"Yeah, sure." Gio pulled his shirt off, the muscles in his abdomen rippling. He sat down on the end of the bed and unlaced his boots. "Playing the field in a two-man station."

"Worked eventually, didn't it?"

Gio's smile grew. "Yeah. Point taken."

Jason tugged his own shirt off, and unzipped his jeans before pushing them down and stepping out of them.

"Nice," Gio said, standing up and moving into his space. He rested one hand against Jason's hip, and Jason's breath caught. He'd missed the simple intimacy of touches like this. This wasn't fast and desperate like they'd been in the shower. Gio's motions were slow and deliberate, and his gaze seemed almost thoughtful.

"Just two blokes getting off." Gio's careful touch belied that, and Jason pushed the worry that maybe it was more than that to the back of his mind. He didn't want to think about it now. Didn't want to fuck it up before they'd even started.

Gio brushed his other hand against where Jason's dick was straining against his underwear, and Jason pulled him closer. He flicked open the button on Gio's fly and unzipped his pants. Gio caught them as Jason tried to tug them down, and hitched them awkwardly back up while he fumbled with the button on the cargo pocket on his left thigh. He dug out a tube of lube, and then let his pants drop.

Jason resisted the urge to check he absolutely had locked the door, and then took his underwear down.

There was no almost-manic tiredness in Gio's eyes tonight. His dark gaze was intent, and he swiped his tongue over his bottom lip as Jason stripped. "Yeah," he whispered.

Jason gripped Gio's jaw. He angled his face upward, and then their mouths were pressing together. Heat rushed through Jason as Gio's lips opened and his tongue licked slowly into Jason's mouth. Jason thought of their first kiss: frantic, messy, a mistake. This one was incredible.

Gio slipped a hand behind Jason's head, guiding him gently as their mouths met again. Jason groaned, pulling Gio closer. He felt

Gio's erection pressing against his thigh, and the sudden wave of pure want that flooded through him was almost overwhelming. Gio drew back, and then stepped out of his underwear.

God, he was beautiful. How had . . . how had someone *hurt* him? It was unthinkable.

Gio sat on the end of the bed, tugging his dick almost absently as he stared up at Jason. Jason sat beside him, and curled towards him. They kissed again, urgency rising between them.

Gio was warm, his skin gleaming.

"Lie down, Jason," Gio whispered in his ear.

Jason lay back, and sighed as he felt that skin-on-skin contact he needed. Gio slid a hand up Jason's chest, trailing his fingers through coarse hair, catching a hardening nipple between his fingers and squeezing it. Jason jerked in surprise.

Gio smiled at him and leaned down for another kiss. His dick was hard and hot against Jason's thigh, leaving a sticky trail in the hair there.

Jason stretched and rolled over.

Gio slid a hand down his spine. "You good to keep going?"

"Yeah." Jason's body stiffened as Gio's hand swept over the curve of his arse before sliding into the warm crease of his body. Jesus. It had been so long since he'd had someone do this for him. He closed his eyes and let himself sink into the sensation.

Gio pressed his fingers against Jason's tight opening. He slipped a fingertip inside, and Jason shivered.

It seemed to take forever for Gio to work him open. Jason wasn't sure how much was Gio being overly careful, or if he was just a bloody tease. Jason shifted impatiently, but it was years before Gio got two fingers inside him, and eons before he began to scissor his fingers, and then crooked them, clearly looking for Jason's prostate.

Jason jerked, then shifted restlessly on the bed. "Oh, oh god!"

Gio gave a satisfied hum and leaned down to bite his shoulder gently.

Jason flushed, squirming underneath him. The biting thing felt good. Really fucking good. It went straight to Jason's already-hard dick, trapped underneath him, and he wanted to get his knees under him, get into position, get *fucked*.

Gio—a tease, definitely a bloody tease—worked his fingers for a few more minutes, and then moved back onto his knees.

Jason rolled his shoulders before getting his hands and knees under him. He moved forward then, and rested his forehead on his folded arms. He heard the crinkle of tearing foil, a sound that took him straight back to university, and shivered. Gio curled one hand around Jason's hip. The other . . . Jason twisted his neck to see Gio gripping his dick tightly and pressing slowly forward.

Jason remembered to bear down as Gio notched the head of his dick up against Jason's entrance. There was a moment of resistance, and then Gio's dick was pushing carefully inside his body.

Jason groaned.

Gio echoed him. "Okay?"

"Yeah." Jason rocked back against him. Gio was moving at a snail's pace, pushing in a fraction, drawing back, and pushing in again. "I'm not gonna bloody *break*."

Gio's huff of breath might have been a laugh, and it warmed Jason. Then Gio thrust forward, and Jason groaned as he felt Gio's balls come to rest against his arse. He rolled his hips and clenched, and Gio moaned.

Jason had missed this. Not just the feel of a dick in his arse—although that was pretty bloody incredible—but this letting down of his barriers, this closeness. He'd known he was lonely, but he hadn't realised how acutely until now, until this moment when the sheer feeling of having someone again, of having *Gio*, threatened to overwhelm him. He squeezed his eyes shut for a moment, twisting his fingers in the rumpled sheets.

Gio withdrew, and then thrust slowly back in. Jason gasped and shuddered as Gio's dick rode against his prostate. His own dick throbbed, and his balls tightened.

"Come on," Jason said, shoving a hand underneath himself and gripping his dick. "Come on, Gio. Faster."

Gio picked up the pace. He groaned as Jason clenched around him, and his fingers tightened almost painfully on Jason's hips.

"Jason." His voice cracked as he moved faster. "Jason!"

Jason gasped for breath as a shiver ran up his spine, and need, hot and urgent, coiled as tight as a spring in his balls. "Gio!"

Jason's whole body jerked as he came all over the sheets underneath him, Gio snapping his hips quickly. A moment later Gio was coming too, breath warm and ragged against Jason's sweat-damp skin.

Jason sagged onto the mattress, and Gio followed him down. He pressed his mouth against the skin between Jason's shoulder blades, the tenderness of the gesture making Jason's breath catch, and then rolled away.

In the sudden quiet, Jason could only hear the thumping of his heart. He turned over onto his back, resisting the urge to reach for Gio, and watched the blades of the ceiling fan turn slowly above them. What now? Jesus. What the hell was the protocol for a moment like this? For two blokes getting off together.

He blinked to clear his vision. "Do you want a beer?"

Gio stretched. He flashed a quick smile that Jason wasn't sure how to read. "I should probably, ah, clean up and head home."

"Yeah," Jason said, swallowing down the unexpected stab of disappointment. That made the most sense. "Sure."

After Gio had left, Jason went and emptied the bathroom bin, and then treaded down the stairs to dispose of the contents in the wheelie bin. The last thing he needed was for Taylor to find a used condom. That would open up a whole discussion Jason really wasn't prepared to have. On so many fucking levels.

The cat, perched on top of the tool cupboard, regarded him narrowly and lashed its skinny tail.

On Wednesday afternoon, Jason ran into Patricia Howe in the supermarket.

"Hello, Sergeant Quinn," she said with a faint smile.

Taylor, hanging off the end of the trolley, looked at her curiously.

"Taylor, go get some cat food."

He could see the cogs turning in his kid's brain, his nosiness battling with the fact that he'd just been given tacit approval to keep the bloody cat. His desire for the cat won out, as Jason had known it would, and he abandoned the trolley and scurried into the next aisle.

Patricia watched him go. "How old is he?"

"He's ten."

"Mine are all grown up now." Patricia fiddled with the gold bracelet she wore. The links were delicate. "My daughter lives in Rockhampton. She's said I can go and move in with her and her family."

"Do you get on?"

"Oh, yes." Patricia sighed. "I just don't know how Brian would take that. He's been very good these past few weeks. Very kind and respectful. I don't want to make him upset."

Jason nodded. "But what do you want to do?"

She looked at him, her expression strangely hopeful, as though she was asking for his permission. "I think I'd like to stay with my daughter for a little while."

"Then you should do that," Jason said. "It sounds like she'd be glad to have you."

"Thank you." She laid a hand briefly over his, where it rested on the bar of the trolley. "Thank you, Sergeant Quinn."

"If you need a hand," Jason said, "with anything, call us, okay? It doesn't matter if it's in the middle of the night."

"Thank you," she repeated, clearing her throat and stepping back. "I won't take up any more of your time today. I'll let you get back to your son."

Jason glanced towards the end of the aisle to where Taylor was rushing back to him, a triumphant grin on his face and a stack of purple Whiskas tins cradled in his arms.

CHAPTER FIFTEEN

It was easy to fall into a habit with Jason. Not a routine exactly—their ever-changing working hours didn't allow for anything as rigid as a routine—but certainly a habit. They kept things professional at work. But late at night when Taylor was in bed, or in the middle of the day when he was at school, if neither Jason nor Gio was working, then sex was something that happened.

They didn't talk about fucking when they worked, and they didn't talk about work when they fucked.

"What's going on with you?" Sandra asked one afternoon, eyeing Gio suspiciously. "You look . . ." She waved a hand in his direction. "*Happy*."

"It's a beautiful day," Gio said.

Sandra narrowed her eyes. "No, it isn't."

Gio rolled his eyes. "Fine. It's a horrible day, and existence is bleak, and we all die alone in the end."

Her mouth twitched. "That's more like it."

Sandra wasn't the only one to notice the change in his attitude.

The Richmond State School Fete was held on Friday afternoon. Taylor had been excited about it for days, begging for jobs to do around Gio's house so that he could earn more spending money than Jason had given him. Because they had a cake stall, Gio! A cake stall!

Gio had paid him five dollars to wash his car.

Gio could see the famous cake stall from where he was standing with Vicki at the first aid tent. The afternoon was softening very slowly into dusk. Swathes of wispy clouds, turned pink and orange by the sunset, were draped across the sky like the fairy floss every second sticky kid was waving around. There was a queue at the cake stall, and Gio smiled as he saw Taylor dragging Jason by the hand to join the line.

Jason was on a day off. He looked good in his jeans and a T-shirt, and he smiled at Gio when Gio eyed him up and down as though he knew exactly what Gio was thinking. Gio had to turn away before he laughed.

"You seem like you're finally settling in," Vicki said, raising her voice to be heard over the scratchy PA system. There was some announcement in progress, but Gio had given up trying to understand them. They had become background noise, like the bursts of pop music, the squeals of kids on the dodgy-looking rides nearby, and the hiss of hydraulics and the roar of the motors on the rides themselves.

"I think I am," Gio told her.

"I didn't think you'd last more than a few weeks, honestly."

"Really?" Gio raised his eyebrows.

Vicki shrugged and tucked a curl behind her ear. "You had the look of a man who was wondering what the fuck he'd done with his life. I thought you'd run screaming back to the southeast corner."

"That wasn't an option."

"I guess not." She knocked him companionably with her shoulder. "I'm glad you're settling in though."

"Me too."

A gaggle of small kids approached them, barefoot and scab-kneed. They were familiar, and it took Gio a moment to place them. Janey Ferguson's kids. He'd first seen them the day Jason had taken him around to Janey's place and she'd screamed at them to get to school, and he saw them on his regular visits to the Fergusons' house whenever the neighbours had got tired of the screaming matches and called the police.

"I've got lollipops," Vicki said, "and he's got stickers. Who wants one?"

The kids darted forward eagerly, and Gio handed out some of the Clancy Koala stickers he'd found in the storeroom at the station. The kids moved on again.

"Those poor kids," Vicki said, clicking her tongue.

They were exactly the sort of kids who would fall through the cracks. Their parents were caught in a cycle of abuse that neither of them seemed capable of walking away from, and what sort of environment was that to raise kids in? Evidently not one bad enough for the Department of Child Safety to intervene, because Gio had seen the number of notifications that had been forwarded to them and not actioned. Because there were always kids who needed more immediate help. That was the kicker.

"Gio! Vicki!" Taylor ran up towards him, face flushed. "I got lamingtons! Want one?"

"Oooh!" Vicki leaned forward to take one. She lifted it off the cardboard tray in a shower of coconut, and raised it in a toast in Jason's direction. Jason was a few steps behind Taylor. "Your dad's raised you right, Taylor!"

"Uh-huh," Jason agreed dryly. "Always offer the ladies cakes."

"I'm a cheap date," Vicki said through a mouthful of lamington.

Taylor presented the tray to Gio.

Gio peeled the cling wrap back and carefully eased a lamington free. "Thanks, Taylor."

"After I eat one of these I'm going to meet Kane and we're going to the haunted house." Taylor made a face. "It's not a real house. It's the year-three classroom."

"I'm sure it's horrifying in its own way," Jason told him.

Gio grinned. He set his lamington down on top of one of the campstools Vicki had set up, and peeled a Clancy Koala sticker off the roll. He pressed it against Taylor's shirt. Taylor laughed, so Gio stuck another one on him, and then another one, and another.

"There," he said. "Perfect."

"Dad, tell Gio to stop picking on me!"

"What?" Jason asked. "I didn't see anything."

"Daaad!" Taylor shoved the rest of his lamingtons into Jason's hands. "I'm going to the haunted house now!"

He rushed off, covered in Clancy Koala stickers.

Gio caught Jason's gaze and smiled. Around them, the fete continued into the night.

There were a hundred things to learn in Richmond that Gio wouldn't have been exposed to at a bigger station. Driver testing was one of them. There was no Queensland Transport in Richmond, or within four hundred kilometres, so on a Tuesday morning, Gio found himself climbing into a beaten-up old ute with an incredibly nervous seventeen-year-old L-Plater at the wheel.

Gio checked his paperwork. "Isabella, right?"

The girl nodded and clenched the steering wheel tightly. She hadn't even started the car yet.

Her address was a station some way out of town. Gio relaxed a little at that. He had no doubt this girl had been driving since the time she could reach the pedals.

"Okay, let's head around the block first," Gio said. "And hey, this is my first time giving a driving test, so go easy on me, alright?"

She gave him a shaky smile and peeled her fingers off the steering wheel long enough to turn the ignition. She eased them out onto the road.

"Okay, turn right up here," Gio said.

"I'm not good on right turns!"

"You're doing fine," he assured her. There wasn't much traffic around. "It took me three times to pass my test."

She glanced at him, disbelief written on her face.

Of course, doing his test in Brisbane had been a lot more stressful than this. For starters, every start had been a fucking hill start. Richmond didn't even have a hill. Or a roundabout. Or traffic lights. Gio was pretty sure the only tricky manoeuvre he had to throw at Isabella was a reverse parallel park.

They tried that outside a house in Victoria Street, and somehow ended up at least two metres from the gutter.

"I don't know how that happened!" Isabella looked on the verge of tears.

"Let's try it again," Gio suggested.

Half an hour later, back at the station, Isabella did burst into tears when Gio told her he was going to pass her despite her parallel park.

"You went easy on her, didn't you?" Sandra asked, eyebrows arched, when he'd finally sent Isabella on her way with her documentation to send to Queensland Transport.

He shrugged and didn't answer.

"Huh," Sandra said, and brought him a cup of tea without asking.

Maybe he was finally getting the hang of this country copper business after all.

Gio went jogging most mornings, following the curve of the river. Early enough to catch the dawn, to see the moment the sky lit up in brilliant colour, and the birds woke up. The air smelled of eucalypts, and the sweet powdery pollen of the silver wattles settled like dust on his skin. It was beautiful when the sun rose, and with every step Gio took, every kilometre he ran, it felt like he was finding his feet again at last.

It felt good.

He tried to run for at least thirty minutes every day, but sometimes pushed it out to closer to an hour, depending on what time he had to start work. Today he wasn't working until two, so he aimed for an hour.

He checked his watch when he reached the cluster of red gums that marked the farthest extent he usually ran, and then turned back towards home.

His muscles were aching when he climbed the front steps and let himself into his house. He showered, threw a load of washing on, and made his first coffee of the day. He wondered if Jason was up yet. Wondered what mornings looked like in his house, with Taylor thrown into the mix. Gio pushed his faint sense of wistfulness away. What he and Jason had was casual, and that was fine. He told himself repeatedly that it was fine, and that he didn't need or want more. Imagining himself eating breakfast with Jason and Taylor and fitting into their everyday lives weren't exactly the sort of fantasies Gio had expected to be indulging in when he'd first noticed Jason was a good-looking guy, but then he hadn't expected to like Jason so much. He hadn't expected to find himself hanging on every smile.

Gio was sitting on his kitchen bench, a bowl of muesli beside him, when his phone rang. He set his coffee down and accepted the call.

"Sophie?"

"Hey. You're not at work, are you?"

"No. I just got back from a run."

"Is that all you do there? Run and work?"

"It's a step up from just working."

She hummed. "Do you have any friends yet?"

"I do, actually."

"Friends, or *friends*?" His silence answered for him. "Gio?"

"I've got friends," Gio said. "I've also got an arrangement, which is none of your business."

"Gio!"

"Save the outrage," he said. "You were the one who told me to do it, remember?"

"Yeah, I suggested a friend or a *hobby*." She clicked her tongue. "Who is this guy anyway?"

"He's um . . ." Gio had no idea why he lowered his voice. "My sergeant."

"You're sleeping with your sergeant? Jesus! You don't take long on the rebound do you?"

Gio was sorry he'd mentioned it at all, but Sophie had been needling him about having no social life, and how he needed to put himself out there, and every time he talked to her it was only about his *job* and that wasn't healthy, Gio, and it had just spilled out. "You were the one who told me to find someone!"

"As if this isn't a disaster waiting to happen!" Her breath huffed down the phone. "I mean, Pete was the *one*, and now—"

"Pete wasn't the one," Gio said, his stomach clenching.

"Oh, bambino." Sophie's voice softened with sympathy. "You were going to *marry* him, remember?"

Yeah, Gio remembered. They'd talked about booking a holiday to New Zealand and getting married there. Making it official somewhere, even though it wouldn't be at home. Flights to New Zealand were cheap. They'd planned to invite a bunch of friends, make a real party of it . . .

"Things changed," Gio said. *Pete* had changed.

"That's fine," Sophie said. "But should you really be jumping into another relationship so soon?"

"It's been twelve months."

He could almost see her roll her eyes. "You break up with Pete, and you won't *talk* to me, and then you get a transfer to the middle of nowhere. It's like you became this whole different person overnight!"

Funny what having the ground ripped from under his feet could do.

"Soph, it's not a big deal. It's not a relationship. It's just a *thing*. It's just casual."

She was silent for a long while. When she spoke again, her voice was wary. "Casual? Gio, you don't *do* casual. You never have."

"Maybe that was the fucking problem!"

"What crawled up your arse?" she shot back. "Apart from your *sergeant*?"

Fuck that.

Gio ended the call and turned his phone onto vibrate. He squeezed his eyes shut. He didn't need Sophie's shit today. She always thought she knew what was best and, okay, yeah, most of the time she was right. But not this time. How could she be? She didn't know the truth. She didn't know what had happened on the Coast, and she didn't know why he was in Richmond, and that was good. He didn't *want* her to know. He . . . he didn't want her pity. He'd fucked up, and he just wanted one tiny corner of his life to remain uncontaminated by that.

His phone vibrated with an incoming call, and Gio ignored it.

Fuck her.

Fuck everything.

Gio started at two, and Jason finished at four. They headed out just before three to set up an RBT outside the school. The principal had phoned complaining of parents parking like dickheads—her words. He and Jason parked at the side of the road and left the strobes on the light bar flashing. Gio pulled his reflective vest on, and his cap, and waved their first customer over. Given it was 3 p.m. on a school day, he didn't expect anyone to blow over the limit, but that wasn't the point of the operation. Funny how quickly everyone remembered the road rules when the coppers were right there.

Inside the school, the bell rang. Minutes later, kids appeared. Gio caught a glimpse of Taylor walking with a girl. Taylor waved, and Gio waved back.

They kept the RBT going until the school traffic, such as it was, had died down again. They were packing up when Jason finally asked, "Are you okay?"

"What?" Gio stacked the traffic cones into the back of the LandCruiser.

"You seem off today. Is something wrong?"

Gio shrugged. "I had a fight with my sister." He paused. "No, not even a fight, really. It's just lately she doesn't approve of anything I do. It's no big deal."

"What do you do that she doesn't approve of?" Jason asked, unfastening his vest and pulling it off.

Gio huffed. "Moving here."

Realisation settled over Jason's features. "She doesn't know what happened."

"No."

"Is there any reason you haven't told her?"

"I don't want her to know." Gio shook his head. "I don't want her involved. She's got enough to deal with. I left her with enough to deal with."

Jason was silent.

"My dad has Alzheimer's," Gio said. "It's early stages, but I dumped it all in her lap—the medical appointments, moving him into a home, getting power of attorney, sorting out his finances—all of it." He swallowed past the ache in his throat. "She resents me. You know what, Jason? You're probably the only person who knows me and doesn't think I'm either a coward or a fucking dog."

Jason lifted his hand and reached out as though he was about to cup Gio's cheek.

A truck rattled past them, spitting gravel over the shoulder of the road. Gio flushed and stepped back.

Jason dropped his hand. "That's not true. You've got Taylor, and Vicki, and those teachers you hang around with. You've got Sandra."

Gio snorted.

"Hey. Sandra's abrupt, but she doesn't do bullshit. If she didn't like you, you'd know it."

Gio looked down. "Yeah."

"Come over tonight, okay? If you're still up after ten?"

Gio lifted his gaze. This was breaking the rules, wasn't it? Talking about this now, here, when they were working. This was the lines getting blurred, and neither of them wanted that. This was getting messy. The disaster waiting to happen, just like Sophie had said.

This was a disaster that Gio was going to tumble into, headfirst, breathless.

"Yeah," he said. "I'll be up."

Jason's answering smile was hopeful in ways that Gio didn't even want to begin to articulate, but it filled him with warmth.

CHAPTER SIXTEEN

The soft tread of Gio's footsteps as he climbed the back steps had become something that Jason looked forward to. He checked that Taylor was sleeping, and closed his son's door gently. By the time he'd made his way to the back door, Gio was already waiting there, bathed in moonlight.

Jason unlatched the door and let him in.

Gio glanced down the hallway.

"He's sleeping," Jason said, keeping his voice low. Always doing this at his place instead of Gio's meant they had to make sure not to be too loud. There was a chance Taylor might wake up when Gio was over, but Jason would much rather think up some way to explain why Gio was visiting in the middle of the night, than have Taylor wake up in an empty house and not know where Dad was. Bad enough that he risked that by ducking out on the occasional quick job.

He walked towards his bedroom, aware that Gio was right behind him. The moment they were inside the room, Gio closed the door behind them and clicked the lock.

Jason crowded him against the door and kissed him. He put a hand on his cheek, something he'd been waiting to do all day, and swept his thumb over the delicate skin under his eye. Gio closed his eyes, his long lashes trembling, and Jason licked into his mouth and then pulled back. He tugged on Gio's lower lip with his teeth, leaving indentations in the soft flesh, and Gio sighed.

I could fall into you.

Gio blinked his eyes open, a small, satisfied smile curling his mouth. "Gonna fuck me, Jason? Gonna get that dick inside me tonight?"

"Yeah." Jason slid a hand down the back of Gio's track pants, and Gio jerked forward. His hard dick nudged Jason's thigh, and Jason ground against him in response.

"Fuck me, Jason." Gio knocked his head back on the door. "Come on."

Jason wouldn't have called them practiced yet, but they were becoming familiar with one another's bodies, the way they moved, reacted. He liked learning what Gio enjoyed. He liked learning how Gio tasted. He liked recognising the way Gio's eyes grew heavy-lidded and his mouth hung open when he was close to coming.

"Wanna ride you," Gio murmured. He rubbed himself against Jason's thigh. "Can I ride you?"

"Yeah. Fuck, yeah."

Jason stripped and climbed onto the bed. He shoved his pillows behind him, and shifted back against them. He licked his palm and jerked himself off as he watched Gio undress, enjoying the slight rasp of too-dry skin. Gio took the condoms and lube from Jason's bedside drawer and crawled onto the bed. He sat back on his heels, and tossed the box of condoms at Jason with a wink.

Is this what we want? Jason thought. *Just two blokes getting off together.*

There was a vulnerability to Gio that Jason never saw in the bedroom, and wondered if he ever would. He'd seen it when Gio was injured, or when he was upset, but in the bedroom Gio was cocky and self-assured, which was hot as hell, but Jason knew there was more to him than that. There was a part of Jason that wanted more than Gio was offering. More than Jason had asked for. More than he could ask for now, without risking everything.

Jason's arousal climbed as he watched Gio squirt lube on his fingers and shift his hand behind himself. He studied Gio's face, watching for the moment his expression shifted as his fingers opened himself up. He was gorgeous. His dark eyes. The muscles that shifted smoothly under his olive skin. Jason wanted to rake his fingers down his abdomen, and tangle them in the dark curls that framed Gio's dick. The way he moved as he prepared himself was one of the hottest things Jason had ever seen.

Gio was shameless when it came to his body, to fucking, but still Jason wanted *more.*

Jason shook his head to clear it, then rolled a condom down over his dick.

Gio shuffled closer on his knees, his mouth quirking into a smile as he hitched a leg over Jason and straddled his thighs. He raised himself up, and Jason caught his hips and pulled him forward.

"Gonna give it to me how I want it?" Gio asked in a low voice.

"You know I am."

Gio's wicked smile grew, and he reached back to grasp Jason's dick. He held it in place as he lowered himself down. They both groaned as the head of Jason's dick notched into place, and then Gio sank down heavily.

He was hot and tight and perfect around Jason's dick.

Jason rocked his hips up as Gio began to ride him, a thousand unaskable questions on the tip of his tongue.

Are you okay, Gio?

What are you feeling, Gio?

Do you want more than this?

Because I think . . . I think that I do.

He twisted his fingers in Gio's curls instead, and tugged him down for a biting kiss, and Gio hummed out his pleasure as they fucked.

The envelope sat on Gio's desk at the station for half a day. There was no return address on it, and the postmark was from just over the border in Tweed Heads. Jason didn't see Gio open it. The envelope was there at two when Gio started, and gone fifteen minutes later when Jason passed his desk on the way to get a coffee. Gio's mouth was a thin line as he scrolled through his emails.

"Everything okay?" Jason asked him.

"Yes, Sarge," Gio said, his expression blank.

Jason wanted to stand behind him and try to ease the tension from his shoulders. He wanted to ask what the problem was, but he wasn't sure who would be asking the question—Gio's boss or Gio's friend—or who would be answering it—Senior Constable Valeri or

Gio. He didn't know how to navigate the moment, and so he let it slide.

"See the email about the CPR course?" he asked instead.

"Yeah."

"I'm up-to-date," Jason said. "When are you due?"

"I'll, um . . ." Gio rolled his shoulders. "I'll check."

"Let me know," Jason said. "If you have to go all the way into Townsville for a course, we can shuffle your roster so you get a couple of days off while you're there. Give you a chance to get some shopping done and check the place out."

"Thanks," Gio said, his expression softening.

"Did anyone get more milk?" Sandra yelled from behind the counter. "If someone doesn't go out and get milk, I'm going to kill everyone in this station."

Gio stood, grabbing his keys. "I'll go."

"Thank you, Gio!" Sandra called.

Gio took the envelope out of his drawer, and Jason watched him head for the back door. Whatever the envelope was, he didn't have it when he got back about ten minutes later with the milk.

It ate at Jason all day. He still didn't know how to read Gio a lot of the time, but it was obvious that whatever was in that envelope, it hadn't been nothing. Gio's blank expression reminded him of how Gio had been when he first arrived, and Jason didn't want them to regress back to then. They were friends now, weren't they? He'd hoped that Gio trusted him enough now to come to him with any problem, and more than that, it bothered him that something was upsetting Gio. It ate at Jason because it was clearly eating at Gio as well.

"What was in the envelope?" Jason asked, ten hours later. The night was bright. Insects were chirping and buzzing, and *ping*ing against the window screens.

"Doesn't matter," Gio said, reaching down to pick his shirt up off the floor. His skin shone with sweat, and the muscles in his shoulders bunched as he pulled his shirt over his head. He scooped his jeans and underwear up off the floor, shaking the underwear free of the denim before stepping back into them. "It was nothing."

"Bullshit."

Gio met his gaze and held it. "It doesn't matter."

It was an obvious lie, but Jason let it go for now. He didn't have the right to push, but he'd hoped Gio would decide to open up if he asked. Apparently not though. Jason swung his legs over the side of the bed and reached down for his own clothes. He stood and pulled them on. "You want a beer before you go?"

Gio hesitated and then nodded. "Sure."

They sat on the front veranda in the dark, since turning on an outside light would only attract more bugs. Jason kept a thumb over the lip of his stubbie to make sure nothing flew into the bottle.

Gio's chair creaked as he leaned forward. "I was a good copper. I *am* a good copper." He snorted. "Maybe not a good country copper yet, but I'm getting there."

"You are," Jason agreed.

Gio took a swig of beer, the moonlight illuminating the planes of his face. "I'm not staying in the job just to prove a point, or anything. Like, just to stick it to those fuckers. If I didn't love this job, I would have quit months ago. But this is the only thing I ever wanted to do."

Jason watched him silently.

Gio sighed. "You know when you're a kid in preschool, and they ask you what you want to be when you grow up? I said policeman. I drew this picture and everything. My sister found it and framed it for me when I graduated the academy. I didn't come into it as some starry-eyed idealist though. I knew what to expect when I was starting out: shit pay and shittier hours. I always had this idea that because I was gay, I'd need to work twice as hard to prove myself, but that was fine, because I knew I could do it. And what am I now? Nobody gives a fuck how well I could do my job. All they see is the whiny little bitch who went running to the bosses when his boyfriend dumped him."

Jason took a moment before he responded, unsure of what Gio needed to hear. "Even if that was true, which it isn't, he still deserved to lose his job if he was buying and using steroids."

There was no question in Jason's mind that Gio had done the right thing. A guy in a high-stress job with a short fuse? Add some roid rage to that, and no way in hell should Gio's ex be in any job where he had to deal with the public.

"No, see, they'll forgive that," Gio said. "Not the bosses, but the team. They'll forgive that because Pete was their mate. Because he was a good bloke who made an error in judgement. They feel sorry for him. They fucking *hate* me."

An insect *ping*ed against Jason's stubbie.

"When I was fifteen, our house got broken into," Jason said. "The coppers came around. That was when I decided I wanted to be in the job. It was all very mundane, but I liked the idea that I could help people every day. I think everyone I graduated with wanted to end up in Scenes of Crime—all those CSI shows were huge back then—but I always knew I'd be happiest in General Duties."

"I wanted to end up under State Crime Command," Gio said.

"Homicide?" Jason hazarded.

"Taskforce Maxima."

"Shit." Jason snorted. "Bikie gangs, huh? No wonder you hate it here. Not enough guns, drugs, or criminal syndicates."

"Hardly any organised crime at all," Gio said dryly.

"Yeah, most of it's pretty disorganised," Jason said. "And a fair chunk of it is downright accidental."

Gio's laugh warmed him.

"For what it's worth," Jason said at last, "I'm sorry it wasn't your choice to come here. But I think you're doing a good job."

"Thanks." Gio held his gaze in the moonlight for a moment, then he looked away again. He set his stubbie down on the table—empty, by the hollow sound it made—and stood. "I should head home."

Jason thought about asking him to stay, and if there was any way to frame that question without putting too much pressure on whatever it was they already had here. He didn't want to risk it.

"Good night," he said.

"Good night."

Jason watched him leave.

He sat on the veranda alone after Gio had left, slowly working on finishing his beer. He eked it out, wanting to prolong it while at the same time he didn't want to go inside and get a second one. He was too comfortable to move, and he was on call overnight. He needed to stay well under the limit just in case.

A flash of movement caught his eye, and his heart skipped a beat as the cat appeared at the top of the stairs.

"Jesus," he said. "You scared the hell out of me."

The cat slunk forward, and then sat and maintained a safe distance between them.

Taylor had been on Jason's case for years to get a pet, and maybe Jason should have caved earlier. A dog might have stopped the cat from moving in. But then, the yard wasn't fully fenced, and that was unsafe for a dog—it had been unsafe for a little kid too. When Taylor had been small, he'd been something of an escape artist. Jason had been at the station one day when a council road worker had turned up at the front counter, Taylor on his hip.

"I think this little fella belongs to you," he'd said, bundling Taylor over.

Taylor had apparently been fascinated by whatever work they were doing on the street, and had followed them as they'd progressed around the block.

That was Taylor all over. Inquisitive. Adventurous. Oblivious to hazards. Always diving headfirst into sticky situations. The last one was probably genetic, and as unavoidable as the freckles on the bridge of his nose that he'd also inherited from Jason.

Jason looked over towards Gio's house. There was a light on in the living room, but he couldn't see anyone moving around. He wondered if Gio took showers after they hooked up, or if he just tumbled into bed and fell asleep smelling like sex.

Want was a greedy emotion. Jason had wanted to kiss Gio, and so he had. He had wanted him in his bed, and that had happened too. And now he wanted more than middle-of-the-night hookups and conversations held in the darkness. What would it be like to wake up with Gio in his bed? To start their day together, with coffee and breakfast and adult conversation? That was the type of intimacy he missed the most from marriage. Sex was only a part of it.

Gio had just come out of a bad relationship. He was what? Twenty-six? Jason had a good decade on him, plus change. Further to that, Jason was Gio's boss, he was closeted, and still dreamed of his wife most nights. Jesus, it would be a bloody mess.

But want wasn't rational. And every time Jason ran his hands over Gio's skin, every time he used his mouth to pull up marks, or licked the dip over his collarbones where his sweat made his skin shine, Jason wanted more.

He finished his beer and went back inside, leaving the cat sitting alone on the veranda.

CHAPTER SEVENTEEN

Gio was eating his dinner at the truck stop on Wednesday night when Vicki joined him.

"Don't even talk to me," she grizzled, dragging out the chair beside his so she could sit.

"What's your problem?" He took the top off his steak burger to add more tomato sauce.

"Got a speeding ticket, didn't I?" she growled, stealing one of his chips.

Gio winced.

"It's from last month," Vicki said. "Fuckers set up right on the bend as you're coming up from that rise at Leichardt Creek. You know the spot?"

Gio nodded, surprised that he actually did. "Were you working?"

"Yeah, but I wasn't under a code, so I'm stuck with it." She grimaced. "The points *and* the fine."

"Sorry."

"Those arseholes." Vicki waved her hand at him vaguely. "The traffic guys. Not you and Jason."

Gio made a sympathetic noise around his burger, glad it gave him a reason not to answer beyond that. Down on the Coast if an ambo had bitched about a speeding ticket, he would have told them to harden the fuck up. What did he care? He wouldn't have known them, and so what if they met up over the occasional job? Maybe it would have been different if he'd been in General Duties, but Gio had been in the Tactical Crime Squad back then, and they'd had a very different mind-set. He'd loved how competitive it was there. It was only once he'd left that he'd realised how toxic that environment had been. How cutthroat. It hadn't been about teamwork. It had been about winning, and fuck everyone else. Fuck other sections, fuck General Duties, and fuck outside agencies completely. It didn't work like that here, given that he and Vicki tended to shadow one another on their evening and night shifts. For safety, but also for company.

Vicki's radio gave a hiss of static. A moment later, her Comms was calling her.

Gio grabbed one of the chips she'd purloined, and his radio blared to life as well.

"VKR calling Richmond two-eight-nine."

Gio dropped the chip, wiped his fingers on his pants, and stood up. He moved away from the table so that their respective Comms operators weren't talking over one another, and then reached for the microphone clipped to his epaulette. "Go ahead, VKR."

He listened to the details as the operator relayed them, and wrote the job number on his hand.

"Copy that, VKR. Show me proceeding."

He looked regretfully at his burger and chips, and then at Vicki. "Fergusons?"

She nodded. "Let's go."

There was a part of Gio that would always be surprised how violent people could be, how filled with hate, and how quickly they could lose their shit. He thought it at every domestic violence incident or disturbance that he went to. He'd thought it the first time Pete had been crowding over him, his face twisted up with anger, spraying spit in Gio's face as he'd just fucking bellowed at him. And Gio, who had been trained to bring someone down in a fight, had just frozen in utter shock. He'd let it happen simply because his brain couldn't process the fact it *was* happening. He'd never felt such a disconnect.

When he pulled up outside Janey Ferguson's place a few minutes after getting the call, Janey was standing in the front yard screaming, and one of her kids was pulling at her sleeve. The boy was no more than seven or eight. Gio remembered him from the fete. He'd given him a Clancy Koala sticker.

"Mum," the boy was saying. "Mum."

The neighbours' curtains snapped shut as Gio approached.

"Janey?" he called out. "Janey, what happened?"

He angled his torch towards her. She was wild-eyed—drunk, possibly, or high. She clamped her mouth shut when the light hit her, and moaned instead.

"Janey, are you hurt?" Gio asked her. "Janey?"

"Mum," the boy said, tugging at her sleeve again. "Mum?"

Gio took the boy by the shoulder and pulled him out of her reach. "What happened, mate?"

The boy sniffled. "Dad came over."

"Is he still here?" Gio asked, angling the torch towards the house.

"He went again." The boy showed Gio a gap-toothed grimace.

"Anyone else here apart from you kids and your mum?" Gio asked.

The boy shook his head.

Okay. Gio could deal with Janey on his own. He didn't need to bother calling Jason out for this.

"Did you see your dad hit your mum?" Gio asked the boy.

He was aware of Vicki approaching, lugging her kit. Apparently that was enough to get Janey's attention.

"Who the fuck called youse?" she yelled at Vicki. "I don't need the fucking ambulance! I need the fucking useless fucking coppers to go and get my fucking money back off that *cunt*!" She screamed the last word loud enough for the entire neighbourhood to hear it.

"Did Harvey assault you, Janey?" Gio asked.

"No! But if he comes back here, I'll fucking stab him!"

"And I'm out," Vicki said. "She's all yours, Gio."

Gio nodded at her, keeping his eyes on Janey. "What happened, Janey?"

"How fucking thick are you?" Janey screamed at him. "I fucking *told* you! Harvey stole my money!"

"You keep screaming at me, and you'll be the one coming down to the station," Gio said. "Do you understand?"

Janey wailed, and then moaned like some sort of landed sea creature. Her upper lip shone with snot, and Gio's stomach turned. "I w-want my money back!" And then she was sobbing.

Gio took a step back and focussed on the kid again. "Are you kids okay?"

The boy nodded staunchly.

"Have you got a grown-up you can call to come and look after you?" Gio asked.

The boy's expression dissolved into tears. "Don't take Mum away!"

"Mate, I'm not taking your mum away." Unless she took a swing at him, which seemed increasingly likely. "I just want to make sure there's a grown-up here who can keep an eye on everyone, alright? Including on your mum."

No fucking way was Janey Ferguson in any condition to care for her children. Whatever the outcome of tonight's incident was, Child Safety would be getting another notification.

"Auntie Lyn lives in Cooper Street."

"Okay," Gio said. "Let's go inside and call Auntie Lyn."

The boy nodded and scurried towards the front steps. The rest of the kids were peering out at them warily, skinny fingers curled around the doorjamb. One of the older girls had a baby seated on her narrow hip.

"Janey," Gio said. "Janey, we're going inside."

Janey tugged at her hair and keened and moaned.

"Get inside, Janey," Gio said. "Get inside, and then you can tell me what happened."

"I told you!" She stumbled towards the front door. "I already fucking told you!"

Gio followed her, casting a glance toward the house next door. The curtains twitched. He spared a thought for the people who had to live beside the Ferguson house, and then redirected that thought to the kids who had to live in it.

"Esme, right?" he asked the oldest girl. The name seemed like an odd fit. It brought to mind old ladies with walking frames, not twelve- or thirteen-year-old girls.

The girl nodded.

"Can you go call your Auntie Lyn for me? Tell her she needs to come over, please."

Esme nodded, shifting the baby to her other hip before going to find a phone.

Gio steered Janey into the kitchen. "Sit down."

She slumped into a chair at the tiny table.

The house was the same mess as always: Rubbish piled up in bags beside the bin because nobody had bothered to take it out. Flies hovering over the sink. The stinking nappy bucket in the corner. It was a mess, but not the sort of mess that warranted an emergency removal of the kids.

"Now tell me what happened tonight," Gio said, crossing his arms over his chest. "And don't just yell at me. I need details. I need to know if there was any assault, and I need to know exactly what happened."

Janey's story came out in sobs. Her anger had flooded away now, replaced by tears. She'd invited Harvey around, and they'd been drinking, and then they'd got into a fight and he'd taken her money and her cigarettes. Sixty dollars, and half a packet of Winfield Blues. But Gio was satisfied there'd been no violence. There was nothing here he had to arrest Harvey Ferguson for tonight. It was the usual breach of the no-contact conditions on the Domestic Violence Order.

"Okay," he said. "Janey, I can't take a complaint of theft from you when you've been drinking. But I'm working tomorrow, and I'll come and see you then."

She looked up at him through tear-stained eyes. "But what about my cigarettes?"

They were probably long gone by now. "If I find Harvey tonight, I'll try and get them back. But if he comes around here again, you have to call me and tell me. You have to call triple zero, because he's breaching his order."

Breaching it because she kept inviting him around.

He understood it though. The need to believe that this time would be different. He didn't want to admit he had anything in common with someone like Janey Ferguson, but that was a lie. He'd believed Pete when he'd said it wouldn't happen again, even when he'd been to so many fucking DV incidents in his years on the job that he'd known it was bullshit. Total bullshit, but he'd chosen to believe it. Set aside all his instinct, all his knowledge, all his experience, and made the conscious fucking choice to delude himself.

And Janey, he guessed, had exactly the same hard-won experience.

"Weren't you going to go to Gympie?" he asked her. "Wasn't that the plan?"

"What's the fucking point?" she mumbled.

Gio didn't have an answer for her, but he waited with her until her sister arrived. He made sure she was settled before he left.

Gio didn't find Harvey Ferguson during the remainder of his shift, but he did swing by the truck stop again and order some hot chips with extra chicken salt. He was paying for them when he caught sight of the Smoking Kills signs that hid the cigarettes from view.

"And a packet of Peter Jackson Silver," he said. "In the twenties."

He'd never been much of a smoker. He hadn't done it since his uni days and couldn't remember how the hell he'd ever afforded it. But tonight it seemed like a slightly better option than falling into a bottle after his shift. And it really was that kind of a shift.

He was back at the station at ten, and locked up and heading to the house by a quarter past. He checked his phone to see if there was a message from Jason. Nothing yet, but usually Jason waited until he saw Gio's lights come on before he texted.

Gio didn't bother going inside. He sat on the front steps and lit a cigarette.

Okay, so that was disgusting.

He persevered though, and the foul taste soon gave way to a pleasant head spin, and he remembered that yeah, this felt good.

Life was made up of snapshots. The job was. Gio was supposed to be able to compartmentalise. He was supposed to leave work at work, and not bring it home. Keep his snapshots of head wounds and body parts and blood splatters and crying kids in a shoebox under his bed, hidden away. Those weren't the snapshots he was meant to keep on display. He wasn't supposed to shuffle them together with the snapshots of friends and family and days at the beach, and sunlight and smiles bright with laughter. And maybe he hadn't, right up until Pete had hit him, and just like that the walls had tumbled down and his worlds had bled together.

Gio closed his eyes and held the cigarette between his shaking fingers.

"Rough night?"

"Jesus Christ!" Gio flailed backwards, his heart thumping fast.

"There's that situational awareness all the kids are talking about," Jason drawled, leaning on the rail at the bottom of the steps. His expression was hidden in the darkness. "You okay?"

"Yeah. Just, um . . ." Gio squinted at the ember on the end of the cigarette. "Falling back into bad habits."

Jason trod up the steps, and Gio shuffled over to make room.

Jason sat and knocked his shoulder against Gio's. "Rough night?" he asked again.

Gio paused a moment to consider the question. "You know, it really wasn't. Just more of the same from Janey Ferguson." He took another drag on the cigarette. "Harvey had already left by the time I got the call. There wasn't any assault, only the breach, and maybe a stealing complaint if she goes through with that when she sobers up."

Gio froze as Jason's hand settled on his back, moving gently up and down his spine.

Was this walls tumbling and worlds bleeding together?

"Did you get the breach put on?" Jason rubbed his thumb over the knot of bone at the top of Gio's spine.

Gio clamped his lips around the filter on the cigarette and sucked in a burning lungful of smoke. He held it for a moment and then let it shudder out of him. "Yeah. Gonna chase Harvey up tomorrow and charge him for it then."

"See if you can get him in custody first thing," Jason said, lifting his hand for just long enough to move it to Gio's neck. His fingers were warm against Gio's skin. "The earlier you get it done, the better your chances are for a halfway meet with a Charters Towers crew. Save you driving the whole way."

Gio nodded and relaxed into Jason's touch. "Yeah. That's what I figured."

Jason kept one hand on the back of Gio's neck, his thumb brushing against the short hairs at Gio's nape. With his other hand, he plucked the cigarette from Gio's fingers, stubbed it out in a shower of sparks against the metal rail of the stairs, and flicked the butt away into the darkness.

Gio rolled his eyes.

Then two of Jason's fingers were pressing against his jaw, turning his head towards him, and Jason's mouth was on his, and Gio didn't give a fuck if Jason threw the entire packet over the edge of the stairs. He closed his eyes as they kissed and didn't want to think about why they were stinging.

Jason drew back slowly. "Is it hard for you to go to DVs?"

Gio swallowed. "Part of the job."

Jason stared at him in the darkness. "That's not what I asked."

"Sometimes it is." Gio shrugged. "Not always."

Jason ran his thumb along Gio's jawline, as though he thought his touch could draw the words out.

Maybe it could.

Gio held his gaze. "If I could make a mistake like that, like *him*, then how can I ever trust my own judgement again? When it happened, I didn't know who he was. I didn't know who I was either."

"It's not your fault."

Gio snorted and turned his head away. "Yeah, I *know* that. I'm not a fucking idiot. I've read the same pamphlets and done the same courses as you, remember? I've sat there and twiddled my thumbs while some woman from the Domestic Violence Resource Centre wearing a patchwork skirt turns up and lectures a whole room of coppers on how we have to stop victim blaming." He scowled into the darkness. "I *know* that."

"Are you sure about that?" Jason asked.

Gio curled his hand over the top of the rail to haul himself up. "Yeah. I don't know what this is here, but it's not what I'm looking for tonight."

Jason caught him by the wrist and pulled him back down again before he could find his feet. "Then tell me to shut my fucking mouth if it's none of my business."

Gio searched his face in the darkness. "It's none of your business, Jason." He leaned closer. "Shut your fucking mouth."

"Yeah." Jason reached up and tugged his fingers roughly through the longer section of Gio's hair, where his curls were more pronounced. "I'll shut my mouth, Gio."

The blood thrummed in Gio's veins, and his skin prickled. "Fuck me tonight?"

"Is that what you want?" Jason's voice was low.

"Yeah, that's what I want."

"Okay." Jason released his hair. "Come over when you're ready. I'll leave the back unlocked."

Gio nodded.

This time when he rose to his feet, Jason didn't stop him. They parted on the stairs. Gio climbed up them, while Jason walked down. The boards on the veranda shifted under Gio's boots. He dug his keys out of his pocket and let himself into the house. He reached inside and slid his hand up the wall, looking for the light switch and flicking it on.

Gio went to the kitchen first, and emptied his pockets onto the bench. He held the packet of cigarettes in his hand for the moment, staring at the lurid warning picture on the front that honestly looked less like a diseased lung and more like a dried apricot, and then threw the packet in the bin. The last thing he needed was to get addicted to them again.

He thought of Jason and wondered if he was exchanging one addiction for another. He wondered which, on balance, was worse for him.

He showered and brushed his teeth.

He changed into basketball shorts and a baggy shirt.

He picked up his keys again and locked the house behind him.

Jason was waiting.

CHAPTER EIGHTEEN

Sandra gave Jason an odd look when he arrived at work at two the next day, still wearing a faint smile that was a hangover from the night before. *I know you don't like Gio much*, he imagined telling her, *but the things he can do with his tongue!*

"Where's Gio?" he asked. "Did he catch up with Harvey Ferguson?"

"No." Sandra readjusted her glasses. "He's out at a trespassing complaint. He went around to all of the usual haunts this morning, but Harvey's apparently laying low."

"He'll turn up."

"That's the problem," Sandra agreed. "He always does."

Jason nodded.

"Your mail's on your desk," Sandra said. "And Len and I are going to dinner tonight at the RSL. It's his birthday."

Jason froze.

"I told you about this last week," Sandra reminded him. She pursed her lips. "I love Taylor, Jason, but I'd prefer to go for a nice meal with my husband on our own."

"Yeah, of course." Jason headed for his office. "I'll sort something out for Taylor."

He winced as she muttered under her breath about not just sorting it out for tonight, in a voice that he knew she'd intended him to hear. He escaped into his office and closed the door behind him.

Yeah. He needed to sort something out. For tonight, and . . . and for the future. Sandra was obviously at the end of her rope, and Jason couldn't really blame her.

He sat at his desk and composed a text to Kane's mother asking if Taylor could stay at their place tonight. He'd asked a couple of times in the past, but he didn't want to push it because Taylor wasn't a kid who had a big group of friends. He seemed to be wired to only have one friend at a time. It had been Kane for about two years now, and Jason didn't want to complicate that. He didn't want Taylor to lose a friend because the friend's parents felt they were getting taken advantage of.

Sometimes Jason felt as unqualified to successfully parent as he had on the day Taylor was born. He still remembered when Taylor was a few months old and he and Alana had taken him to his first playgroup. Jason had walked into violent disturbances with armed antagonists and felt less intimidated. All those *parents.*

"What are we supposed to do?" He'd fiddled with the straps on Taylor's pram just to look busy.

"We smile and nod, Jason. We smile and nod."

Jason exhaled heavily as he sent the text to Kane's mum. It was a lot to ask. *Hey, can my kid stay with yours after school? And can you feed him and put him to sleep somewhere comfortable until I come and get him at ten? Possibly later, if anything goes to shit.*

He worded it slightly better than that. He hoped.

God. Sandra was right.

He'd swing by Saint Patrick's tomorrow maybe, and ask the ladies there if they could recommend anyone who was looking to pick up some extra cash, and who didn't mind if Taylor sometimes had to stay overnight. It would hopefully be a step in the right direction. Right up until he had to break it to Taylor, probably. He wasn't going to be happy at all about staying with someone he didn't know.

Jason sighed and began to go through the stack of mail on his desk.

Most of it was unimportant. A *Certificate of Thanks* from the school for Gio's presence at the fete. An invitation to the next council meeting. An angry letter from Mrs. McKinney about her neighbour. Mrs. McKinney had been writing letters of complaint about her neighbour for over thirty years. Jason supposed he was glad she put pen to paper, and didn't call. He'd go and visit her later just to smooth down her feathers.

He inspected his next envelope. *OIC, Richmond Police Station, Richmond, QLD, 4822.*

Jason opened it, and a sealed packet fell onto his desk.

Ratsak.

And scrawled across the packet in black marker: *for your rat problem*.

Jason stared at it for a moment, the blood roaring in his skull. Then he rose from his desk. "Sandra? Sandra!"

She opened his door. "What?"

"Get me the station camera and an evidence bag."

Sandra's eyes widened as her gaze fell on the Ratsak. "What the hell is that?"

"Fuck them," Jason said, rage coiling in his gut. "We don't take their shit up here. They want to bring me into this? They're fucking welcome."

Nobody—*nobody* fucked with Gio.

Not when Jason had promised he had his back.

Sandra hurried away, and Jason picked up his phone and dialled. Gordy, the DDO in Townsville, picked up after only a few rings and listened quietly while Jason told him about the rat poison.

"Well, there's no way to prove it was them," he said.

"It's postmarked Southport."

"That's not *proof*."

Jason's anger rose. "Gordy, what—"

"Jesus Christ. Don't tell me I have to explain evidentiary standards and the burden of proof to a bloody sergeant of police?" Gordy gave Jason a moment to seethe. "Of course it's them. You know it and I know it. You just can't *prove* it's them. That's how intimidation tactics work."

"So what? I'm supposed to take this?"

"You're very angry," Gordy said. "This isn't the first thing, is it?"

"It's the first thing directed at me," Jason said, thinking of the dog treats Gio had received, and whatever had been in the envelope he hadn't let Jason see.

"Then put in your report," Gordy said. "And I'll back you in taking it as far as it goes. So long as you know, it's not going to go far."

"Are you fucking serious, Gordy?"

"Perfectly," Gordy said. "Jason, there are two outcomes here. Maybe an investigation gets them to back off, or maybe it doesn't. But I'll tell you right now that there is no way an investigation will identify the culprits. They wouldn't have sent it if it could be traced."

"So I'm supposed to just cop it?" Jason asked, rubbing a hand over his forehead to try to stave off the headache he was sure was coming. "Gio's supposed to just cop it?"

"Don't put words in my mouth, Sergeant," Gordy said, his tone hardening. "I already told you to put in a report, and I already told you I will back you as far as it goes. And when the investigation inevitably fails, then my advice would be for Senior Constable Valeri to get himself a psychologist and a solicitor, and sue the Service for failing to provide a safe working environment."

"Fuck me, Gordy!" Jason shook his head. "Seriously? He doesn't want a fucking payout. He wants to do his job!"

"They push him far enough, and he'll change his tune," Gordy said. "The bullies want him gone because they think he's a dog, and the bosses want him gone because they think he's a troublemaker. Pretty soon a payout will start to look like a good option."

"Not to Gio," Jason said. "Not while I've got his back."

Gordy was silent for a long moment, and Jason wondered if those words had conveyed more than he'd intended. Then Gordy hummed. "Your attitude's changed since last time we talked."

"Last time we talked you told me there are more than two sides to every story. I finally heard his."

"Okay," Gordy said. "Then send me your report."

It was a laid-back shift. Jason refused to use the q-word to describe it, even in his head, because that was a sure way to turn everything to shit in a heartbeat, but it was definitely the opposite of busy. He stopped in to see Janey, and found her sober and surprisingly cooperative. She said she didn't know where Harvey was staying—not that Jason believed that for a second—and promised she'd call if he turned up. They talked more about her plans to move to Gympie to live with her mum, and Jason pushed a little harder, certain that he could get funding off some department or another to help with moving costs. By the end of the visit, Janey looked almost convinced.

"You could do that?" she asked, her hope clearly warring with her suspicion. "You could get bus tickets for me and all the kids?"

"Yes, Janey, I can do that."

Janey chewed her lower lip.

"Give me your mum's number," Jason said. "Let me call her tomorrow and talk to her about it, okay?"

Janey seemed to waver.

"Come on," Jason said. "It'd be good for the kids, Janey. Don't you want them to be better off?"

It was a blatant fucking guilt trip, but Jason didn't care as long as it worked. And the kids would be better off with their parents at opposite ends of the state. Living with their grandmother would be more stable than this.

Janey got her phone and read the number out to him.

Jason was feeling like he'd actually accomplished something by the time his shift ended. With Patricia Howe thinking of moving to Rockhampton to live with her daughter, and Janey Ferguson almost convinced to go to Gympie to live with her mother, that would be at least two victims of domestic violence removed from the immediate reach of their abusers. Not a perfect solution, but Jason could only work with what he was given.

And speaking of not-perfect solutions . . . Jason had stopped by Saint Patrick's and spoken to several of the ladies there, and they'd suggested a few people who might be willing and able to watch Taylor from time to time. Jason planned to follow their suggestions up when he got the chance. Hopefully by the time he'd found someone, and vetted them, he would have figured out some way to tell Taylor what was going on. He knew exactly how Taylor was going to react as well. This was probably going to cost Jason as much in iTunes gift cards as it would in babysitting fees.

He picked Taylor up from Kane's house at just past ten, thanked Kane's parents, and headed home. Taylor climbed straight into bed—Jason wasn't sure he'd entirely woken up on the drive—and crashed out again.

Jason sent a text to Gio and got to work on Taylor's school lunch. He was scraping Vegemite over the SAOs when he heard Gio climbing the back steps. The screen door squeaked open.

"Hey," he said as Gio appeared in the kitchen doorway.

Gio scratched his stomach, his T-shirt riding up. He gave a sleepy smile. "Hey."

"Were you asleep?" Jason grabbed the bread to make Taylor's sandwich for big lunch. "Sorry."

"'S'okay." Gio stepped into the kitchen, and leaned against the bench. "This is better than sleep."

"Watching me make sandwiches? Yeah, it's pretty hot."

Gio's smile grew, and colour rose in his cheeks. "It is, actually, in a weird way."

Jason set the butter knife aside and reached out for Gio. He caught his fingers in the elastic of Gio's track pants, and pulled him close. "Yeah?" He kissed him. "Is this doing it for you?"

He registered the movement over Gio's shoulder a fraction of a second too late.

"Dad?" Taylor asked, wide-eyed. "Dad, what are you doing?"

Shit.

Gio stepped away from him, keeping his back to Taylor. He shot Jason a frantic look.

Shit shit shit.

"Hey, mate," Jason said, his heart thumping wildly. "I thought you were in bed."

Taylor looked from Jason to Gio and then back again. He gripped the doorjamb with his skinny fingers. His forehead was creased. "Dad?"

"Just a second, Taylor." Jason wasn't panicking. He wasn't. "Gio, I'll, um, I'll see you tomorrow, okay?"

"Yeah." Gio backed away, keeping his gaze averted. "See you then, boss."

Even Taylor scrunched up his nose at that.

Gio escaped out the back door.

Jason stared at his son. Ten years old and the most terrifying thing Jason had ever faced. Because he couldn't lose Taylor. Not over this.

Taylor stared back, his eyes big. Then he unpeeled his fingers from the doorjamb and stepped inside the kitchen. "Dad," he said tentatively. "Dad, I know what gay is."

Jason glimpsed the faint scar on his chin.

"You are ten. *You don't have any facial hair."*

Taylor took another step towards him. "I know that it's okay to be gay."

You are ten. How are you so bloody smart*?*

"I'm not gay, Taylor," Jason said, keeping his voice steady. "I'm bi. That means—"

"That means you can love Mum and Gio," Taylor said, his voice hardly more than a whisper.

"Gio's my friend," Jason said, a burst of fear fluttering in his gut. Love. Alana. Those things were worlds bigger than his sexuality. Those were things that deserved their own discussion, and not one that was tangled up in what had happened with Gio. He didn't know how to tackle this. "I don't— I'm not replacing your mum, Taylor."

Taylor flinched so suddenly that Jason panicked for a moment that he couldn't have said anything worse. Maybe Taylor hadn't even worried about that until Jason had put the thought in his head. Jesus. What the bloody hell was he *doing*?

"Mate, I feel like I need to have two really big, really different talks to you about this." Jason put a hand on Taylor's shoulder. "And one of those talks is about being bi, and what you think about that, and the other talk is about Gio, and what you saw happening tonight."

Taylor chewed his bottom lip, his storm-cloud eyes narrowing with worry. "And it's a school night too, Dad!"

"Yeah," Jason said, swallowing down tears of relief. Because his kid, Jesus. If Taylor figured being up late was the biggest crisis of the night, then maybe everything wasn't as fucked up as Jason feared it was. "It's a school night too."

Taylor wrinkled his nose, and Jason pulled him into a grateful hug.

They stayed up and talked for way longer than was advisable on a school night. They sat on the couch, with a movie playing on the TV so that Taylor had something to watch if he didn't want to look at Jason while they talked. Taylor didn't seem bothered though. He asked about boys and girls, and if Jason liked boys one time and girls another time.

"It's like you and ice cream, Taylor. Even if I'm eating chocolate ice cream, I can still like strawberry at the same time."

They had ice cream.

"You can like other things apart from ice cream too," Taylor said, licking his spoon.

"You can like whatever you want to like," Jason agreed.

Taylor pondered that for a moment. "I don't like rice pudding."

"How did this turn into a discussion about desserts?" Jason asked, elbowing Taylor in the ribs. He almost regretted not following the dessert conversation when Taylor turned the subject back around.

"Is Gio your boyfriend?" he asked.

"That's not something we've talked about yet," Jason said.

"Why not?" Taylor wiped his mouth with the sleeve of his pyjama top. Then he looked outraged. "Dad! You have to ask someone if they want to be your girlfriend or your boyfriend before you kiss them!"

"Oh, that's how it works." Jason couldn't help his smile. He slung an arm around Taylor, and almost wore the plate of ice cream for his trouble. "Listen, mate, about Gio . . . it's really important that you don't tell anyone about us, okay?"

Taylor narrowed his eyes. "Why?"

Because I don't know how he feels. Because there is so much else going on with him. Because this is a small town. Because if you come out in a town like this, you need to know someone else has got your back. Someone apart from your ten-year-old son.

"Because it's complicated, mate, and I wish I could give you a better answer than that, but it's just complicated. With work, and with the people in town."

With you.

Did Gio even want someone like Jason? Jason was a hard sell. Not just because of his job—at least Gio would have no trouble understanding the pressures that came from that—but because of his son. His first priority would always be his son. And that was a hell of an ask for any potential new partner.

"I like Gio," Taylor said at last, shovelling another mouthful of half-melted ice cream into his mouth. "He's cool."

"Yeah," Jason said. "He's pretty cool."

It was past midnight when Taylor went back to bed. Later, after finally finishing packing Taylor's lunch for tomorrow, Jason passed his room and found him hiding under the covers with a torch on.

"Taylor," he said. "It's *so* late. Come on."

Taylor threw the covers back, pointing the torch towards him. The beam arced across the ceiling before it hit Jason in the face. "I was reading."

"Bedtime," Jason said, shielding his eyes.

Taylor muttered under his breath and flicked his torch off. "You used to be cool, Dad!"

"I was never cool, mate."

Taylor's snort of laughter followed him down the hallway.

Jason brushed his teeth and went to bed. He sent a text to Gio: *Sorry about tonight. I'll see you tomorrow.*

He looked at Alana's smiling face in her photograph and, like always, felt the ache of no longer having her in his life. Of no longer having her by his side, when he didn't know what the fuck he was doing or how the hell to brazen it out.

"Smile and nod, Jason," he heard her say. *"Smile and nod."*

CHAPTER NINETEEN

Gio started work at eight and spent the first half an hour washing the cars. Rust-coloured mud covered the concrete by the time he'd hosed out under the wheel arches, and Gio's shirt was wet with water and sweat. He had a spare inside. Or, if not, at home. At about eight thirty he saw Taylor leaving for school. He looked like some sort of water bird with his long skinny legs and his bulky backpack. He made his way slowly across the grass-stubbled yard, dragging a stick through the dirt for the benefit of the cat that watched him avidly, following him at a safe distance.

Gio waited until Taylor had made it to the road and headed towards the school, and then he turned the water off, coiled the hose up, and walked across to Jason's house. He climbed the steps and made it onto the front veranda just as Jason opened the door.

"Hey," Gio said.

Jason looked almost nervous. "Hey. I thought Taylor had forgotten something."

"Is he okay?" Gio stuck his hands in his pockets.

"He is, yeah." Jason smiled slightly, colour rising in his cheeks. "So, ah, yeah, we had *that* talk, and the good news is that Taylor thinks you're cool."

Gio raised his eyebrows, surprised. Of all possible outcomes, that wasn't one he'd expected.

"He wants to know if you're my boyfriend," Jason said.

Gio lifted his chin and held Jason's gaze. "Don't . . ." He exhaled heavily. Then inhaled and started again. "Is he asking, or are you? Because that's not a question you get to hide behind your kid."

"Then I'm asking too." Jason ducked his head and scrubbed a hand over his hair. "I'm asking first."

Some of the tension that Gio had been holding bled away. "You mean spending time with you when we're not fucking?"

Jason flushed. "Yeah."

Gio tilted his head. "Openly?"

Jason nodded slowly. "Um, except maybe not right away? Give it some time, see how it goes? Coming out in this town—not just as bi, but coming out in a relationship—there's no stepping back from that. We'd need to be really sure about it."

Gio considered that for a moment. He'd always said—*always*—that he wouldn't date anyone in the closet. There was too much associated bullshit that he didn't need. He wasn't going to get sidelined in his own relationship, and forced to play a friend, a flatmate, a guy from work. That wasn't who he was.

But . . .

But things were different here. They had to police this fucking town, and they had to have a united front to do it. Not all compromise was capitulation, was it? Except now his tension was back, and his stomach was in knots.

"Okay," he heard himself say, despite it. This might be a hell of a gamble, but he was willing to make it. He wanted to believe that Jason was worth it. He wasn't certain he had that faith in anyone anymore, but he wanted to believe he did, that there was still some residue of hope and optimism inside him that Pete hadn't quite managed to beat out of him. And if Gio was ever going to take a risk again, then why not now? Why not on Jason?

Jason raised his eyebrows. "Okay?"

"We see if it works," Gio said, his heart beating faster. "If it does, we do it openly. If it doesn't, nobody else needs to know."

Jason's sudden smile was almost enough to make Gio think he'd made the right choice.

Almost.

Three days. It took three days to go to shit. Somewhere in those three days—sitting down for dinner with Jason and Taylor, watching a movie together when the meal was over, and staying overnight instead of sneaking out in the darkness—somewhere, Gio started to feel at home. Not just with Jason, but with Taylor too. Somewhere in those three days he showed Jason how to make proper bolognaise sauce, in return was treated to one of the best home-cooked steaks he'd ever eaten, and learned that they'd changed the way maths was taught since he'd been in school and that he was totally fucked up by year five homework. Gio hadn't even realised how lonely he'd been until suddenly he wasn't.

They talked more in those three days than they had in the entire time Gio had been in Richmond. About Gio's dad, and Sophie, and Pete, and the shit that happened down on the Coast, and Gio learned about Jason's family as well. His parents in Cairns—Gio got the impression that relationship was strained. Jason also talked about Alana's parents down in Victoria. Alana's brother, who lived in England. Cousins Taylor would probably never meet, and the weird guilt Jason felt over that, even though Alana and her brother hadn't been close to begin with.

Gio fell easily into the spaces that Jason opened up to him.

Three days.

Gio got the call about the assault on Castlereagh Street at 1 a.m. on Friday morning. He was dealing with a noise complaint out on Racecourse Road, but wrapped that up quickly and headed back into town. The ambulance was already parked outside the address on Castlereagh Street when he arrived, the strobes flashing against the weatherboard façades of the neighbouring houses.

Vicki had beaten him to the scene and gone in first.

And it only ever took a second for a job to go bad.

"Hey!" Gio yelled as he approached the knot of people jostling Vicki as she knelt over the prone woman on the ground. "Hey, back off!"

He elbowed through them and stood over Vicki. He caught a glimpse of her expression: fear and relief battling for dominance.

"Back off," he repeated, one hand on his spray. Just in case. There were six of them, and they were drunk and belligerent. "Let her work."

The drunks circled.

"Who called these cunts anyhow?" one of the drunks snarled, spittle flecking his grey whiskers. He puffed his chest out. "Who the fuck called youse anyhow?"

"Back *off*," Gio said again, flicking the pouch holding his spray open with his thumb. He widened his stance, adrenaline flooding through him.

"*Yah*!" The drunk spat on the ground. "Fuckin' copper cunts."

"Vicki," Gio said, not taking his eyes off the guy. "Get out of here."

Gio heard glass breaking.

One of the other drunks lunged suddenly, and Gio leapt back. He was on his back foot, off-balance, and the second drunk was coming at him with a broken bottle. He caught the man's swinging arm, and tried to force him back. For someone of his age and wretched condition, the man was surprisingly strong. Gio saw the grubby old fist of the drunk's free hand in his line of vision, but couldn't let go while the man was still wielding the broken bottle in his other hand.

There was a flash of white when the fist connected with his mouth, and then Gio was on the ground. He couldn't see a thing, but the drunk still had hold of him. The man was on top of him, and he *stank*, and Gio realised he was tugging at something on his belt.

Adrenaline coursed through him, and he tasted blood in the back of his throat.

Vicki was screaming into her radio: "Urgent assistance! I need urgent assistance!"

Gio let go of the drunk's arm, and brought his knee up sharply. He didn't care what he hit—kidneys, stomach, groin. He just wanted to hurt him long enough to get the man off him. There were more hands pulling at him now, and kicks aimed at his ribs. The first drunk was still on top of him.

Gio reached for his taser. He needed to put some volts through this arsehole. There was dirt and sweat in Gio's eyes, and he couldn't see properly, but he felt the drunk's bony hands around his throat. The man was trying to choke him.

He had to get out from under him before he blacked out. He pushed at the drunk, and saw a flash of frizzy blonde hair over the guy's shoulder. Vicki was trying to wrench him free too. Together they managed it, and then Gio scrambled backwards on his knees. He drew his firearm.

"Back off!" he rasped, spraying blood. "Back the fuck off!"

His head throbbed, everything hurt, and three minutes ago he'd been standing on his feet. He didn't know exactly what had happened, or how it had happened so rapidly.

He kept his firearm pointed at the drunks, afraid to blink. He panted for breath, Vicki on her knees behind him, and refused to let his hands shake.

The wail of the approaching siren was the most beautiful sound in the world.

The drunks broke and scattered like cockroaches, leaving only Gio, Vicki, and the unconscious woman behind.

Gio didn't reholster his gun until Jason was by his side.

"Shit," Jason said. "Are you okay?"

Gio tilted his head up. "Yup," he said, not risking a nod. "Glad you got here so quick."

"Shit, Gio," Vicki said. "I'm sorry. I totally misread it. I shouldn't have gone in. I should have waited."

"'S'okay," Gio said, still waiting for his heart to stop trying to beat out of his chest. "It's okay."

Jason helped him to his feet.

To the hospital to get checked out and cleaned up, then the station to put his weapons in the safe; Gio was familiar with the routine at this point. It was almost dawn by the time Gio and Jason were walking across the yard towards home. He wanted to get into a hot shower to get rid of the taste of sweat and antiseptic. He wanted to curl up with Jason and fall asleep with him. Except . . .

"Jason," he said, the word a little distorted by his busted lip. He pointed at Jason's front steps.

Taylor was curled up at the top of the steps, wrapped in a blanket like a burrito.

Jason's face fell.

"Go," Gio said. "Look after him. I'll be fine." He smiled, despite the sour taste at the back of his throat.

How long had Taylor been sitting there waiting for his dad to come home before he'd fallen asleep?

How often did it happen?

And was Gio supposed to keep pretending it wasn't an issue?

Three days.

Gio was dreaming of sunlight shining on skyscrapers. Steel and chrome and glass, and the glittering ocean stretching out beyond the horizon. It was so bright he couldn't stare at it for long. The sand, white as chalk, burned the soles of his feet.

He woke up when his phone rang.

"Senior Constable Valeri," a man said. "DDO Gordon. I thought I told you to stop getting flogged."

"Um." Blinking around his bedroom, it took Gio a moment for his brain to come online. The headache probably didn't help. "Sorry, boss."

"So you bloody should be," the DDO said. "How are you feeling?"

"Not too bad," Gio said, closing his eyes against the glare of the day.

"Good," the DDO said. "And while I've got you, any more unsolicited mail you get out there, I want to know about it."

"What?" Gio opened his eyes again, his heart skipping a beat as he thought of the Schmackos.

"Keep a log of it," Senior Sergeant Gordon said. "Understood?"

"Yes, sir." Gio's hand shook. He'd told Jason that he didn't want to report it. He'd *told* him.

"Get some sleep, hey? And I mean it this time, Valeri. Stop getting flogged."

Gio had no idea how he kept his voice steady. "Okay, boss."

The senior sergeant ended the call.

Gio climbed out of bed. He was numb. Some of that was fatigue, probably, but some of it was the anger building in his gut. Strange. It was there—he could *feel* it—but it was distant, disconnected somehow. His mind hadn't worked out how to process it yet, what to do with it. Or maybe he'd just used up all his adrenaline last night and had none in reserve to fuel a burning rush of rage. His anger was contained. It was cold.

He pulled on jeans and a T-shirt, and stumbled into the bathroom to splash water on his face. His split lip was swollen, but it could have been worse. Vicki was okay, and that was the important thing. Gio could save the upcoming crisis of confidence over getting assaulted twice in the space of a few scant months for later. Was he projecting an attitude that immediately put people offside? He remembered one of the women from his graduating class at the academy years ago.

"Now she," one of the trainers had said, *"is going to take a few punches before she learns."*

Gio poked at his split lip and wondered if he had somehow developed the same sort of abrasive personality that made people want to punch him in the face.

That was to worry about after.

He returned to his bedroom and grabbed his phone. It was just past eleven. He shoved his feet into his unlaced trainers, locked the front door behind him, and set off towards the back of the station. Both police vehicles were still there.

Good.

The sensor on the back door cheeped as Gio held the tag on his keys against it. He opened the door when the lock clicked, and stepped inside the cool of the air-conditioning. He strode through to the small dayroom.

"Gio!" Sandra called from the counter. "Shouldn't you be in bed?"

Gio caught sight of the CCTV monitor beside her computer. There was someone in the cell. He headed down the hallway, and peered in the window in the cell door. It was the guy who'd assaulted him.

Good.

"Gio?" Sandra called. "What the hell is your problem?"

Gio walked towards Jason's office. He opened the door without knocking, and Jason looked up from behind his desk. "Gio?"

"You want to tell me why the DDO knows I've been getting mail?" His eyes stung, and he didn't know if it was just from lack of sleep, or if maybe his anger wasn't as cold as he'd thought. "I told you I didn't want to make a complaint about it! I *told* you!"

"You're not the only one getting mail, Gio!" Jason rose to his feet.

"What?"

"They sent me something too."

"What'd they send you?"

Jason's brow furrowed. "Ratsak."

Gio let out a strangled laugh. "Succinct. To the point. Not exactly subtle though."

He thought of Coop, for some reason. Coop, always with a smile on his face and a smart-arse comment on the end of his tongue. Had it been Coop? Coop, who'd sat beside him one night when they were doing surveillance on this guy, and proudly showed Gio pictures of his wife's ultrasound. That was where it hurt the most. Coop had been his friend. They'd all been his friends.

Jason walked around his desk. "Gio."

Gio stepped back. "It still doesn't give you the right to get involved!"

"*They* got me involved." Jason's tone was steady.

"And now you've dragged me back in!" Gio shook his head. "You should have just left it alone! They baited you, and you took it, and now they'll escalate!"

"Gio, they can't touch you here." Jason put a hand on his shoulder.

"Oh, fuck off!" Gio shook him off. "Don't patronise me. I *told* you! They had photographs of my niece's day care!" He sucked in a shaking breath. He'd thought Jason understood, or at least that he respected Gio enough to abide by his decision. But here Gio was again, getting dragged back into the middle of the shit-storm he'd only barely clawed his way out of, and it was Jason doing it to him this time. The betrayal burned more than he wanted it to, because it wasn't just Gio's trust that had been broken, it was his fragile hope as well. He'd thought they were building a relationship. He'd thought that maybe there was a future in it. Not now though. Not fucking now. "You had no right to do that, Jason. No right."

"It's workplace bullying," Jason said.

"This is about my family, Jason! My *niece*!" His voice cracked.

"If I don't report it, I'm complicit in it."

Gio choked out a bitter laugh. "Oh, so now you want to follow the letter of the law, do you? *You*?"

Jason's expression shuttered.

Gio wanted to hurt him as much as he was hurting.

"What section of the Criminal Code is it?" he asked, his voice raw. "Three-sixty something? Something about leaving a child under the age of twelve unattended for an unreasonable amount of time?"

"Don't." Jason's voice was cold.

"Don't what?" Gio asked. "If I went round to Janey Ferguson's house and found out she'd left her kids alone for hours at night, you'd expect me to report it. Wouldn't you?"

Jason didn't answer.

"Wouldn't you?" Gio demanded.

"If I hadn't left him alone last night, who the hell knows what would have happened to you and Vicki."

Gio shook his head. "Don't pretend last night was the only time, Jason. Don't pretend you've never ducked out for a noise complaint in the middle of the night and left him sleeping. Don't pretend you don't know what could have happened that day with the microwave if I hadn't been next door."

There was a line. There was always a line with any person, and Gio had known from the start exactly where to find Jason Quinn's. The man lived and breathed for Taylor. It was the easiest thing in the world to reach inside Jason and hurt him the way he'd hurt Gio.

Gio lifted his chin. "If I don't report it, Jason, then I'm complicit in it."

He didn't flinch. Not even when he saw the flash of anger in Jason's eyes. Not when it took him right back to his apartment on the Coast and it was Pete standing in front of him instead, and if Gio knew one thing in the world, if there was one truth on which he could balance everything he knew, it was this: he'd crossed the line and he was going to get his second fist in the face in less than a day.

Jason was going to punch him, but Gio wasn't going to flinch.

Jason's storm-grey eyes blazed. "Get out."

Gio stared at him.

"Get the fuck out of my office, Senior Constable Valeri." Jason's chest rose and fell. "Get the fuck out of my sight."

"Yeah." Gio shook his head, his smile more of a sneer. "Sure thing, *Sarge*."

He slammed the office door after him as he left.

Sandra stared at him, mouth open, as he stormed out of the station.

It wasn't until he was halfway home again, surrounded by scrubby grass, that the fear caught him, and he struggled to catch his breath.

Fuck it.

Fuck Jason, and fuck the job, and fuck everything.

And fuck his life, most of all.

CHAPTER TWENTY

Jason waited for the call. From Gordy, probably. Maybe from higher up. The career-ending call that would tell him Gio had put in a report to Child Safety, naming Taylor as a victim. There was a good chance it wouldn't stick. Not with Gio's reputation as the guy who solved personal disputes with official complaints. And Jason was pretty sure that Sandra wouldn't sell him out, but that didn't mean it wasn't *true*. He couldn't provide Taylor with the level of care he needed—and the level of supervision the law required—and he hated himself for it.

"What section of the Criminal Code is it? Three-sixty something?"

Jason could have told him.

Section 364A(1).

A person who, having the lawful care or charge of a child under 12 years, leaves the child for an unreasonable time without making reasonable provision for the supervision and care of the child during that time commits a misdemeanour.

It came with a maximum penalty of three years imprisonment.

It wouldn't come to that. In the end, Jason probably wouldn't even be charged with anything. He would be asked, behind the scenes, if he thought he might be better off in another line of work. Friendly tones at first, before they piled the pressure on. The exact same pressure they'd applied to Gio, most likely, because everything would have been so much easier if Gio had just gone away.

And Jason really wanted to hate Gio for threatening to report him, but Gio was absolutely right.

"If I went round to Janey Ferguson's house and found out she'd left her kids alone for hours at night, you'd expect me to report it. Wouldn't you?"

Yes.

Jason didn't get a pass because of his job, or his personal circumstances, or because he made an effort to be a great dad the rest of the time. He didn't get a pass for leaving his ten-year-old son alone in the house for hours some nights. It was neglect. Not the barefoot, dirty sort of neglect that the Ferguson kids wore, but neglect all the same, and nobody should get a pass on that.

Jason spent all of Friday waiting for the call.

He did a halfway meet with Charters Towers for the prisoner who'd assaulted Gio and Vicki the night before, handing him over on a dusty stretch of highway where there was room to pull over onto the shoulder. The air smelled of diesel fumes and dust. Insects chirped.

The crew from Charters Towers loaded the prisoner into the back of their pod and then they stood around and talked for a few minutes while Paula, the sergeant, had a cigarette. She was middle-aged, bird-thin, and had short-cropped greying hair. Her partner—a fresh-faced guy in his twenties—towered over her.

"So what's the drum?" Paula asked, exhaling a cloud of smoke into the air.

Jason thought of Gio sitting on the steps that night, and how lost he'd looked. "Same same."

Paula leaned on the side of the pod. "Living the dream, huh?"

Jason snorted. "Something like that."

The hot breeze picked up dust and laid it down again in sheets across the highway, and Paula filled him in on some of the news from Charters Towers: transfers, retirements, and at least one messy divorce thanks to a messy affair.

"So his wife's fucked him off, and so's his girlfriend," Paula said, and let out a cackle. "The dickhead." She tossed her butt into the dirt and ground it out with the toe of her boot. "That's what you get for playing away from home."

Jason nodded.

"Oh well," Paula said at last, straightening up. "Drive safe."

"You too," Jason said.

He wondered if they would have been as sociable if Gio had been with him.

He wondered how long it would be until he got the call from Gordy, letting him know just how fucked he was.

The call didn't come.

On Saturday Gio had a day off, so when Janey Ferguson phoned the station that morning wanting to talk to the police, the details were passed on to Jason, who was starting at two. The call had diverted through to Policelink, and then Comms, and by the time Jason got the message, it had been through several layers of unintentional encryption. He sighed as he got the garbled incident details from an apologetic Comms operator, and as soon as he'd finished writing down the details, he changed into his uniform, dropped Taylor off at Kane's house for the day, and headed around to Janey's place.

Janey was sitting at her rickety kitchen table, dressed in her ratty old dressing gown, with an overflowing ashtray in front of her. She put one cigarette out as Jason arrived, and lit another one straightaway.

"I want to go to Gympie," she said. "I want to get away from Harvey once and for all." Her bottom lip, cracked and dotted with sores, trembled. "Being around Harvey's not good for the kids."

Jason had been telling her that for years.

He sat down opposite her. "Okay."

Janey crossed her skinny arms over her chest. "Mum said we can stay with her."

"That's good."

Janey looked at him suspiciously, as though she thought he was going to pull the rug out from under her feet at any moment. "And that charity can get me and the kids bus tickets?"

"Absolutely." Jason reached into his pocket for his notebook. He set it on the table and flicked it open. "The woman at the DV Resource Centre I've been talking to is called Tracey. She knows all about you and the kids. I'll give you her number."

Janey pressed her mouth into a thin line. "What about my furniture?"

There was probably nothing in the house that was worth salvaging, but Jason kept that thought to himself. "Tracey said they can pay to get that sent down too. Janey, this is what Tracey does. She can answer all your questions if you give her a call."

"On a Saturday?" Janey scoffed.

Jason wrote Tracey's number on the back of one of his cards, and slid it across the table. "Call her. She'll answer."

"It's that easy, huh?"

"I never said it was easy," Jason said. "When you talk to Tracey, she's going to tell you that the most dangerous time in a violent relationship is when you leave it. So it's my job to make sure that Harvey stays in line. It's up to you if you tell him or not, but this is a small town. He's going to find out when the removalists' van turns up. So my advice is to let me tell him."

Janey snorted. "Youse still haven't found him from the last time!"

"Yeah," Jason said, and held her gaze. "So how about you tell me where he's laying low?"

Janey jutted out her chin.

"Come on," Jason said. "You tell me where he is, and I can have him in custody for the last breach while you and the kids are getting on the bus."

She snorted again, and then stubbed her cigarette out. "I'll think about it."

"You do that," Jason said, rising to his feet. "And call Tracey."

Janey nodded at him warily as he left.

Jason spent the afternoon coordinating things with Tracey. If they could get Janey to agree, they could get her and the kids on the bus as soon as Tuesday. Janey and the kids would be better off down south, and it'd certainly make Jason's job easier if Janey and Harvey weren't assaulting each other with depressing regularity.

He picked up Taylor from Kane's place at about three, and drove him to Sandra's.

Taylor chewed his thumbnail on the drive, his forehead creased.

"What's up?" Jason asked him.

Taylor turned his face towards him. "Can't I just go *home*?"

"No, you—"

"Or I can drive around with *you*!" Taylor exclaimed.

"I'm working, Taylor."

"I'd stay in the car and everything, Dad! Please!"

"No." Jason swallowed. "No, mate, you can't do that."

Taylor scowled and slumped in his seat. He refused to speak to Jason when Jason dropped him off at Sandra's house, and Sandra herself gave him a narrow look as she ushered Taylor inside.

Jason drove back towards the station.

Taylor hated him.

Gio hated him.

And Sandra, clearly, was done with his bullshit.

Gio's lights were still on after Jason had finished work and collected Taylor, so Jason waited until Taylor was asleep before he walked over to Gio's. He climbed the back steps and knocked on the frame of the screen door. The screen rattled.

The television was turned off, and a moment later Gio appeared. He looked sleep rumpled and sore. Jason wanted to rub his thumb gently along his split lip and soothe the pain away.

Gio opened the back door. "Sarge."

"Don't," Jason said. "Not that shit again."

Gio raised his eyebrows.

"Two days," Jason said. "For two days I've been waiting to get a call saying you've put in a report to Child Safety about me. But you haven't put one in, have you?"

"Why?" Gio's expression gave nothing away. "You thought I'd do it because I'm a dog?"

"No. I thought you'd do it because you have every right to do it. Everything you said was true." Jason's throat ached. "I'm fucking up. I can't do it. I thought I could, but I fucking can't."

He'd told himself he was ready. Told himself there was space in his life now for somebody new, after Alana. He'd told himself that Gio could have been that person. But maybe the timing had just been wrong. Or maybe it hadn't, but the person had. Maybe he and Gio should never have tried to be anything more than colleagues. And the stupid thing was, he still wanted to reach out and touch him, to see if it would all somehow fall into place again if he did.

"Not nice, is it?" Gio asked bitterly. "Knowing there's a shit-storm coming right at you."

"I'm sorry." Jason shoved his hands in his pockets. "I should have talked to you before putting in the report about the Ratsak. But Gio, Jesus, it's not just that I have an obligation to report bullying, it's that it made me bloody furious, okay? It made me furious that they're still coming after you. You're here now, and they've got no fucking *right*."

Gio was silent for a moment, and then he shrugged. "I don't need you to fight my battles for me, Jason."

"I know that." Jason drew a deep breath. "And I should have talked to you first. But I couldn't ignore it, Gio. Not professionally, and not personally either."

Gio huffed out a breath. "And around and around we go."

"I'm sorry." Jason wanted to card his fingers through Gio's curls. He wanted to suck up marks on his skin and drag his mouth against the scrape of his stubble. He wanted to listen to the way Gio laughed and squirmed under Jason's touch, but he kept his hands by his sides. "Maybe . . . maybe there was no way this was ever going to end well. I'm sorry. I hope we can still work together."

Gio's dark eyes were unreadable. He jerked his chin in a nod. "Yes, Sarge."

Jason had no right to ask for anything more. He nodded, and then turned and walked away.

Monday morning dawned overcast, and Jason wondered if they had more flooding to look forward to. He got Taylor off to school, and spent the morning getting the house into order: vacuuming, scrubbing the grout in the shower, replacing the washer in the leaking tap in the kitchen sink, and getting some washing done. The cat glared at him malevolently from the top of the tool cupboard.

He went and bought groceries, and a ten-dollar iTunes card for Taylor. Ten dollars in a vain attempt to assuage his guilt.

The kid had to get armour for his dinosaurs, right?

Jason started work at two. He arrived at the station a few minutes early. Gio was sitting at his desk, and Sandra was leaning over his shoulder pointing at something on the screen. Google maps.

"Hey." Jason nodded at them.

"Jason," Sandra said.

Gio nodded. "Sarge."

"I was just showing Gio where Dingo Creek Station is," Sandra said.

"They've had a break," Gio said. "Weapons' safe broken into."

"Huh," Sandra said. "That's what they say, but half these cockies don't even lock the damn things in the first place."

"True," Jason muttered. "Dingo Creek's right next door to Windermere, the Howes' property."

"Next door in this place can mean a hundred k's though," Gio said. "And I'd rather not get lost on my way there and become the subject of a search and rescue."

Sandra snorted and patted him on the shoulder. "It's important to keep your goals realistic, city boy."

Gio laughed. He had a beautiful laugh. Jason had missed it.

"If you want some company, I'll head out with you," Jason said.

Gio's laugh faded. He looked faintly surprised that Jason had offered. "Sure. I was just going to call them this afternoon, and leave it for tomorrow."

"Okay," Jason said. "Well, the offer still stands for tomorrow."

Gio nodded, a faint flush of colour rising in his cheeks. "Thanks, Sarge."

Jason went to his office and opened his email. He glanced up when Sandra entered and set a cup of coffee on his desk. She peered at him over her glasses.

"I don't know what's going on with you," she said at last, "but I would very much appreciate it if you sorted it out."

"Yeah, I—"

"Oh, Jason, that 'you' was plural." She raised her eyebrows. "As in, you and Gio both. I'd tell you not to shit where you eat, but I have a feeling I'm a little late when it comes to dishing out advice, aren't I?"

Jason froze. "Was . . . was it obvious?"

"Drink your coffee," Sandra said, "and give yourself an uppercut in the meantime. I know you, Jason. Of course it was bloody obvious." Her expression softened. "You looked almost happy for about half a second there. It's been a while."

Jason swallowed around the ache in his throat.

"Drink your coffee," she repeated, and left the door ajar when she walked out.

Jason stared at his emails, wondering vaguely at the wisdom of marking them as read when he wasn't actually taking anything in, but experience had taught him at least ninety percent of them were bullshit. He closed his email, opened QPRIME, and checked his outstanding tasks. Tick-and-flick stuff, mostly, but nothing he felt like tackling quite yet. There were some new tasks that had been generated overnight and sent to Jason as the OIC. Jason went through them, and forwarded several to Gio. There was nothing too complicated in them. Finalising crime reports. Chasing up overdue statements or withdrawals of complaint. Tracking down a witness for an incident that had occurred in Blackall several months ago, who had now moved here. Admin stuff.

They could work together still.

Jason could be Gio's boss and his friend without needing more.

Jason worked until he heard Taylor's voice coming from the dayroom. He walked out to meet him, and found him seated at the spare desk, unzipping his backpack and pulling his homework out. Taylor was chattering away at his usual rate of knots, and Gio was listening with a faint smile on his face.

"And then Cassidy's friend Becky told Kane that Cassidy likes me," Taylor said. "But Cassidy's the one I threw up on that time, so *that* can't be right."

"Well, Cassidy probably knows that was an accident," Gio suggested.

"I dunno." Taylor chewed his bottom lip. "If someone threw up on me, I'd be pretty annoyed about it still."

Jason snorted. "Clearly Cassidy's a better person than you are."

"Dad!" Taylor exclaimed, obviously caught between outrage and delight. "You're supposed to be on my side!"

Gio laughed.

"Jason."

Jason wasn't sure what it was about Sandra's voice that immediately caught his attention. Her tone was low, almost whispered, as if she couldn't push out enough air behind the word. He didn't even know how he'd heard it over Taylor.

"*Jason.*"

It caught him because he'd never heard Sandra sound afraid before.

Jason held up his hand to forestall whatever Taylor was going to say next, and stepped through the open doorway into Sandra's workspace behind the front counter.

The grill was locked open. It didn't matter, because it was a fucking grill. Open or closed, it wouldn't have provided any protection at all against Brian Howe and the Tikka T3 Lite he was currently pointing at Sandra from the foyer.

Brian turned as Jason appeared, swinging the barrel of the rifle around to face Jason.

"You cunt," Brian said. "You fucking *cunt*."

"Put it down, Brian," Jason said, and how the hell was his voice so calm? How was it, when Sandra was right there beside him, when *Taylor* was only metres away?

"She's gone! Patricia's gone and left me!"

The most dangerous time in a violent relationship.

"Put it down, Brian," Jason repeated, his heart pounding.

"You ruined my fucking life!" Brian said, his voice hardening, and in that moment, Jason knew there was nothing he could do to stop this. His blood turned to ice.

No.

No no no.

Taylor.

Brian fired.

CHAPTER TWENTY-ONE

"You ruined my fucking life!"

Gio grabbed Taylor by the wrist, and thrust him behind him. "Get under the desk. *Stay* down."

Taylor scurried to obey. Gio unholstered his Glock, and held it out in front of him. He couldn't see into the foyer from the dayroom, and he could only see a fraction of Sandra's workspace behind the counter. He couldn't see Jason or Sandra.

A shot rang out.

Gio heard a body hit the floor.

He stepped into the doorway.

Brian Howe with a rifle. Sandra standing there. And Jason was on the floor, blood pumping out of his chest. It took a fraction of a second to take it all in, and to act, while at the same time his brain was making the connection between the stolen firearms from Dingo Creek Station and this moment.

Gio fired. Once. Twice. He aimed for Brian's body mass, just like he'd always been taught. Once, twice, and then Brian was down, screaming and moaning and bleeding everywhere, and Gio vaulted over the counter and into the foyer, because Brian was down and he had to *stay* down. He kicked the rifle out of Brian's reach, watching his hands, not his face. Hands.

The Glock was shaking in Gio's grasp. He grabbed his radio.

"VKR, Richmond Station. Urgent." He sucked in a shaking breath, gaze still fixed on Brian's hands. Brian's fingers twitched. "*Urgent*!"

"Richmond Station, go."

"I have—" His hand shook so much his thumb slipped off the microphone button for a second. "I need an ambulance, VKR. The sergeant's been shot. The offender's been shot too. Oh fuck." A sound like a sob tore out of his throat. "I need *help*, VKR."

"Jason," he heard Sandra say, her voice ragged. "Jason!"

"Richmond Station," the operator said. "I need the condition of the—of the people who've been shot."

"Sandra?" Gio couldn't look away from Brian, whose fingers were still twitching weakly. Maybe he was dying. Maybe Gio should put pressure on his wounds. But he couldn't make himself move. He kept his thumb on the microphone button. "Sandra, is Jason breathing?"

"Yes!" she called back, her voice thready.

His thumb slipped again.

"—hear him asking if Jase is breathing!" he heard the operator shouting at someone in the background. "VKR to Richmond Station, was that a yes?"

"Yes," Gio said.

"What about the offender?"

Brian's fingers weren't twitching anymore.

"No," Gio said, cold flooding his body and leaving him more numb than before. "He's dead."

Gio watched as blood pooled out from underneath Brian, dark against the grey marbled linoleum floor of the foyer. Did all government buildings have such ugly fucking furnishings? The police recruits in the poster on the wall smiled down at Gio, and he wanted to laugh at them.

This? he wanted to ask. *Is* this *what you're selling?*

He reholstered his Glock and bent down to pick up Brian's rifle. He set it on the counter, and then used the fob on his keys to open the door into the dayroom.

"Gio?" Taylor wailed from under the desk.

"Stay there," Gio said, his voice cracking. "Just stay there, Taylor, please."

He stepped around into the workspace behind the front counter.

Sandra was kneeling beside Jason, her hands pressing against the wound in his chest. His blood was pumping out from underneath her fingers. His face was pale. His mouth was moving, but Gio couldn't make out any words. His eyes were wide with shock.

From somewhere outside, Gio could hear an approaching siren.

Hurry the fuck up, Vicki.

"Dad?" Taylor asked, appearing in the doorway. He burst into tears. "Dad?"

"This is a two-man station," Jason had told him that first night. *"If things turn to shit, it's just us. Even coming lights and sirens, the nearest backup is about two hours away. Longer than that if they're on the other side of their division."*

The crew from Hughenden made it to Richmond in a little over an hour and twenty minutes, and all Gio could think was that they must have fucking flown down the highway.

Jason was at the Richmond hospital now, and Gio didn't know how bad he was. Gio was at the station with a dead body in the foyer, and he didn't know what the fuck he was supposed to do.

The sergeant from Hughenden introduced herself and Gio forgot her name immediately. She took Gio's firearm off him, taped off the crime scene, and told her senior constable to take Gio to the hospital.

"Don't say anything, Valeri," she warned him. "Not until you get a union rep."

Gio nodded, too numb to care. Too numb to think about five minutes from now, let alone the weeks and months and possibly years of an investigation stretching out ahead of him.

It felt like just a moment ago he'd been laughing with Jason and Taylor, and then—

And then—

And then this. Somehow the universe had skipped some steps, because *that* didn't become *this*. Not on a lazy Monday afternoon in a small town in the middle of nowhere.

The rescue chopper was landing in the paddock across from the hospital when they arrived, and Gio's heart skipped a series of beats. *He's alive. He's still alive.* They wouldn't have sent the chopper all the way from Townsville for a corpse, only for a medivac.

When Gio and the senior constable from Hughenden got inside the hospital, Taylor was crying. He tore himself out of Sandra's grasp a minute later when the crew from the rescue chopper wheeled Jason towards the exit.

Gio caught him.

"Dad!" Taylor screamed, struggling to get to Jason. "Dad!"

Gio tightened his grip on the kid, and tried not to think about how Jason's blood was soaking through his shirt onto Taylor. He must've got it on him when he was helping Vicki back at the station.

"You can't go in the chopper, Taylor," he said. "You can't, okay? They're taking him to Townsville. They're gonna look after him there."

Taylor kicked and screamed.

A neighbour had come to the station. A *neighbour*, like he was just popping in to see what was going on after he'd heard the commotion. Only in Richmond could a neighbour hear gunshots from the police station and set out towards the noise.

"You," Vicki had told the startled man. *"You're driving the ambulance for me."*

Taylor and Sandra had been packed into the front of the ambulance, both of them pale and crying. Gio had waited behind at the station—the crime scene. He had locked the doors of the station and had sat outside in the sun, while Brian Howe's blood congealed on the shitty linoleum inside, his radio blasted frantic bursts of noise at him, and the crew from Hughenden thrashed the hell out of their vehicle to make it to Richmond in an hour and twenty minutes.

How . . .

How had any of this happened? There were too many separate pieces for Gio to put together. Too many to make sense of.

How was he even now standing in the hospital foyer? Because when he blinked, he was right back at the station, and Brian Howe was pointing a rifle at Sandra. When he blinked, there was blood everywhere.

"Taylor," he said, holding the struggling boy. "You can't, mate. You *can't*."

Taylor, still crying, turned and buried his face in Gio's neck.

The chopper crew wheeled Jason outside.

"No," Gio said when the doctor came to check him. "No."

He refused to let go of Taylor.

The senior constable from Hughenden tried to take a breath sample, but Gio couldn't suck enough air into his lungs to push it out again.

"Take blood," Gio told him. "Just get them to take my blood."

Taylor clung to him tightly.

"It's okay," Gio murmured to him, rubbing his back. *Liar liar liar.* They both stank of Jason's blood. "It's okay."

They sat and waited, and Gio tried not to blink. He stared at the posters on the far wall while Taylor sobbed against his neck. They sat for what felt like hours. The nurse who took Gio's blood tried to talk to Taylor, to coax him away with a promise of biscuits and chocolate, but he refused to look at her. At some point, he fell asleep with Gio's arms still around him.

The senior constable from Hughenden had Rihanna's "Work" as his ringtone.

"Fuck," he said when it blasted out in the small waiting room in the hospital. He stood up. "Shit. Sorry." He answered the call. "Madison."

He turned away from Gio and Taylor, and moved a few paces down, as though that would give him privacy.

"Boss," he said. "Boss, I need to get his kid to Townsville." He listened to whatever he was told, and then said, "Any news?"

Taylor, awake again, tensed in Gio's arms.

"Okay," Madison said. "Yep." He ended the call, and then turned back to them. "They're landing in Townsville soon, and he's going straight into surgery."

Taylor lifted his tear-stained face towards the guy. "Is my dad gonna be okay?"

"I don't know." Madison's expression was solemn. He shifted his gaze to Gio. "The crews from the Towers are almost here. Branch is coming too. The DDO says one of the GD's can take Taylor. A Townsville crew is heading out to meet them and take him to the hospital."

Jesus. Taylor was going to be handed off to different coppers all the way to Townsville.

"Let's get you both back," Madison said.

Afterwards, Gio was just as unsure of the sequence of events in getting home as he was for the shooting. Someone had brought Taylor's backpack from the station and used his key to get into Jason's house. There was a bag packed and waiting for Taylor, and clean clothes to change into. Jason's blood had soaked through Taylor's clothes though, and Gio talked him into having a shower. Taylor panicked when he took his shirt off and saw his dad's blood on his skin, so Gio sat on the hallway floor outside the bathroom while Taylor showered with the door ajar.

The living room was filled with unfamiliar coppers. There was a never-ending procession of them. Gio didn't know who any of them were, really, or where they'd come from.

It was dark outside now. When had that happened?

"Giovanni," one of them said, crouching down beside him. "I'm Chris. I'm a union rep from Mount Isa. The bosses are going to be here soon, and Ethical Standards are on their way. The media too. So I know the last thing you want to do is go through this now, but we need to, okay, to get it sorted out before they all want a piece of you."

Gio nodded.

"You need to get cleaned up as well," Chris said. "And I'm going to have to bag your uniform."

"Yeah."

"Okay," Chris said. "Let's go to your place, and get you locked down."

"Taylor needs—"

"We're looking after Taylor," Chris said. "Let's look after you too."

Gio waited around long enough to say goodbye to Taylor. Taylor appeared very, very small as they loaded him into the back of a police car and drove off into the night.

Chris stayed by Gio's side. He was plain clothes: an older guy, with a beard, and a face that was starting to show the effects of sun damage. The faint smell of cigarettes clung to him. Not a smoker himself, Gio guessed, but a man who spent a lot of time around them.

He spent the night on Gio's couch, a makeshift office set up on the coffee table.

Gio stared out his front window towards the back of the station. There were lights on inside, and more police cars pulled up around it than he had seen since he'd been on the Coast. The undertaker arrived at a little past midnight.

At two, there was a knock on Gio's door.

Chris let them in. Two inspectors, and the assistant commissioner.

"He's out of surgery," one of the inspectors said. "Still listed as critical. We'll know more in the morning."

They took it easy on him, or at least it felt like that. Gio had been in enough interviews with bosses to know the personas they projected—friendly, supportive, encouraging—were no indication that they weren't planning to fuck him over in the wrap-up. Chris took control of the questions when Gio couldn't.

"Don't answer that," he said several times. And, "Senior Constable Valeri has been awake now for almost twenty-four hours, and he's been through a traumatic incident. He's in no condition to answer all of your questions tonight, sir."

"Did you instruct Brian Howe to drop his weapon?" the assistant commissioner pressed.

So that was how they were going to get him.

Gio opened his mouth to answer, but Chris held up his hand. "Brian Howe had just shot a police officer and had his rifle pointed at a civilian staff member. Giovanni's quick actions saved Sandra's life, and his own."

Gio closed his mouth.

He wondered if Taylor was in Townsville yet. He wondered who was looking after him, and if they'd let him see Jason yet. Critical. What did that mean? That the surgery hadn't done what it was supposed to do? They'd been laughing at the station, and then—

He flinched as he felt his finger tighten on the trigger all over again.

"Don't answer that," Chris said, pulling Gio back into the now.

Gio nodded. He hadn't even heard the question.

Chris fielded the rest of the questions. There weren't many. The bosses left with the promise of returning in the morning and walking Gio through the scene at the station. He didn't know how he'd manage. Could he remember exactly what he'd done, exactly what he'd thought, exactly where he'd been standing? And by tomorrow the bosses wouldn't be his biggest problem. Not with Ethical Standards also on their way.

They could fuck him over in a heartbeat, but Gio was too tired to care.

"Try and get some sleep," Chris advised him.

Gio retreated to the darkness of his bedroom.

He couldn't sleep. His exhaustion could barely take him to the edge before he was jolted back again by flashes of horror. Jason's blood. Brian's twitching fingers. Taylor's screams. And how could he look the investigators in the eye and tell them he'd done the right thing when he couldn't remember the exact sequence of events? What should he have done differently? Should he have told Brian to put the rifle down? Was that something he was supposed to have done, even though Brian had already shot someone? Because Sandra had been in Brian's sights, and Taylor had been in the station too. A civilian and a child. What if Brian hadn't put the rifle down? What then?

Should he have told Taylor to run out the back instead of hiding under the desk?

Why had he told him that at all, when he hadn't really known what was going on until he'd stepped out behind the counter? Had he known on some instinctual level? Or had he just seen too many movies?

He closed his stinging eyes and tried to sleep.

Opened them a minute later as fear gripped him again, this time followed by a blast of realisation. He fumbled for his phone. What time was it? Three? Four? Maybe the shooting hadn't hit the news last night, but it would by this morning.

He scrolled through his meagre contacts and hit Sophie's name.

Her voice was thick with sleep. "Gio?"

"It's so late," he said, his voice breaking. "But if I didn't tell you, you'd be worried."

There was a low murmur in the background of the call. Ian. Sophie shushed him. "What is it, Gio?"

"Jason got shot," he said. "He's pretty bad. And I—I shot the guy who did it. He's dead, Soph. I killed a guy."

"Oh my God!" Sheets rustled. "What happened?"

Gio almost wished Chris was here. *"You don't have to answer that."* But even Chris would be no match for Sophie in big-sister mode.

"He shot Jason," Gio said. "So I shot him."

"Oh, bambino." Sophie made a sound that was half horror, half frustration. "Why are you so far away? What can I do? What do you *need*?"

Her voice wasn't enough to comfort him, only to remind him of the thousands of kilometres between them. He scrubbed at the hot tears on his face. "Soph, everything's such a fucking mess. Everything I touch goes to shit, and I don't know what to do anymore."

"Oh, bambino," she whispered. "Come home. Can you ask them to send you home?"

He squeezed his eyes shut. "No."

She was silent for a long while, only the faint whisper of her breath in his ear. Then she sighed. "Gio."

His stomach clenched. "I don't want to fight, Sophie. Not tonight, please."

"What about . . ." She paused. "His name is Jason?"

"Yeah. Jason."

"Is he going to be okay?"

"I don't know." Gio cleared his throat. "He's critical. I don't really know what that means. They said we should know more in the morning. He's got a son. Taylor. He's ten. He was there."

"Oh my God."

He was crying now, and there was no way to hide it from her.

"Gio." She sounded like she was crying too. "Oh, bambino. It's going to be fine. It's going to be fine, I promise."

There was something in her tone that hit exactly the same pitch as Gio had when he'd had Taylor clinging to him like a limpet at the hospital. And Gio heard the exact same voice in his head that he had then: *Liar liar liar.*

But hollow comfort was better than none.

CHAPTER TWENTY-TWO

Nothing hurt. Pain might have clued Jason in quicker to where he was and what had happened as he slowly blinked awake, but nothing hurt. There was a woman sitting beside his bed. Her head was tilted forward, her chin resting on her bosom, and she was sleeping.

Mum?

Why was his mum—

The memories flooded back thick and fast, hitting him in a barrage and breaking over him. He sucked in a breath, except he *couldn't*, and *there* was the pain that made everything fall into place. A sharp, stabbing pain that seemed to be centred in his chest, pushing his ribs down, ripping through his lungs. A strangled whimper escaped him.

His mother was awake instantly. "Jason! Don't move! Don't move!" She grabbed the call button hanging from the rail on his bed and jabbed at it, wincing. Then she reached out and put her hands over his, and he noticed how swollen her knuckles looked, and how twisted her fingers were. She'd had arthritis for as long as Jason could remember.

"Taylor?" he rasped.

"He's staying with one of the police officers here."

"Gio?"

"I don't . . ." His mother frowned, her forehead creasing. The lines around her eyes were more pronounced than when he'd seen her last, her hair a shade lighter with grey, her shoulders more rounded. "I don't know who that is, Jason."

A nurse came in then, and Jason's mother moved back while the man checked him over. Jason tried to pay attention to what the nurse was saying, but he was already drifting away again. Taylor was safe. He held on to that. Taylor was safe.

But was Gio okay?

The universe faded into blackness around him.

He woke up again sometime later, to a different nurse checking his catheter and changing the bag. It seemed darker than before, although the room had no window. Had the light always been this low? Maybe it was night, and this was their concession to it.

The nurse caught him watching her, and flashed him a smile. She moved what looked like a small plastic controller up to where his left hand was resting. "Press this whenever you want pain relief. Don't worry, you can't have too much."

Jason didn't know if he wanted pain relief or not, but he pressed the button anyway, and sank back into sleep.

When he woke up next, the room was brighter, and he was in definite pain. He pressed the button, and it softened the edges of his pain enough to breathe. He took the time to really take in his surroundings. The bed. The catheter tube snaking out from under the blankets. Other tubes too, draining away bloody fluids. Jason lifted his left hand. There was a cannula taped to the back of it, hooked up to a saline drip. Jason let his left hand fall onto the bed again, and inspected his right hand. It was unencumbered. He brushed it slowly over the blankets covering his chest. He could feel tubes taped in place, and a bulky dressing on the right side of his chest. A part of him wanted to press down on it to see if he could discover the dimensions of the injury underneath, but the still-rational part of his brain told him that was a stupid fucking idea.

There was a television hanging from the ceiling above his bed. It was on, the volume muted. It was playing an ad for a rug warehouse, the salesman leering manically at the camera. *Rugs! Rugs! Rugs!* The address of the place was at Domain on Duckworth Street. Jason blinked at the screen.

So he was in Townsville Hospital?

There was a narrow counter on the wall opposite. It was bursting with flowers and balloons. How the hell long had he been out?

When the nurse came in to check on him, Jason asked, "What happened?"

"I'll go and get the doctor, and she can—"

He grunted. "No. What happened at the *station*?"

Taylor was okay, but what about Gio? What about Sandra? And what had happened to Brian Howe? Because Jason hoped to hell that fucking arsehole was sitting in a cell somewhere. He thought Jason had ruined his life? Jason hadn't even fucking *started*.

The monitor beeped as his heart rate rose.

"Take it easy," the nurse said. "I'll get someone to come and see you."

Jason closed his eyes for a moment and licked his dry lips. He was cold, and bone weary. He opened his eyes, and then wiggled his toes just to make sure he could.

The door to his room opened, and a barrel-shaped middle-aged man stepped through. He was wearing a scowl, as though Jason had personally offended him by getting shot.

"G'day, Jase," he drawled.

"Hey, Gordy." Jason wet his lips again.

"Well, look at you lying around, you lazy bugger."

"Yeah, that's me. Lazy." Jason fought for breath. "What happened?"

"Sandra and Valeri are fine." Gordy had dark bags under his eyes, and Jason wondered how long he'd been waiting around at the hospital. "Valeri shot Brian Howe. Fatally."

"He okay?"

"Fatally," Gordy repeated, deadpan.

"Gio." Jason tried not to laugh. It would hurt like fuck. "Arsehole."

"That's Senior Sergeant Arsehole to you, thanks very much." Gordy grunted. "I haven't spoken to Valeri. His union rep's got him locked down tighter than a nun's knickers, which is a good thing. It's a total clusterfuck, as per the standard operating procedures of the Queensland Police Service, but there's no reason he can't come out of this smelling like roses. They might be falling over themselves down south hoping this is what'll fuck him up for good, but word has it the assistant commissioner is going in to bat for him with the commissioner."

"Good," Jason said, pushing the word out with some difficulty. He pressed the button for more morphine. "Gotta have his back, Gordy. Someone's gotta have his back."

And maybe Jason couldn't be that guy anymore, but someone had to be.

He dozed off into sleep.

Jason was too tired to really care what the doctors told him. He had broken ribs and a collapsed lung, although of course the doctors gave it to him first in words that showed why they were the experts and Jason wasn't: hemothorax, bruising of the lungs, subcutaneous emphysema, tearing of the thoracic wall, and a fracture of the breastbone. He was looking at a recovery time of between one and three months. Longer than that to be considered fit for more than desk duties.

He was alive though. That seemed to be the thing worth focussing on.

"Daaad!" Taylor screeched as he burst through the door to Jason's hospital room. He flung himself towards Jason's bed, and Jason braced for what was going to hurt like fucking hell, only to be spared at the last minute when the woman escorting Taylor caught him by the collar of his shirt and hauled him back.

"Come here," Jason said. "Gently, mate."

Taylor leaned over him, burying his face against Jason's shoulder and sobbing quietly. "I thought you were *dead*!"

"I'm sorry," Jason told him, tears stinging his eyes. "I'm so, so sorry."

Taylor refused to leave his side for the next few days. He was staying with Melinda, Jason learned. Jason had met her on a few courses, and had liked her. She was a senior constable in Intel, and a peer support officer who'd put her hand up to look after Taylor while he was in Townsville. She lived close to the hospital, and had kids of her own. She was nice, and her husband was nice, but Taylor wanted to go *home*. Who was feeding the cat, Dad?

The HSO from District Office who came to check in on Jason made sure she spoke to Taylor as well, but Jason was fairly sure he didn't need a trained psychologist to diagnose Taylor's sudden clinginess, and his regression to almost babyish behaviour. And Jason didn't do a lot to dissuade him either. He was feeling pretty bloody clingy himself. He convinced his nurses to put all the tubes and apparatus to his right side, so Taylor could cuddle up on his left.

Things with his parents were awkward. While Jason was grateful they'd made the trip down from Cairns, he couldn't help but think of the last time he'd seen them, after Alana's funeral.

"You can't look after him on your own, Jason," his mother had said, her face twisted with desperate hope. *"Let us take him for a while."*

"Get the fuck out of my house."

They'd never liked Alana. Well, that wasn't exactly true. They'd liked her fine up until the weekend they'd surprised Jason with a visit to Townsville, and had walked in to find Alana in bed with Graham.

"I just don't know, Jason. I just don't know why you'd want to go out with a girl who's also sleeping with someone else."

"I'm sleeping with him too, Mum."

On his wedding day, his father had taken him aside and helped him adjust his tie. He'd smiled at Jason and patted him on the shoulder, and Jason had smiled in return, jittery with nerves.

"It's not too late to back out, son."

He hadn't totally cut them out of his life. He'd sent birthday cards and Christmas cards, and received them in return. It had been enough. He'd had no intention of welcoming them back into his life until they showed his wife some respect. And then, when she was gone, they'd swooped in like vultures. Like the slate had been made clean now that Jason had buried Alana, and bygones could be bygones. He knew they blamed Alana for forcing Jason to take a side. It had never occurred to them to blame themselves.

They were solicitous now, careful not to mention Alana. They bought Taylor presents, and fretted over his clinginess with Jason.

"Dad, he doesn't want to go to the park," Jason said. Taylor was tucked in against his side, playing a game on his iPad.

"Oh, he shouldn't stay cooped up in here all day," his dad said with a forced laugh.

"He doesn't *know* you."

His mother clicked her tongue. "And whose fault is that, Jason?"

Jason raised his eyebrows. "You tell me, Mum."

She couldn't answer that.

Taylor set his game aside when his grandparents left, and reached for the controls for the bed. He eased them up slowly, and they watched the television for a while, and caught that same crazy ad. *Rugs! Rugs! Rugs!* Then Taylor shot Jason a worried glance.

"Dad, if you'd died, who would I live with?"

"Your mum's parents." Jason lifted his hand and scrubbed his knuckles gently against Taylor's hair. "You remember visiting them that time? They live on the farm in Victoria."

Taylor wrinkled his nose. "I think I remember a cow?"

"Yeah," Jason said. "A dairy cow licked your face and you cried."

"I *cried*?"

"You were four, and it took you by surprise."

Taylor's expression grew anxious. "Dad, I don't know them either."

"Mate, I . . ." Jason swallowed. "I can't promise you that nothing bad is going to happen again. I wish I could, but I can't. But it is my fault you don't know Grandma and Grandpa O'Keefe as well as you should. When I get better, how about we go and visit them?"

Taylor nodded solemnly. "What about Gio?"

A jolt of surprise ran through Jason. "What about him?"

"Will he come with us? Is he your boyfriend?"

"No." Jason rubbed his hand carefully across his aching chest. "That didn't work out."

Taylor chewed his bottom lip. "He's still our friend though, right?"

"Yeah," Jason said, and hoped it was true. "Gio's still our friend."

Jason thought a lot about Gio in that first week after surgery. Every time a stranger appeared in his room and introduced themselves as a fellow copper, bringing along books, or magazines, or stuff for Taylor, Jason thought of Gio.

Everyone always talked about how the police looked after their own. Jason had always seen that as something to be proud of, and his experience now was nothing but positive. Gio's hadn't been, though. Would these same men and women who were taking time out of their schedules to visit some guy they didn't even know, just because he wore the same uniform, have turned against Gio down on the Gold Coast? Jason's hospital room was full of flowers from people he'd never met, from all corners of the state, and all sections of the Service. Jason couldn't help wondering if someone who'd thrown in a few dollars to brighten his room was the same person who'd sent him Ratsak in the mail. Because they'd been a united front on the Gold Coast as well.

It was good that the assistant commissioner was willing to go in to bat for Gio, but Jason worried about more than his job. Was he *okay*? Was someone there for him? Listening when he needed to talk. Sitting with him when he didn't. There were times when Jason clung to Taylor a little too tightly. When, out of nowhere, some switch flicked in his brain and he was staring at Brian Howe all over again. What did Gio see in those moments? And who did he have to hold on to?

He wanted to call, but knew better. The shooting was still under preliminary investigation by Ethical Standards. Any phone calls now might look like they were getting their story straight. The old *Courier Mail* test, where perception was as important as truth.

He missed Gio though. It would have been nice to tell him that.

It was a week before Jason was even able to get out of bed, and that was with a nurse under each elbow. It took half an hour to walk the short distance down the hallway to the nurses' station and back again. Jason had never felt weaker in his life, but he got his catheter removed after proving he could make the walk, and had his first warm shower that evening. The nurse who accompanied him was Kyle. He had glasses and a hipster beard.

"So, this is cozy, hmm?" Kyle teased.

"Please." Jason gripped the handrail. "You think I've never showered with another bloke before?"

Except last time Jason had showered with another bloke, he'd been the one holding him up.

Kyle laughed. "Aren't you just full of surprises?"

The shower felt incredible. Jason's ribs hurt like hell by the time Kyle helped settle him back into his bed, but it was a relief to be clean again, and not stink of antiseptic and blood. He watched as Kyle peeled back his dressing to check his wound. The skin around the sutures was swollen and bruised, in lurid splotches of black and purple, but the wound itself was clean. The drainage tubes still looked disgusting. It made no sense to Jason how there could be actual tubes stuck into his lung that didn't cripple him in agony. They weren't comfortable, but he found he could ignore them easily enough. He really only hurt when he tried to move.

The morphine was *very* good.

On Saturday, his parents went back to Cairns. A part of Jason was sorry to see them go. Another part of him was glad he didn't need to deal with the associated stress anymore. His dad extended a half-hearted offer to come and visit Richmond over Christmas, and Jason agreed it was something they could talk about later. He didn't hate his parents. It would have been easier on some level if he had.

On Sunday, Jason had a rare Taylor-free morning. Melinda had got movie tickets for Taylor and her kids. Taylor fretted about going, but Jason was firm with him. Taylor needed a break. Hanging around the hospital every day was doing him no good.

Taylor barged into Jason's room that afternoon, pink in the face from running all the way from the lift, and climbed onto the end of Jason's bed and gave him a scene-by-scene account of the movie.

"We're having Subway for tea," he said. "Melinda's getting it now. Did you know there's a Subway here? In the *hospital*?"

Like it was the height of civilisation.

Melinda came by to collect him a few minutes later.

"I'll see you tomorrow, Dad." He left the superhero cup he'd got at the movies for Jason to use.

On Monday, Jason gave his statement to the investigators, in between his thoracic ultrasound and his latest blood work. He had a union rep with him as a matter of course, but it was obvious nobody was here to screw him over. They all wished him a speedy recovery before they left, and promised the Service would support him during his recovery.

The nights were the worst. They were interminable. Jason dozed more than he slept. He was bored with being stuck in bed all the time, but at night there was nobody to help him get out of bed and walk up and down the hallway for a while. And if he tried it himself, he usually managed to tangle all his tubes up.

He thought a lot about Gio at night. He thought about how Gio had felt skin to skin. He thought about how Gio had kissed like he was asking a question Jason didn't know how to answer. He thought about how every step had been something of a misstep, a stumble, a mistake—not because they'd taken those steps, but because they hadn't figured out how to move without tripping one another up. They hadn't talked enough. Neither of them had been brave enough to ask if it was more than physical.

He'd been like this with Alana too. When the thing with Graham had fallen through, he'd been afraid to lose her as well. She had always been able to read him like a book though. She'd laughed and told him that he wouldn't get rid of her that easily.

He'd spent too many hours in hospital rooms like this one.

"Please don't leave me," he'd whispered to her towards the end, clutching her hand.

Her fingers had been thin and cold, her bones as brittle as a bird's.

"Please don't leave me."

He still hated himself for having said it. It had been selfish. Cruel. But Alana had only smiled, her eyes shining with tears. *"I love you."*

She hadn't wanted him to be lonely. She'd told him not to be. Made him promise, although he'd hated saying it, that he'd find someone else when he was ready. And Jason thought that maybe he had been ready, except then he'd gone and fucked it all up. He'd been too afraid of losing Gio to lay everything on the line, and then he'd gone and lost him anyway, before they'd even really started.

Jason closed his eyes briefly, rubbing his hand gently across his aching chest.

He fucking hated hospitals.

He wanted to go home.

CHAPTER TWENTY-THREE

Jason's house was empty, and Gio hated it.

Richmond had never felt more suffocating than it did following the shooting. Gio wanted to drive to Townsville to see Jason, but he was on lockdown until Ethical Standards was finished with him. He couldn't go back to work until they cleared him either, and he was stir-crazy within a matter of days. Chris had advised him not to leave the house until the media left town, but it wasn't the media Gio was most anxious about. A simple "no comment" could shut them down. He wasn't sure that would work for the lady on the checkout at the supermarket, or the man from the newsagency. These were people who had known Brian Howe as well.

He was told not to think about contacting Patricia Howe. Gio wondered if she hated him. She'd loved her husband, even though she'd made the right decision to leave him. And now Brian was dead. Did she blame Gio for that? Did she blame herself? Gio didn't know. He wasn't sure he wanted to know. What were the chances, after all, that she blamed Brian for his own death? Buckley's and none, probably. He wondered if she lay awake at night, wishing she'd never gone to the police in the first place.

It was a mess, *he* was a mess, and Jason's house was empty.

A constable from Mount Isa and a senior constable from Julia Creek were brought in to cover Gio's and Jason's absences. Sandra hated them.

"They're hopeless," she grumbled when she visited Gio a few days after the shooting. "The tall one, the ranga, has set the alarm off at least twice a day. How bloody hard is it, Gio?"

Gio nodded sympathetically.

"I mean, what the hell is he even doing?"

"His best?" Gio suggested.

Sandra levelled a stare at him. "I liked you better when you weren't a sarcastic shit."

"Liar."

Sandra pressed her mouth into a thin line for a moment. "Anyway, I hear Ethical Standards is packing up and leaving in a few more days, so they won't be bothering either of us anymore."

"Yeah?" Chris hadn't mentioned it, but Gio knew that Sandra had her methods. "They're almost done?"

It felt like they'd interviewed everyone Gio had ever had contact with since coming to Richmond. It was difficult to judge if they were just being thorough, or if they were actively building a case against him.

Her gaze softened as she looked at him. "You didn't do anything wrong, Gio. Don't let them tell you otherwise."

Gio wasn't sure if he believed that—he replayed a thousand different scenarios in his head every minute of the day, and twice as many at night—but he appreciated the sentiment. And if he was no longer to be at the beck and call of Ethical Standards, he would actually be able to get out of town for a while. And he had to do that. He couldn't stop thinking about Jason. He was okay, people kept telling Gio, but Gio needed to see that for himself. Because it felt like every time he closed his eyes, every time he so much as blinked, all he could see was Jason lying on the floor of the station with blood pumping out of his chest.

Four days after the shooting, Vicki turned up to Gio's place with a bottle of Bundy rum.

"I'm on rec leave," she said. "And you're on whatever leave you're on. So get the bloody glasses out."

They both drank too much, and Vicki didn't make a big deal of it when Gio's hands shook too much to pour the rum. She took the bottle back and poured for him. Then she encouraged him to pretend his couch cushions were every ranked officer he'd been interviewed by since the shooting, and to punch the shit out of them.

It was the best he'd felt in days.

Gio woke up the next day with a throbbing head, what felt like a mouthful of gravel, and no regrets.

It was a week and a half before Gio was free to make the drive to Townsville. He'd talked to Sophie about it, and she'd agreed he should go.

"You'll obviously be miserable until you can see he's going to be okay, bambino. Just go. Do some shopping. See a movie. Get the hell out of that shitty little town."

"It's not that shitty."

She scoffed at that.

The drive to Townsville was just over five hours. Gio fuelled up in Charters Towers, and then followed the highway east over the Mingela Range. The red dirt gradually transformed into a scrubby green landscape that wasn't as tropical as Gio had been expecting. The highway widened to two lanes each way as he got closer, and at last the sprawl of warehouses and commercial buildings transformed into the outskirts of a city. Gio saw a few tall buildings in the distance, clustered around the distinctive jutting outline of what had to be Castle Hill.

The traffic thickened around him, and Gio stopped at the first set of traffic lights he'd seen in months. It made him feel oddly homesick for the Gold Coast in a way he hadn't in a while. He followed the flow of traffic onto the Ring Road, and past Lavarack Barracks towards the Townsville Hospital. Getting a park at the hospital was a bitch; another reminder that he wasn't in Richmond anymore.

Gio entered the foyer of the hospital. The air-conditioning was cold, and made his sweaty shirt stick to his back. He approached the information desk, showed his badge, and asked for Jason's room.

He took the lift to the second floor and followed the signage.

He stopped when he reached Jason's room.

Stupid.

What the hell was he doing?

When he'd started driving, he'd had five hours to decide what he was going to say. Except now here he was, and he had nothing. Fucking nothing. He was tempted to turn around and walk away.

Except Sophie was right. He needed to see that Jason was okay.

A shriek of laughter spilled out into the corridor. Taylor.

Gio drew a deep breath, held it for a moment, and then stepped inside the room. Jason was lying in a bed, Taylor crouched on a chair beside him. They both looked over as Gio walked inside.

"Gio!" Taylor launched himself at him in a flurry of skinny limbs.

Gio caught him and hugged him tightly, his chest aching. He looked over Taylor's head to Jason.

"Hey, Gio." Jason smiled broadly, and held his hand out.

Gio set Taylor down, and clasped Jason's hand. His heart skipped a beat as Jason's grip tightened, and his wedding ring dug into Gio's fingers. Gio swallowed; his throat was raw. "Jason."

He sank down into the chair Taylor had vacated, and stared at Jason helplessly.

Jason rubbed his thumb over Gio's knuckles.

He'd missed this. Jason's touch. The simple validation of skin on skin. The comfort that Jason offered him, calming and at the same time frustrating. They'd tried so hard to draw a line between work and off duty, but in the end that wasn't the line that had tripped Gio up. It was this one here. The one between friendship and something else.

"You okay?" Jason asked him softly.

Gio rasped out a sound that was almost like a laugh. "Um, killed a guy. So, um."

"Yeah." Jason's gaze held his.

The weight of that would take a long time to lift, if it ever did. It wasn't a matter of right or wrong. A man was dead because of Gio, and that was big. Too big to wrap his mind around still. He didn't even know how to begin processing it. He was afraid it would change him. He was more afraid it wouldn't. And he didn't know how to put any of that into words.

"Yeah," he echoed instead.

Jason didn't say anything, just squeezed Gio's hand again and warmth spread through Gio. His eyes stung.

"Gio?" Taylor asked, nudging into his space. His eyes were large.

"Yeah?" Gio asked.

Taylor bit his lip anxiously. "Is someone feeding the cat?"

Gio had booked a room at a hotel on The Strand online before he'd left Richmond. After leaving the hospital, he spent twenty minutes relearning how to drive in peak-hour traffic, and then he was standing on the balcony of his room, overlooking The Strand and Cleveland Bay. He breathed in deeply, replacing the antiseptic smell of the hospital with salt air. The sunlight glittered on the water, and Gio followed the progress of a ferry for a while as it cut across the bay towards Magnetic Island. The view could hypnotise him if he let it.

Maybe later.

Gio returned back inside and showered. When he was finished, he checked his phone for messages and found one waiting: *We're downstairs!* He took the lift down, a smile on his face before the doors even rolled open to reveal Sophie standing in the foyer, Chloe on her hip.

Sophie rushed forward when she saw him, ignoring her luggage, and wrapped herself around him in an awkward hug that left Chloe squashed between them.

"You've got me for two days, Gio," she said when she finally released him. "Let's talk."

They walked on The Strand in the late-afternoon sunlight, and bought gelati. Chloe wore most of hers. They found a bench to sit on that overlooked a statue of a dugong that was perfect climbing size for a toddler, and Gio found that somehow the shooting was easier to talk about if he could watch Chloe and not look his sister in the eye. Some of that was probably guilt. Some of it was worrying about what expressions would pass over Sophie's face.

Sophie linked her fingers with his. "You did the only thing you could, Gio."

"I don't know." He was safe to voice his doubts with her, he knew. "What if it wasn't? What if he would have put the rifle down if I'd told him to?"

"He'd already shot someone," Sophie said. "What did he have to lose by shooting everyone else too?"

"You think he would have done it?"

"I think there's no way to know for sure," Sophie said after a moment. "But on the balance of probabilities? I think there's a good chance he would have. And I think you know that too."

Over at the dugong, Chloe squawked as she slid off its back and tumbled into the grass. She immediately tried to climb it again.

"Look at me, Gio," Sophie said.

He turned his head to meet her gaze.

Her face was solemn, her eyes wide. "There's something else, isn't there? Something you aren't telling me?"

"I . . ." Gio drew a breath. "Yeah. I need to tell you about Pete."

"You should have told me," Sophie said later that night.

Gio stared at the play of lights on the ceiling of the hotel room. "I couldn't."

"He was *hurting* you!"

They kept their voices low. Except for Chloe crashed out in the portacot on the floor, they could have been on one of the long road trips their parents used to drag them on during school holidays. They'd driven from Brisbane to Melbourne once, and spent overnight in some tiny hotel in some tiny town Gio had never heard of before. He and Sophie had shared a room, and felt very grown-up. And sometime in the night their old roles had fallen away, and they'd talked as friends, as equals, and Sophie had told him about a boy she'd slept with, and how it hadn't been like her friends had said it would be, and she felt dumb because he'd talked her into it when she wasn't ready. And Gio, fourteen years old, hadn't known if he was supposed to get angry, or if he was only supposed to listen and tell her it wasn't her fault. Instead, in an effort to share a secret for a secret, he'd blurted out that he thought he might like boys. In *that* way. He'd panicked afterwards that she'd hold it against him, or that it would be weird in the morning at the very least, but they were closer than ever afterwards. And all because of a night spent talking in a shitty hotel room with ugly orange curtains.

"That's why I couldn't tell you, Soph," he said, his throat aching. "Because you would have wanted to *do* something."

There was a sudden rustle of sheets, and then Sophie was climbing into his bed with him. "God, Gio, of course I would have! To him, and to all of them!"

She breathed heavily for a moment, clearly angry, and Gio had a sudden flash of a memory from half a lifetime ago: Sophie in her school uniform, her fists balled and her eyes blazing as she stared down some kid who'd punched Gio at the bus stop. *"You leave my brother alone, you little fuck!"*

"They don't know what he did," Gio whispered. "They think it was just about the steroids, and that I shouldn't have dobbed him in."

"Don't you make excuses for them," Sophie shot back, fierce. "Even if that had been all he did, he still deserved to lose his job."

"They shouldn't have involved you." He shook his head. "I had a picture of Chloe on my desk. I'm sorry."

"Don't you apologise for what they did! But don't ever think you need to protect me, Gio!"

"Soph . . ."

"No," she said. "No, if I'm being threatened, or my child is being threatened, then you *tell* me, Gio. You tell me, and I will make so much fucking noise to the police, to politicians, to every journalist who will *listen* that those fucking arseholes you thought were your friends will regret ever crawling out from under their rocks to harass you. Because the police can't threaten to fire me, Gio, and they can't transfer me, and they can't tell me to keep quiet either!"

Gio swallowed around the lump in his throat. "Soph, I need to keep you out of it."

"Is it still happening?" she asked him.

He was silent for a long time. Too long, evidently.

"Gio!"

"Just leave it. Please, Soph. I'm dealing with it."

"Are you really?"

Gio closed his eyes briefly and thought back to his fight with Jason. It might as well have happened in another lifetime. "Jason put in a report. It's being investigated."

"And will that make them stop?"

Gio sighed. "I don't know."

They rested in silence for a while.

"I have wasted a lot of months being angry with you, Gio," Sophie said at last, her voice quiet and close to breaking. "I thought you were selfish, leaving me and Ian to deal with Dad. I wish I'd known you felt you didn't have a choice. I wish you'd told me."

"I couldn't." His eyes stung. "I didn't know how."

"I know." Sophie moved closer to him, shifting onto her side and throwing an arm over his chest. "I love you, bambino. Please don't lie to me again."

Gio closed his eyes. "I love you too. And I won't, I promise."

Gio spent a week in Townsville after Sophie and Chloe had flown home again. He had a few appointments at District Office. The assistant commissioner said that Ethical Standards had assured him that Gio would be cleared to go back to work by next week, although they would also be referring the case to the CCC—standard procedure—and there would be a coronial inquest held in the next few months as well. The assistant commissioner told Gio he had his full support, and Gio tried to believe it. Gio also had several meetings with the HSO. She'd checked in a few times by phone since the shooting, and it was good to put a name to a face at last. She talked to him about what to expect in the next few weeks and months, in terms of both psychological and physical symptoms. Gio took all the pamphlets and tossed them into the front seat of his car. He thought about throwing them out, but he didn't. He read through them at the hotel.

He visited Jason every day at the hospital. Jason was getting more and more frustrated being stuck there, which Gio guessed meant he was healing.

"I want to go home," he grumbled. "I want to sleep in my own bed. God knows Taylor's missed enough bloody school."

Taylor, sitting on the floor doing a word search in a magazine, looked up and grinned.

"And Sandra's on my case about this kid she knows," Jason said.

"What kid?"

"Some friend of the family. She's seventeen, and she's just got a job at the supermarket. She starts a week from Monday. Her parents live a couple of hours out of town, so . . ." Jason grimaced.

"That could work," Gio said cautiously.

"Maybe." Jason sighed. "I'm half expecting Sandra will have her moved in by the time I get home."

"That sounds like something Sandra would do."

"If a girl comes to live with us, I'll have to wear pants all the time," Taylor piped up. "So will you, Dad."

"That's . . . that's not going to be a problem, mate." Jason shook his head. "Anyway, there'd be someone in the house overnight if I got called out on jobs. Not that that's going to be an issue for a long bloody while yet."

Gio watched the careful way he rubbed his chest. "It'll be sooner than you think."

Jason exhaled.

"Pants," Taylor intoned ominously, and then bounced to his feet. He sidled around Jason's bed. "Can I get some chips from the vending machine? And some Maltesers?"

"*One* thing," Jason said, and nodded at the drawer.

Taylor dived in and grabbed his wallet. "Thanks, Dad!" He helped himself to a five-dollar note and headed off down the hallway.

Gio turned his head to watch him go. When he looked back again, Jason's storm-grey gaze was fixed on him. Gio leaned back in his seat. "I'm probably heading back in a few days."

Jason raised his eyebrows. "You're not sticking around here?"

"Someone has to be there to explain to the newies about bingo night."

Jason smiled. "I thought they'd have to lever you out of Townsville with a crowbar."

Gio shrugged. "Richmond's sort of grown on me."

Jason's smile widened. "Yeah, it does that. Alana and me, we said we'd be there three years at most. But then it gets in your blood somehow, and you can't imagine heading back to a city."

A few months ago, Gio could never have imagined it. But now, when he thought of the mornings he'd spent jogging by the river as the sun came up, illuminating the eucalypts and setting the sky behind them on fire, he could believe it. It was big country, but it didn't make Gio feel small. It made him stand taller.

"You'll make a country copper of me yet," he said.

Jason's smile faded into something almost wistful. "Did we fuck it up?" he asked quietly.

"What?"

Jason's mouth quirked. "Nah, it's nothing."

Gio shook his head. His heart pounded. "Bullshit. Say what you mean, Jason."

"The thing with us," Jason said. "Did we fuck it up?"

"We really did," Gio said, and tempered his words with a slight smile.

"I'm sorry." Jason's expression was grave. "About the way I handled things with the Ratsak. I got angry. I got ahead of myself. I should have talked to you first."

"Don't." Gio closed his eyes briefly. When he opened them again, Jason was holding his gaze. "Not when we both know you would have done your job and reported it anyway."

Jason didn't answer, but his expression tightened.

"I'm sorry too," Gio said. "For threatening to report you over Taylor. It was a low blow."

"The difference is, you didn't report it."

"You were right though." Gio shrugged. "And maybe nobody will be able to prove anything, but it might get them to pull their heads in."

"Last time we talked about this, you were dead certain it'd get them to escalate."

"I'm done with being bullied." Gio's heart beat faster. "Fuck them. You've got my back, right?"

"Yeah, I've got your back." They sat in silence for a while, and then Jason quirked his mouth into a brief, regretful smile. "So, the thing with us. We fucked it up."

"Yeah," Gio murmured. "But if you wanted . . ." He swallowed. He felt as though he were standing on the edge of a precipice, ready to leap. He didn't know if he would fall, or if he would fly. But he was tired of standing there. "If you wanted," he said, "we could try again?"

Jason pressed his lips together tightly for a moment, and then cleared his throat. "I'm not an easy sell, Gio. Me and Taylor, we're a package deal."

"I know that."

Jason dropped his gaze to his hand. The light glinted off his wedding ring. "I'm still in love with my wife."

Gio laced his fingers through Jason's. He lifted Jason's hand and pressed his mouth to it. The gold band was cold in the air-conditioning. "I know that too."

Jason's expression transformed. His bottom lip trembled. A muscle in his cheek twitched. His eyes widened as though he couldn't understand what he was seeing when he stared at Gio. He looked achingly vulnerable.

"I think we could have something," Gio said. "Something real. And I want to try again."

Jason's throat clicked as he swallowed. "I want that too."

Gio stood and leaned over him. He slid his fingers into Jason's hair, and pressed their mouths gently together. The kiss was too cold, too dry, and tasted faintly of the antiseptic smell that permeated the entire hospital. It was as perfect as Gio needed it to be. Not an ending, but a beginning.

They could both use a new beginning.

CHAPTER TWENTY-FOUR

Six Months Later

The sun had set already, but the cockatoos in the rain tree at the bottom of the paddock were still calling out to one another in curious, questioning notes that ended with a chorus of raucous squawks. It was cold. The heat of the day had vanished the moment the light did, and Jason shivered as he crossed the yard. He climbed Gio's back stairs, almost tripping on the cat that lounged there invisible in the dark.

Gio's back door was unlocked. The smell of fresh coffee wafted out onto the cold night air.

Jason stepped inside. "Hey."

Gio leaned in the kitchen doorway. He was still in uniform. "Hey. Is Taylor in bed?"

"I told him that if he didn't get to sleep on time, the camping trip was off."

"Harsh," Gio said with a grin. He stepped back into the kitchen.

Jason followed him, and then crowded him up against the bench, corralling him in with his arms while Gio fiddled with the coffee machine. He leaned in and bit the side of his neck gently, and Gio jerked.

"Are you trying to give me third-degree burns?" Gio asked, elbowing Jason in the ribs.

"I'm trying to give you an erection," Jason said, sliding his hands down Gio's chest and tugging at his belt.

Gio snorted. "I just spent eight hours drinking shitty coffee from the shitty machine in the station. I need a decent caffè macchiato before I even think about an erection, thanks."

"You are such a coffee snob," Jason said, pressing a kiss to the curls at the nape of his neck before releasing him.

Gio turned around, smiling. "It's part of the package, Jase. You should thank me for teaching some refinement to your skippy arse."

Jason curled his hand around the back of Gio's neck. He pulled him in for a kiss. "Drink your fancy bloody coffee, then."

Gio's smile widened.

Jason gazed out of Gio's kitchen window over to his own house. There was a low flickering light in the living room. Holly liked to watch TV in the dark. Having Holly living with them was working well. There was someone there at night if Jason was called out, and Holly's parents were happy she wasn't living alone in town. Jason wasn't sure what made him such a safe bet, whether it was because he was a police officer, or because it was an open secret in town that he and Gio were together. It was the sort of thing that nobody had really addressed—nobody sober, at least, and most of the drunks had quickly learned that their arrests went much more smoothly if they shut their mouths on that particular topic—but people knew. For every sideways look Jason got, he also got a few smiles and nods and, once, an entire tray of lamingtons made by one of the ladies from the Catholic Ladies' Auxiliary at Saint Patrick's.

"For you and your young man, dear," she'd said, patting him on the arm, and she hadn't been talking about Taylor.

Gio drank his coffee. It was a mystery to Jason how Gio could put away so much caffeine and still sleep at night. He seemed to manage it though, moulding himself easily to the curve of Jason's body. Some nights it was Jason who didn't sleep. Some nights he lay awake staring into the darkness and listening to Gio breathe. Some nights he wasn't sure how they'd made it to this place where everything was quiet and soft and right, but Jason didn't want to question his luck. They were at a place now where it worked, where *they* worked. They were at a place where they had room to build a future together.

"How was work?" Jason rearranged the magnets on Gio's fridge.

"Nothing to report, boss." Gio's tone was only half-teasing.

They still got the occasional unmarked package in the mail—probably just an attempt by Gio's ex-colleagues to prove that they were untouchable—but Jason was satisfied that the investigation had put the wind up those arseholes and that the harassment was dying a slow death at last. Gio might still be hated down on the Coast, but in the police service's Northern Region he was a fucking hero. Which was good. With the inquest into the shooting coming up soon, he could use that support.

And then maybe—finally—they could put everything behind them and get on with their lives.

"Glad to hear it," Jason said.

Gio set his cup down in the sink with a soft *clink*. "I need a shower. Are you staying over?"

"Yeah."

Gio flashed him a smile. "Good."

He padded down the hallway, peeling off his shirt as he walked.

"Don't be too long!" Jason called after him, and Gio laughed.

Jason headed for Gio's bedroom and sat on the edge of the bed, listening to the pipes squeal as Gio turned on the shower. He unbuttoned his shirt, fingers grazing over the scar tissue on his chest. Jason was still reluctant to touch it. He didn't know if the tenderness in the scar was imagined or not. He'd healed, but he'd spent so long learning to move without exacerbating the injury that sometimes he still didn't trust himself to take a deep breath, or to twist his torso when he moved. His first fight at the pub after going back on active duty? He'd suddenly imagined a fist in the chest, and for a second he'd been frozen to the spot. Then Gio had moved in front of him, and he'd been able to breathe again. To act. To do his bloody job.

Afterwards, Gio had said, *"Do you think that never happens to me, Jase?"*

They had each other's backs. They were solid.

Jason shrugged his shirt off and then stood to unfasten his jeans. He shoved them and his underwear down, and then climbed into Gio's bed. There was a paperback lying on the bedside table. Something by that Turkish writer that Gio loved and Jason barely understood. Jason flicked through a few pages and then set the book aside. He heard the pipes shudder off, and a few minutes later Gio appeared in the doorway wearing a towel.

He raised his eyebrows at Jason. "So, I believe you said something about an erection?"

"Drop the towel and get your arse over here," Jason said.

"Yes, Sarge," Gio said with a laugh, and did just that.

The ute bounced over the rocky ground, sending up swirling plumes of dust behind them. Taylor, buckled into the middle seat, whooped and crowed, while Gio gripped the handle above the door.

City boy.

Okay, so Jason might have overplayed the idea of a campsite. Clearly Gio had been expecting somewhere with some actual amenities, or at least a road to take them there. They'd turned off the road about an hour back, the track had run out soon after, and Gio was looking increasingly dubious.

"We're sleeping in the middle of nowhere tonight, aren't we?" he asked as they bounced over another hillock. Spinifex scraped the undercarriage of the ute. "You want me to die of a snake bite."

"It's winter, Gio. There won't be any snakes."

"I'll bet that's exactly what the snakes want you to believe."

They arrived at the campsite a short while later. Taylor immediately went scrounging for firewood, and Jason unloaded the back of the ute. Gio looked around dubiously.

It wasn't much to look at during the day. Just a small bluff overlooking the curve of a creek bed. The creek bed was bone-dry in winter. On the other side of the creek bed, the flat countryside reached out for the horizon. The hillocks and ridges of the earth were smoothed out by sheer distance. A few clumps of trees dotted the landscape, their white trunks stark against the red dirt.

"Wow," Gio said.

"It used to be an inland sea," Jason said. "A million or so years ago. Now come and help me get set up."

"Did you bring a tent?" Gio asked. "I'm not seeing a tent."

Jason hauled the swags out of the back of the ute. "We don't need a tent. It's not going to rain."

"Seriously?"

Jason laughed. "Trust me, Gio. We'll be fine."

Taylor came stomping back with an armful of firewood. He dropped it beside the ute. "Can I go looking for fossils, Dad?"

"Stay in sight of the ute," Jason warned him.

The uniformity of the landscape could be dangerous. Jason had headed up enough search parties to know that even the most experienced locals could get lost out here. He'd heard stories of people finding massive fossils uncovered by the wind and the weather, or sheltered formations with indigenous rock paintings on them, who after finding their way back to their vehicles were never able to locate the places again. There were stranger things too. Once, he'd been sent out to search for a bloke who'd been mustering and was overdue. The bloke's quad bike had died, it turned out later, and it had taken him hours to make it to high enough ground to get a signal on his phone. When the bloke had managed to call in at last, Jason had driven to where he'd thought he was, and turned the lights on the police LandCruiser on.

"Can you see the lights?" he'd asked.

"Yeah. Yeah, I see them. Yeah, you're coming right for me."

Jason had been stationary at the time.

"Well, what the hell was I looking at?" the bloke had asked when Jason had eventually found him.

Jason had figured there was no way either of them would ever know the answer to that.

He watched for a moment as Taylor scrabbled down into the creek bed and then climbed out the other side, and then turned his attention to building up the fire. It was too early to light it yet, but he wanted to be ready by dusk. The temperature would drop the second the sun slipped below the horizon.

"Alana and I used to come out here," he said, clearing a place for the fire.

Gio crouched down beside him, sweeping some brush away.

"We used to roll our swags out here and watch the stars for hours." He smiled at the memory. "We had to tether Taylor up with one of those toddler leashes so he didn't wander off in the middle of the night."

"That sounds like something Taylor would do," Gio said with a laugh.

"Well, not much has changed, that's for sure." Jason checked to see that Taylor was still in sight, and then turned back to Gio. "Thank you."

"For what?" Gio asked softly.

"For coming with me even though you obviously hate camping."

Gio ducked his head, flushing.

Jason rose to his feet, and held a hand down for him. "It's beautiful when the stars come out, I promise."

"Huh," Gio said, looking at Jason with his head at an angle.

"What?"

"Turns out that you, Jason Quinn, are a *romantic*."

It was Jason's turn to flush. "Shut up."

"And now it's gone." Gio's smile was brilliant.

"Shut up," Jason said again, and reeled Gio in for a gentle kiss that left them both breathless.

Behind them, the late-afternoon light turned the red dirt golden.

Dear Reader,

Thank you for reading Lisa Henry's *Two Man Station*!

We know your time is precious and you have many, many entertainment options, so it means a lot that you've chosen to spend your time reading. We really hope you enjoyed it.

We'd be honored if you'd consider posting a review—good or bad—on sites like **Amazon, Barnes & Noble, Kobo, Goodreads, Twitter, Facebook**, **Tumblr,** and your blog or website. We'd also be honored if you told your friends and family about this book. Word of mouth is a book's lifeblood!

For more information on upcoming releases, author interviews, blog tours, contests, giveaways, and more, please sign up for our weekly, spam-free newsletter and visit us around the web:

Newsletter: tinyurl.com/RiptideSignup
Twitter: twitter.com/RiptideBooks
Facebook: facebook.com/RiptidePublishing
Goodreads: tinyurl.com/RiptideOnGoodreads
Tumblr: riptidepublishing.tumblr.com

Thank you so much for Reading the Rainbow!

RiptidePublishing.com

RIPTIDE PUBLISHING

ACKNOWLEDGEMENTS

Thanks, as always, to my wonderful beta readers and fellow authors: J.A. Rock, Sofia Grey, Jaqueline Grey, and M. Caspian.

ALSO BY
LISA HENRY

Adulting 101
Sweetwater
He Is Worthy
The Island
Tribute
One Perfect Night
Fallout, with M. Caspian
Fall on Your Knees (part of the *Rated: XXXmas* anthology)

With J.A. Rock
When All the World Sleeps
Another Man's Treasure
When All the World Sleep

Playing the Fool series, with J.A. Rock
The Two Gentlemen of Altona
The Merchant of Death
Tempest

With Heidi Belleau
Tin Man
Bliss
King of Dublin
The Harder They Fall

Writing as Cari Waites
Stealing Innocents

ABOUT THE AUTHOR

Lisa likes to tell stories, mostly with hot guys and happily ever afters.

Lisa lives in tropical North Queensland, Australia. She doesn't know why, because she hates the heat, but she suspects she's too lazy to move. She spends half her time slaving away as a government minion, and the other half plotting her escape.

She attended university at sixteen, not because she was a child prodigy or anything, but because of a mix-up between international school systems early in life. She studied History and English, neither of them very thoroughly.

She shares her house with too many cats, a green tree frog that swims in the toilet, and as many possums as can break in every night. This is not how she imagined life as a grown-up.

You can email her at lisahenryonline@gmail.com
Or check out her website at lisahenryonline.com
Got Twitter? Follow her at twitter.com/LisaHenryOnline
Hanging out on Goodreads? So am I:
goodreads.com/author/show/5050492.Lisa_Henry
Facebook: facebook.com/lisa.henry.1441

CPSIA information can be obtained
at www.ICGtesting.com
Printed in the USA
LVOW12s1934090118
562393LV00005B/892/P

9 781626 497115